An Unfair Division

Suspense & Romance You Can Fall For

L. J. Vant

All Around Publishing, Inc.

Warning: The reproduction and sale of this book without authorization is illegal. All rights reserved: No part of this book may be reproduced or transmitted in any means or in any form without written permission by the publisher.

An Unfair Division
Copyright © 2022 by L. J. Vant

First Printing: June 2011 by Publisher BookStrand
Original printing under author name Zequeatta Jaques
Reprinted April 2022 under pen name L. J. Vant after extensive revision

Cover art created by Zequeatta Jaques
All art and logo copyright © 2022 by All Around Publishing, Inc.

This book is a work of fiction. References to real establishments, people, events, locales, or organizations were used by the author only to provide a sense of authenticity, and used fictitiously. The characters, and all events and dialogue, are a product of the author's imagination and should not to be taken as factual.

ISBN: 978-1-7344314-5-2

Printed in the U.S.A.

Publisher
All Around Publishing, Inc.
www.allaroundpublishinginc.com

Other books by L. J. Vant
Across All Boundaries

Prologue

Augusta County, Virginia 1983: Time continues to flow and no matter the era, people can and have displayed shocking behavior. Let's read ahead and see where this story goes.

"Arg!" the woman cried. Head thrown back, neck stretched tight, she clenched at the iron bedrail behind her. Her huge, extended belly tightened as a third contraction gained speed. She twisted on the bed, and the serrated knife of the contraction lessened, and with its tenuous passing, the woman's body eased. Her fingers loosened from the bedrail she'd gripped so tightly. Suddenly, she clawed at the rail again.

"Ah...!" she screamed. The empty room resounded with her cry as the contraction held her within its grip. Pain clawed through her as she pushed down hard. Her teeth sank deep into her bottom lip and blood dripped from the puncture wounds.

She wanted to get rid of the things inside of her, hoped to live long enough to see *his* face when he realized what she'd done. The woman grasped his image to her, the hatred she felt for him intense. Her face grotesque, she labored to expel her first burden and then her second.

Blood gushed between her spread legs and quickly dispersed around her.

"Please. Please, find me," she gasped. She closed her eyes in exhaustion. She knew she didn't have long to live.

"Come. Come see what you have caused with your betrayal. Come see the damn things you wanted so badly," she whispered into the empty room.

****

Blake quickly strolled into the mansion inherited from his father. He had returned earlier than planned from the tour of his estate holdings. The feeling of unease he'd experienced all that day had finally caused him to rotate the Jeep he drove and head it toward home.

His friend, Chad who rode with him, understood his concern.

Blake knew that something was wrong when he walked into the overlarge home. The stillness of the mansion hit him with the full force of it. Taking the stairs two at a time up the large, and winding staircase, he hurried to the master bedroom where his wife should be resting. Slamming the bedroom door back with the force of his scared entry, he was startled to find his butler and a housemaid stood in the room.

Their heads jerked up at his entrance. The note they'd intently been reading forgotten as they stared wide-eyed at him. Blake noticed that the maid quickly stepped away from the butler and the paper he gripped.

"Where's my wife?"

The butler's hand shook as he held out the personal stationary he held. "She says in this note that she's in labor and hopes by the time you find her, that she and your babies are all dead."

Blake sucked in his breath in disbelief. Snatching the note, he quickly scanned it. Pain ripped through him at its written content. So much hatred held inside that his wife was willing to kill two innocent babes just to torture him? *No*, Blake denied his harsh thought even as it lingered, *herself maybe, but not her own flesh and blood. Belinda wouldn't harm her own babies.*

"When did you last see my wife?" he asked, pinning the butler with a hard look. Belinda couldn't have gone far, not in her condition.

His butler turned toward the housemaid. "Maybe two or three hours ago, wouldn't you agree?"

The housemaid gave a quick nod and refused to look at Blake. She hunched her shoulders at his hiss of anguish at his realization at the amount of time that had elapsed.

"You!" Blake ordered the butler, "Send someone for the doctor, and then wait by the CB base in my office. When I find my wife, I'll radio to let you know where to bring the doctor." At the butler's look of pity directed his way, Blake wanted to smash the man's face in.

Without waiting for a nod of understanding, Blake turned toward his silent friend who'd followed him into the house. "Come with me, Chad. I may need your help."

With Chad close behind him, Blake hurried out the bedroom door and from the mansion.

The plantation's Jeep roared to life on his first try, and throwing the vehicle in gear, Blake floored the gas pedal under his foot. *Where could Belinda have gone?* he wondered as tires spit gravel at his speed. Chad struggled to shut the door on his side of the Jeep. Blake realized that wherever his wife had gone, she would've made sure she had time to deliver the babies before he could get to her. She would die without the proper care, and she knew it.

Their doctor had warned she would have complications with the twins' births. Yet, against their doctor's advice, she'd insisted on carrying the babies to full term.

Blake hit the steering wheel with the palm of his hand as his fury coursed through him, fury, because he'd believed Belinda these past few months, and with that belief, he had let his guard down. Belinda had begun to talk of the babies she carried with what he'd believed was genuine, maternal instinct kicking in. And when she'd told him one evening, she wished for them to try to work through their differences, he had gladly and foolishly jumped at the chance. Maybe after the twins' birth, she had told him softly, they could begin their married life over again.

Dumb, stupid! Because of the guilt he felt over the sorrow he'd caused her, he'd desperately wanted to believe her.

Suddenly, Blake realized where his wife had gone. He slammed his foot down on the Jeep's brakes and spun the vehicle to the left. He watched as if from a distance as Chad quickly grabbed hold of the careening vehicle's roll bar with this sudden action. Blake hit the gas pedal once again with his foot as he changed and ground the gears of the Jeep. Belinda had gone to *the cabin*, the cabin where she'd known her lover. The love of her life, someone Blake had paid a huge sum of money to leave his plantation and disappear. Someone who'd greedily taken what was offered only to show up five years later. Someone who was now dead.

At the sight of the cabin thirty minutes later, Blake's heart lurched. His wife's red sports car sat before the cabin's sagging porch. Bringing the Jeep to a sliding stop before the front of the cabin, Blake hoped that he'd reached his wife in time. *This time she will get the help she needs,* he vowed. *This time*, he would bring up the subject of divorce, and if it was what she wanted, there would be no more resistance from him. Anything to right the wrong he'd done. Grasping his CB mouthpiece from the dash of the Jeep, Blake pushed its speaker button. "John, you there? This is Blake."

"I'm here, sir."

"Bring the doctor to the cabin on the east side of the plantation. Yes, yes, exactly," Blake replied to the butler's halting repeat of his directions. "Hurry!"

Pushing open the door, and then taking a deep breath, Blake stepped from the vehicle. He watched Chad follow his actions. They both started toward the cabin where it had all begun. A cabin Blake now realized he should've ordered torn down years ago.

Opening the cabin door, its rusted hinges squeaking, Blake abruptly halted. Shock paralyzed him to where he couldn't move. Belinda lay upon a blanket spread over the dusty old mattress, a mattress, she and her lover had made love upon behind his back. Blood heavily covered both the blanket and her thighs. In sick horror, Blake realized that two, tiny babies lay face down between his wife's spread legs.

Chad cried out beside him, "See if the babies are alive!"

Blake couldn't and didn't move. Chad shoved him forward, and stumbling, Blake moved toward the iron, four-poster bed his wife lay upon. Startled out of his daze by his longtime friend's hoarse cry of anguish, Blake saw Chad snatch up one of the babies from the bed and begin to administer to it. Quickly, scooping up the other newborn, Blake gently turned the tiny thing over within his arms. Opening its mouth with his thumb and forefinger, he scrapped out the mucus and blood that had collected within the small cavity of the baby's mouth. The baby sucked in air and then gave a mewling howl of outrage.

Blake raised his head, and he watched Chad carefully help the other infant to breathe. Relief surged through him when the tiny thing Chad held let out a cry of rage.

"Blake."

Turning, Blake looked down toward his wife.

"I knew you would come. I hung on," she whispered. "I hung on just so I could see the horror on your face. Here are your precious babies. I despise and hate you. I always have...."

Holding the tiny, blood-covered babe upon his hand, Blake felt his world shift at Belinda's cruelty displayed. The woman he loved watched him as he fought his emotions.

She smiled her slow, sweet smile when he lost his battle, and his tears wet his face. Belinda gasped her final breath even as she kept her gaze locked with his. Deep down, Blake knew she'd wanted to see his expression of hurt before she let loose her hold on life.

****

Six years later 1989: Our life path, is it random, chosen, or do the actions of others determine our destiny?

"Daddy! Daddy! Caite's trying to twist the head off my baby doll. She says it will hurt my baby bad!"

Raising his eyes from the stock report he'd been reading, Blake watched the screaming child who ran toward him to where he sat in his chair in his home office. His mouth twisted in self-mockery. *A rich man am I in money, but not life,* he bitterly thought. As usual, he'd sold his shares of stock just in time, before the company he'd invested in heavily announced a sharp dip in their profit earnings; but the children his wife had birthed and that he'd wanted so badly were not his, but her lover's. Blake hoped if there was life after death, that Belinda was aware of her fatal error in believing her lover's lie of being unable to have children. He hoped she writhed in daily agony that she'd almost killed the children she would have dearly loved if she hadn't believed they were his.

When the doctor informed the babies brought to the hospital the night of their birth would need blood transfusions, and that their blood type was rare, something had clicked in Blake that night. He knew that blood type wouldn't answer his sudden nagging question, but a DNA test would. The doctor that night had studied him for a moment, until with a shake of his head, he'd finally nodded in agreement at his request for the test to be done.

When the results were revealed, hatred coursed through Blake for the first time for his wife, hatred for her and the man she'd loved. He wanted to love the twins, but something died in him that day. He saw to the twins' basic needs. However, as far as loving them, it seemed that he couldn't feel any emotion no matter how hard he tried.

Six-year-old Taite silently clutched her doll to her as she watched him. *Where is this child's nanny?* Blake thought with irritation.

"Daddy?" she hesitantly asked. Her tears threatened. With aggravation, Blake reached out his hand for the tattered doll she held. Taite turned when her sister belligerently walked into the room, and she inched closer to Blake. When Blake laid a hand on her shoulder at her movement, she sighed and gave her sister a look of what he could only interpret as sheer triumph. For a moment, Blake felt amusement swell within him before the emotion faded.

He watched as Taite frowned heavily at her identical twin sister. She stuck her tongue out at her. Blake lightly tapped the end of that tongue. He shook his head indicting his disapproval of her behavior and he leaned closer to her.

"Caite can't hurt your baby doll, Taite. So, there is no need for your dramatics, understood?" Blake watched the child give a hesitant nod to him. He continued. "Now as for your sister and her destructive behavior, she will have all her dolls taken from her for a week. Is that understood, Caite?"

Turning toward the child he'd raised as his own, Blake felt startled for a moment. The look held in Caite's eyes was something he didn't think a six-year-old should have. Suddenly, the child blinked, and the veiled challenge directed toward him vanished. "I understand, Daddy," she said before she grinned impishly and then flounced closer. "Taite's such a cry baby, though. And the thing's head needs to be pulled off. It's dirty and old. Besides, she has a lot of other baby dolls to play with."

Chapter 1

Twenty years later
Taite's story

"I thought we agreed to meet at six this evening to work out?" Looking in aggravation at her sister, Taite stepped off the treadmill she had been running on for the past twenty minutes. She dabbed at the sweat on her forehead with the white gym towel she'd picked up. The old-fashioned lyrics of Jingle Bells, Taite's favorite song, played in the background of the Gym and Fitness Club.

Caite grinned as she pulled her naturally, burnished copper-colored, shoulder-length hair back and put it up into a thick ponytail.

Her white sports shoes and red workout pants and matching top, looks good on her, Taite thought as she watched her sister. Christmas was just around the corner, and Caite seemed to be in the spirit of things. Her ponytail holder had the imprint of Christmas trees on it.

"I'm twenty minutes late because I offered to help my new boss with setting up her office."

"Kissing up already are you, sis?" Taite questioned.

"It doesn't hurt to get chummy with the boss. She might throw some good sales my way," Caite slammed back.

Taite laughed, her aggravation leaving her as she straddled a stationary exercise bike. She watched Caite mount another one alongside her.

"Besides, you know the old man has cut me off," Caite added. She adjusted the bike's seat position and then the pedals tension resistance.

Taite shook her head at her twin as she watched her. "Oh…poor…you…. Dad set us both up with our own condos and supported us for six years while we earned our MBAs, and then when we decided what we really wanted to do was to get into the real estate business, he didn't even bat an eyelash."

"Oh...no...he didn't bat an eyelash," Caite drawled with a frown. "He just dryly stated he wasn't going to buy us the business, and what we needed to do was to go to work for someone."

"Talking about working for someone, did I tell you the real estate broker I work for was bought out?" Taite stopped peddling as she looked at her sister.

"No. Is it going to affect your job?"

"I don't know. I hope not, but it could with sales down."

"When did you find out about the sale?"

"The owner told us the news this past Thursday. He's retiring, he said, going to move to Florida. He said the new owner is not supposed to take over until the week after next."

"Don't expect the old man to help you out if you lose your job," Caite snipped. "And you know I'm always broke, so don't look at me to help tide you over."

Taite frowned. "Unlike you, sis, I do try to put money back for a rainy day. And I don't steal from the old man to get what I want."

"Well, aren't you just the Goody Two-shoes," Caite sharply replied as she draped the towel she held around the back of her neck.

Thoughtfully, Taite watched her sister. Giving a shrug she turned back to her exercise bike. Her sister didn't need her advice, nor would she listen if she tried to offer it. Another half hour of exercise and she would be ready to go home. She had the whole weekend before her to relax and to get caught up on her housework, and she didn't want to get into an argument with Caite and ruin her first weekend off in a long time.

****

Stepping into her quiet condo, Taite tossed her keys into the shallow bowl that sat on the glass-topped entry table.

"Hey, Sexy, I'm home," she called out. She kept a watchful eye down the tiled entryway as she slipped her exercise shoes from her feet and then hung up her heavy, winter coat. Her laughter pealed from her when her tan cocker spaniel darted around the hallway corner, running full blast toward her.

Sexy was her nickname for the dog. Sexy's real name was Toto. Or that was what had been written on the adoption papers when she'd adopted him as a puppy four years ago. Taite liked the name Sexy better.

"Did you miss me? You gorgeous male you." Bending down, Taite petted her beloved dog. "Let's get something to eat and afterwards I'll take you out for your walk. We can look at the Christmas lights. Now what do we want tonight, any requests?"

Taite looked down at her pet as if he should answer. When he just wagged his tail, she laughed and walked on into the kitchen.

"Mm…how about spaghetti for me and a bowl of dog food for you, sound good?" Sexy wagged his tail.

Washing up, Taite quickly set out the ingredients for her supper and then scooped out a cup of dog chow for Sexy. He kept a watchful eye on her activities as he ate. Quietly, he lay at her feet when she sat down to eat her own meal.

"Let's go," she stated when she finished.

Jumping up, Sexy trotted to the front door. He wagged his tail eagerly when Taite walked up to him.

"You're a good boy. Yes, you are," she crooned. Leaning down, she patted the top of his silky head and snapped the leash that she held onto his collar. Reaching for her coat, Taite opened her front door. In a bold and uncharacteristic move, Sexy darted into the hallway toward the open elevator doors, his leash jerked from her fingers.

"Sexy, wait!" Taite called out, startled. She took off in hot pursuit.

Her elderly neighbor stepped out past the elevator doors and he turned and smiled at her. Taite slid to an embarrassed stop as Sexy darted past him and on into the open elevator.

Amusement lined her neighbor's face.

"Honey, you know I'd wait for you any day," he drawled.

Taite noticed the lone man in the elevator look from her to her neighbor and then back to her with obvious distaste. She didn't recognize him. Jerking her gaze from the stranger's steady stare, Taite smiled tightly at her neighbor. "You know darn well that I wasn't talking to you, Bill."

"Too bad for me," her neighbor stated before he turned. A chuckle could be heard as he walked away.

Feeling her face flame at the stranger's silent regard, Taite stepped into the elevator and grabbed Sexy's leash. She frowned down at her pet. She couldn't fathom what had come over him. Sexy had never before done anything resembling the kind of behavior he'd just displayed. Even now, he sat quietly beside her, back to his well-behaved self.

"I take it your dog's name is Sexy," the stranger drawled as he looked down at Sexy and then back up toward her. The elevator doors slid shut with a quiet click.

Taite's heart gave an unexpected little jump when her gaze connected with dark, coffee-colored eyes. She swallowed—her throat suddenly dry. Unable to answer, but with a small nod given, Taite reached out to hit the button that would take her to the lobby of the building. She noticed that the third-floor button was lit. Apparently the stranger was either visiting someone on the third floor or he was the new owner of the previously vacant condo on that level.

"Maybe you should take your dog to obedience school. It's not good having animals running loose. Some of us have small children. I wouldn't have taken kindly to it if your dog in his or her excitement had jumped on my child."

Taite felt her anger rise at the man's sharp tone. Yet something within her fell at the realization that the attractive man before her was married. Confused at the sharp, conflicting emotions, Taite avoided his direct gaze, her eyes locked on Sexy. Her dog cocked his head at her and returned her look. He gave a slow thump of his tail, as if to say *"chicken"*.

Straightening her spine, Taite glanced up at the man.

"Sexy has been to obedience school and is usually very well behaved.

I don't know why he is so anxious to go out this evening. I have a walker who comes by during the day. So, he gets his exercise."

The man grunted with disbelief as he shuffled the coat draped over his arm. Without another word, he walked from the elevator when its doors opened.

Taite watched the man's long, unhurried strides take him from her. She could tell that he took care of himself physically. He was a well-built man, muscled, although not overly so. Even with the lingering anger she held at his tone toward her, her fingers itched to touch the thick, coal-black head of hair he sported. The slight curls which brushed against his pristine-white shirt collar seemed to call out for her fingers to feel what Taite knew with certainty would be a silky softness.

****

Pierce could sense the gaze of the pretty young woman watching him as he strode away, before the elevator doors closed blocking her view. He didn't know why it had angered him when he'd believed the woman called out to the elderly gentleman who'd rode the elevator with him. He had glimpsed the woman before when he'd toured the condo he had decided to buy, although she hadn't noticed him at the time. She had been with another elderly man on her way out of the lobby area. It was her shoulder-length coppery-colored hair that had caught his attention that first time. He had to admit the rest of her was damn fine, too. Too bad it seemed that she preferred elderly gentlemen.

Opening the door to his new home, Pierce looked around at its interior. He liked what the new decorator had done with the rooms. She had changed the original decorator's dark and gloomy theme to a lighter and airier feel. Just what he needed, he realized. The condo wasn't overly large, only a two bedroom, but it was spacious enough for him and Lacy. At the thought of his Lacy, her babysitter walked out from the smaller of the two bedrooms. The elderly lady smiled at him.

"I just put her down for a nap. She played hard all day long."

"Thanks, Emma. I can't tell you how much you agreeing to watch Lacy for me relieved my worries."

Emma shook her head at Pierce. "I was so saddened when my nephew told me what happened to your wife. Although it has been two years, that sort of thing hurts for a long time, doesn't it?"

"Yes, yes it does," Pierce replied as he walked Emma to the front door. Before she turned to go, and with a sad smile directed his way, she promised she would be back early the next morning. Shutting the door behind her, Pierce went back into his living room. Sitting down in his leather recliner, he tiredly stretched out his legs. The light, burgundy-colored end-pillows on the couch opposite from where he sat had been bought to perfectly match the chair he reclined in.

With Emma's mention of Lacy's mother, Pierce felt his resentment rise. It was a resentment he'd fought every single day for the past two years. The unjustness of the death of his wife ate at him. Why had the fates allowed someone as beautiful and as good as his wife to be killed, and yet the other driver survived? He shouldn't have. Both vehicles had been mangled to nothing.

Abruptly standing, Pierce walked into his kitchen to find something to eat. *If there is a god, that god certainly isn't a fair one*, he thought as he rummaged through his cabinets. He'd had only four years with his wife before her life had abruptly been cut off. Two years into their marriage was when he'd received the phone call that had ended his own life.

But at least I still have Lacy, he thought. His beautiful, rambunctious Lacy had been a newborn when her mother had died.

Turning, Pierce gazed at the picture of his wife that hung between the large bay windows in the living room.

"I miss you, sweetheart," he stated. His hunger forgotten, he went to check on their child.

Chapter 2

Taite laughed at Sexy as the dog watched her get dressed for work the following Monday morning. She could have sworn the animal shook his head at her when he saw her pull out what she called her "Reel in the Sale Outfit". It was an outfit she wore only for her male customers. Yes, the scooped neckline was lower than what she normally wore. A *lot* lower, Taite had to admit when she glanced toward the mirror again. But hell, her recent customer was so obvious in his flirting with her, and he'd continued to drag out the buying of the home she'd shown him for so long that she decided today would be the day he would buckle under. Her motto, *Sign on the dotted line please,* would begin to lose face with her coworkers if she didn't get his signature soon.

Leaning down, Taite patted the top of Sexy's silky head as she walked past him. "Don't judge. I have to make a living or you don't eat."

Her only response was a sad look as Sexy dropped his head down to his front paws. He didn't make a move when Taite walked out from the bedroom and on to the front door.

"Bye, Sexy," she called out as she left. She clicked the condo door shut and locked behind her.

Briskly walking into her office, Taite smiled at her male coworker who lazily raised his hand in greeting toward her through his office window as he sipped his morning coffee.

The main office lobby area was decorated with its usual annual, two large Christmas trees. The glass-fronted panes of everyone's offices also spruced up by the hired professional decorator. The boss's favorite pre-recorded, Christmas carol's rotated and played softly in the background. It was definitely that time of year. Laying her leather briefcase on top of her desk, Taite opened it and took out the papers she would need that day.

Her coworker and brief boyfriend at one-time stood and walked to her door. He dropped a broad shoulder against the inside of her doorframe. "Wearing your 'Reel in the Sale Outfit' today, I see."

Taite laughed at Mickey's deliberately drawled Texan accent, which sounded just like their elderly boss. "The man will either sign today, Mickey, or he needs to go on down the road. I have other customers interested in that house. I've only put up with him this long because he put in a much higher bid than my other clients and the owners are not in any particular hurry to sell."

"Ah, honey. If only I could show a little cleavage and make a sale."

Taite's laughter rolled from her.

Walking to where Mickey stood, she reached out to run her fingertips down his muscle-bound arm. "I may show a little cleavage to my male customers, Mickey. But you know when it comes to closing a sale with the *female* clientele that you most definitely have the advantage."

Taite's smile stretched wider when Mickey gave her his cocky and charming lopsided grin, and he deliberately flexed his bulging muscles underneath her fingertips.

A loud snort sounded from the lobby area.

Taite looked past her office doorway.

The gorgeous man she'd met in the elevator just the night before had paused in mid-step, and his gaze was trained on her exposed cleavage. Lifting his gaze, Taite noted he zeroed in on her fingers still wrapped around Mickey's upper arm. At the man's obvious disgust, she felt a hot flush spread across the tops of her breasts. It didn't stop there. No. Its heat crawled up her neck to cover her face.

Taite jerked her hand down to her side. With arched eyebrows, the man brushed on past, although for a second, his gaze connected with hers.

"Who was that?" Mickey asked. He turned to watch the man's long stride rapidly eat up the distance between her office and their boss's office.

"I don't know," Taite mumbled, her embarrassment raw. A second time now she had met with the stranger's disapproval, it seemed. She and

Mickey both watched their boss jump up from his office chair to extend a hand out to the stranger. Their boss's door was rapidly shut when the man casually took a chair in front of the desk.

With determination, Taite shrugged off her embarrassment and went to sit down behind her own desk. "None of our business, either, I suppose. But, if he wants to buy a house, he's yours."

Mickey laughed. "What? Not going to use your 'Reel in the Sale Outfit' of yours with him."

Taite grimaced. So, Mickey had noticed the man's disapproval of her. "I need to get to work, Mickey. I have a busy day today, and I want my desk cleared of all paperwork before the end of next week. Even though the boss says that the new owner is supposed to be here sometime after next week, I intend to keep my planned days off as scheduled. I'll just meet and greet the new owner when I come back from my vacation after New Year's."

"Don't blame you, Taite," Mickey responded. "You haven't had a vacation this year yet and the year is almost gone. Is your sister going home with you for Christmas?"

"No. Didn't she tell you that she and Dad are on the outs again? You know how money flows through Caite's fingers like sand. Dad put his foot down on her expenses, so she's boycotting him."

Mickey shook his head as he turned back toward his own office, leaving hers.

Making sure her gaze didn't drift to her boss's office, Taite briskly picked up her phone. Pulling out the handwritten list of names and phone numbers she'd written out the night before, she began to make calls to her clients scheduled to tour homes that day. After several completed calls, she looked up when she heard a quiet cough and exclaimed in delight. Standing Taite rushed around her desk to hug the man before her. "Chad! What are you doing here? Did Dad come to town with you?"

Glancing behind her father's long-time friend and out into the office lobby area, Taite's disappointment was keen at her realization that Chad was alone. She should've known her father wouldn't have come to the big city. He hibernated on that farm of his, growing older and more cankersome as the years passed.

"No," Chad replied. "I couldn't talk Blake into coming with me. I even told him I was going to fish an invitation from you to spend the night at your place. He said he'd just see you when you came down for your vacation."

Closing her door, Taite walked over to lean a hip against her desk. She motioned for Chad to sit in the chair before her.

"So, to what do I owe this unexpected pleasure?" she teased. Taite watched the silver-haired man she adored fidget for a moment. She thought he even blushed. Curiously, she watched his actions.

"I've met someone, and I'm going to ask her to marry me," Chad finally stated.

With astonishment, Taite stood up straighter. Chad was a confirmed bachelor, and at sixty-seven years old, why should he suddenly want to get married? She hadn't even known he was seeing anyone. *Did some young gold-digger manage to turn his head?* Taite wondered. Chad, after all, was a very wealthy man.

"How long have you known this woman?" she asked sharply.

"Long enough."

"How long is long enough?"

"Four months."

"Four months! Chad, I don't know about this." Taite leaned forward, her expression sober. "Why haven't you introduced her to me? Who is she, and where does she live?"

Chad laughed. "That is why I wanted to see you, Taite, so I can introduce her to you. We met quite by accident one evening, as I was leaving your place, it so happens. She lives in your condo building and has for the past year.

"I asked her last week to come to your father's for the Christmas holiday weekend. Your father told me he doesn't care whom I invite. You know how he is. He thinks that I'm a foolish old man to want to get married at my age." Chad gave a self-conscious shrug.

Taite studied her father's close friend. Chad was someone she'd always been able to run to as a child when hurt or confused. The story was that he'd breathed life into her when her mother had gone into early labor and had died before help could get to her. Chad was someone Taite loved dearly. *And dare I say he even loves me back as my father should love me?*

At her thought, Taite felt guilty. Her father loved her she was certain. He just wasn't the type to say it or to show it. She couldn't remember when she'd quit running to her father, trying to draw his attention. She just knew that during her childhood, Chad had managed to fill that father-daughter void. Her sister though, Taite reflected with sadness, was still trying to get their father to say that he loved them. Caite's antics as the years passed grew bolder and more desperate, it seemed.

Shaking off her thoughts, Taite met the gaze of the man who watched her. He worried about her opinion of his recent news. She straightened. "I would love for you to stay with me, Chad. Tonight though, I insist that you take me to meet this woman who's managed to capture your heart."

Keeping her concern for Chad's emotional welfare under tight wraps, Taite watched as he rose to his feet.

"You'll like her, Taite. I'm not some foolish old man. I promise."

Laughing, Taite hugged the man she had many times as a child wished was her father. She drew back from their embrace and she asked, "Do you have the key to my condo with you?"

Chad nodded.

"Then just let yourself in, and I'll meet you there when I get off work."

****

Pierce was unable to keep his gaze from drifting toward the woman he'd run into the night before. He felt that same sharp anger of the prior evening again. He watched as she gaily laughed and then embraced the elderly man who stood in her office. It was the same man who had been with her the first time she'd caught his attention.

He hadn't noticed a woman in over two years, and his sudden, intense awareness of this unknown woman and the anger she caused confounded him. *What in the hell is the matter with me?* he wondered as he continued to watch the two from across the open space of the office lobby area.

Not only did he want to punch the older gentleman now exiting her office, he had even wanted to clout muscle-bound boy when he'd noticed her touching him, and he didn't know either one of the men, much less her, so why this intense emotion? He wasn't the type of man who endorsed violence. There was something about the woman that caused his blood to sing, Pierce acknowledged as he watched her and the older gentleman. She was pretty, he would give her that, and built, *hell yes*, but he'd been with women since his wife's death who were just as pretty, and, visually, had just as much to offer. None though had affected him as she did. Not this way.

The only thing he did know for certain was that the attractive woman and her muscle-bound coworker were now two of his employees out of the twelve in this office space. He watched as the woman guardedly glanced his way when she showed her gentleman visitor out the front lobby area. Their gazes connected for a second as she returned to her office. She quickly turned away and shut her office door.

Shifting so that he couldn't see her, Pierce nodded his head at what the man who sat across from him was saying. The older man was someone who he'd developed a strong friendship with during the haggling of buying this business.

"Paul, don't give it a second thought," Pierce stated in response to his friend's obvious worry at the news he'd just imparted. The change in plans wasn't a cause for alarm as far as Pierce was concerned.

"Lacy and I will be fine over the Christmas holidays. Go and be with your daughter and her husband, since they can't fly out this year. My taking up the reins of ownership a few weeks earlier than planned will not inconvenience me in any way."

Pierce watched Paul recline back in his chair, his relief obvious. The gray-haired gentleman who sat before him stated during the purchase of his business that he was more than ready for retirement at the age of sixty-nine. He had also disclosed that his wife's parents resided in Florida, and she wanted to be close to them during their final years, which was another reason he had for selling out.

Paul was a born and bred Texan from Fort Worth, and even after twenty-five years of living in the state of Virginia, he still had a strong Texan accent. Pierce believed the elderly man was proud of that Texas connection so had made sure that the accent hadn't been lost over the years. At Paul's statement that it was time to go and meet his newly acquired staff, Pierce stood. His gaze once again met that of the woman's.

****

Taite pulled her coat from her shoulders as she hung up the phone she'd grabbed upon walking into her office. The day had been hectic and long. She threw her coat over her office chair as she rubbed at the back of her neck. She could feel one of her rare tension headaches coming on. Her last home for the evening had been shown, and now it seemed the new boss wanted to speak with her before she would be able to leave for the day. It was well past six p.m.

Rummaging in her desk, Taite found the container she haphazardly searched for. She and the other staff had all hurried and put together a retirement party for Paul when they'd unexpectedly been introduced to the new owner of the real estate business and been informed that today was Paul's last. Taite's good-byes had been said to her boss before he'd left that morning. His daughter was having a minor surgery he'd said, but he and his wife wanted to be with her when she went into the hospital. They were catching a flight out that very evening.

As she opened the small container she held and then shook it over her open palm, Taite glanced through the glass partitions that separated the different offices from each other, and she watched as the dark-haired man who now sat in her prior boss's chair studied the papers in front of him. Looking back down toward her hand, Taite, with aggravation, realized the bottle she held was empty of pills. Throwing the container into the trash, she risked a glance toward her new boss again. The man had spoken privately to all the staff throughout the day and had just stated he wanted to talk to her, too, before she left for the evening.

Taite wondered if he was about to inform her that her services would no longer be needed. He had dismissed two employees already that day. True, she had to admit they'd been dead weight for quite some time, but it had still cast a pall over the office. It seemed to Taite she'd intentionally been left as the last person for him to meet with. She and her new boss were the only two people still in the office. Given the man's behavior toward her so far, Taite had a strong suspicion he didn't particularly care for her and he was about to let her know of his dislike.

Feeling her temper begin to rise at the injustice of the possibility of being fired, Taite fought to tamp down her emotion. Slowly, she walked toward the man who waited for her. *Now is definitely not the time to lose my cool*, she silently admonished herself when she entered his office and edgily stopped before him. *Tired, I'm just tired. And I have a headache*, Taite soundlessly chanted as she worked to calm her jittery nerves. Just because the man who sat before her appeared to have judged and found her lacking didn't mean that he planned to sack her. She was a good employee and had made a significant number of sales for the business even with the economy down.

"Did you make the sale to the gentleman that warranted the low-cut dress you're wearing?"

Feeling her face flame at the deep, low-voiced question, which she was certain was a putdown and not an actual inquiry, Taite's temper flared.

"As a matter of fact, I did," she snapped unable to stop her outburst.

If she was going to get fired for no reason, she might as well give this arrogant and…and…judging ass one. Defensively, Taite squared her shoulders. *Go ahead*, she thought. *Fire me! And where is your wedding ring?* she wondered wildly. She couldn't remember if he'd worn one the night before.

For several seconds, the man intently studied the pen he held. Slowly, he laid it down to the top of the desk that he sat behind. He then looked up at Taite, his face set.

"Sit," he commanded, and he motioned sharply to the chair behind her.

Taite stiffened at the abrupt tone and action. With a narrowed gaze, she didn't move. "Look if you're going to fire me, then just fire me and be done with it. I don't need a lecture from you on my wardrobe. I realize, for whatever reason, you don't like me." She watched as dark eyebrows rose in that critical, judging way the man seemed to have. Just as his eyebrows had raised the other two times he and she had collided.

"Oh, the hell with it. I quit!" she rashly wailed.

Whirling as her tears threatened, Taite took off for her office. Vaguely she heard the man behind her scramble to his feet. Jerked around unexpectedly by her arm, Taite fell heavily against a solid chest even as she hissed in outrage. Her new boss, his expression almost comical, stumbled backwards when her full weight slammed into him. Taite's legs and his legs became hopelessly entangled as he crashed against the arm of the chair behind him. The chair slid. Valiantly, he struggled to remain upright. Realizing that they both were going to crash to the floor, Taite tensed and grasped a tight hold to the front of his shirt.

He took the brunt of their awkward fall and seemed stunned, unable to move, after a *"whoosh"* of air exploded from his lungs when his back hit the floor.

"Holy shit," he breathed after a moment had passed. "Quit squirming for hell's sake!" he yelled a second later.

Her embarrassment stinging, Taite instantly stopped her awkward attempt to rise from her prone position. She felt her tears threaten to spill once again.

"Damn! Damn! Damn!" she cried unable to control her outburst. She had worked hard these past two years in an attempt to prove to her father that she could make it on her own. Now she'd have to search for another job, which meant she would have to dip into her savings until she found one. Something she didn't want to have to do. Her father would look at her with an expression only he could give. It signified disappointment and made her feel awkward and terrible. The man below her moved.

"Lady, all I wanted to tell you before you went off the deep-end was that I don't expect you to prostitute yourself for a sale. I wasn't planning to fire you, although now, I'm strongly tempted."

"Prostitute!" Taite yelled as she half rose. Her elbows locked into place, she glared down at the man who lay beneath her. "Listen here, mister. I may occasionally don this dress to pull a deal though, but let me assure you, I do not prostitute myself. This would be prostituting!"

Quickly bending, Taite smashed her mouth onto the man's. Her hips fit snug against his and she ground them against him. Somewhere in the back recesses of her mind, Taite noted that she enjoyed the forced kiss and their snug fitting-bodies. She opened her mouth further, experimenting. Her deliberation became centered on the feel of firm lips under her own. Known for her ability to stay cool under pressure, Taite didn't recognize herself or her loss of control, nor was she able to pull back or even stop what she'd started.

With a moan, she grasped a tight hold of the black hair she'd longed to caress the night before. Just as she'd imagined, it was silky soft, and the short curls lapped around her fingers as if they enjoyed her touch.

In a flash, Taite found herself flipped onto her back and the kiss taken over. A hand worked its way up the inside hem of her dress line to begin to pull at her pantyhose top. The man she had attacked groaned hoarsely with need. Taite could feel that need. For a moment she melted and wrapped her arms tightly about his neck, until she remembered. She wrenched her mouth from his.

"Wait," she cried. "Wait, please. I didn't mean...I mean I didn't... Please, don't do this. You're married." At her tortured words, the man above her abruptly stilled, his breathing harsh, loud within the quiet office.

When their gazes met, Taite's eyes watered. She knew her expression held her fear and confusion as he quietly studied her. His hand clenched against the silk of her pantyhose-covered thigh. Slowly, he removed it from beneath her dress. Reaching up, he jerked her arms down from around his neck.

"I think it would be best if you considered yourself fired," he stated before he rolled off her to stand.

Jumping up, Taite avoided looking at the man who stood so rigidly beside her. Quickly, straightening her dress, she scampered from his office. Gathering her coat and purse, she hastened out the front lobby of the building without a backward glance.

****

Pierce watched as the woman he now knew as Taite Carpenter practically sprinted from the empty lobby and out the front office doors of the building he now owned. Reaching down, he jerkily set the chair they'd knocked over back to its rightful place. *What in the hell just happened here?* he wondered in startled confusion. One minute, he'd planned to tell the woman what a good job she'd done over the past two years, and in the next moment, he was rolling on the floor with her like some damned animal. It was her scared plea for him not to complete his actions that had finally made him come to his senses.

Pierce sank down onto the office sofa as his confusion continued to course through him. *Hell; and damnation.* He wasn't so hard up for the feel of a woman that he should have lost control as he had. He brought his forearms up to rest them on his knees and he studied his trembling hands.

What was it about this particular woman that made his insides jump and his blood to sing? When she'd squirmed on top of him, trying to rise from her prone position, he'd become as rock-hard as an inexperienced virgin.

Her *"Reel in the Sale Outfit,"* he'd overheard some of the staff jokily state was what she wore that day, *certainly reeled me in*, he thought with a shaky breath. If she hadn't cried out, he didn't know what he would have done. *Hell, yes, I do*, he thought an instant later. He would have screwed her right there on the office floor.

Chapter 3

When she reached her car, Taite quickly slid behind its steering wheel and then locked the car's doors. Trembling, she laid her forehead against the steering wheel and promptly burst into tears. With horror, she realized that she'd actually bit the man's bottom lip. Baffled as to what in the world had come over her, she cringed in acute embarrassment. She knew she'd been tense and worried all that day while showing her listed homes to her clients, but to act so rashly? It just wasn't like her. The man she'd run from must think her a complete and certifiable nut case.

Jumping when her cell phone rang, Taite quickly wiped at her face. She looked at the front of the phone to see who was calling. Sniffing, she tried to gain some measure of control.

"Chad?" she questioned when she finally answered the phone.

"Taite, honey, listen. I'm not going to be waiting for you when you get home. I'm over at Emma's right now. The man that she babysits for has called and asked if she could watch the baby for a couple more hours. Of course, she told him no problem, feels sorry for him. It's a long story. I'll tell you all about it when I get home."

"Geez, Chad, she's babysitting. Are you dating a high schooler?" At the deathly silence on the other end, Taite knew her smart-aleck comment had stunned him. "I'm sorry," she quickly amended. "I didn't mean that. I've just had a very bad day, and I'm all out of sorts. I promise, I didn't mean that."

"We'll talk later," Chad responded before he abruptly hung up.

Taite grimaced. Not only had she lost her *freaking* mind, but now she'd hurt the one person who'd always stood beside her. Starting her car, she punched the number for her sister on the cell phone she still held. "Can you meet me at the gym in about thirty minutes?"

****

Changing their clothes in the gym's locker room, Caite howled with laughter when Taite informed her as to what had happened that evening. With embarrassment, Taite avoided the curious glances of the two women who came out of the gym's sauna and walked into its shower area.

"I don't know why I expected sympathy from you," she exclaimed angrily. "Anytime something horrendous happens to me, you seem to think it's funny. With us being identical twins, all the articles written say that you should feel some of what I'm feeling."

Taite watched her twin quickly sober. Caite frowned heavily at her.

"Bullshit on all the articles written! You and I both know that we don't feel anything the other feels." With those harsh words ringing, her sister flounced away.

Taite sank onto the slatted, wooden bench that was behind her. She waited for her anger to subside. Why had she even thought to confide in Caite? It seemed that her sister always had to compete with her, and when she stumbled, it only amused Caite. Standing, Taite decided to forget her planned workout and to forget Caite. She needed to go home and to hibernate for a while, decide what to do now for a job.

****

"What do you mean, you got fired today?"

"Just what I said. I got fired. Actually, I got fired for assaulting my new boss."

Taite fidgeted with her embarrassment felt when Chad looked at her with a dumbfounded expression on his face. The fork full of food he'd just raised stuck in midair never making it to his mouth. Taite guessed she shouldn't have blurted out her news quite so bluntly. However, they'd both had a lot to share that evening, and really, she just didn't know how else to bring up the subject of what had happened to her that day.

When Chad brought Emma over to meet her after she had arrived home, she'd found that she liked the older lady immensely. The infant girl Emma was babysitting that evening was an adorable child and one who'd instantly wanted Taite to hold her when she'd met them at the door. Laughing, Taite had let the child pull at her hair as Chad introduced his Emma to her. And Emma had agreed to Chad's proposal of marriage. She was a handsome woman who fit Chad perfectly. *They looked good together,* Taite thought, recalling how striking they'd appeared when Chad, standing next to Emma, had introduced her. Chad with his silver hair was always dignified looking and dressed upscale. Emma's hair had been cut stylishly short and colored dark. Taite could tell that she liked to stay well-dressed just as Chad did.

It seemed that Emma was a retired grade-school teacher who lived with her nephew, and who babysat for people within the condominiums. She stated that she babysat because she loved children, but had never had any of her own as she'd never married. She was a lively woman who seemed to have a great sense of humor.

Taite had echoed Chad's wish, when Emma had risen to leave, for her to come with him to her father's estate for the Christmas holidays. Taite knew that Chad wanted Emma to have a chance to get to know her father and for her to meet his two spinster sisters before they married. His two sisters could be a riot, and you knew where you stood with them. If they didn't like you, you darn sure knew it.

Coming out of her thoughts, Taite smiled tightly at the man who continued to stare at her in his confusion. She and Chad had prepared their supper together after Emma and the child had left. Taite leaned toward Chad. "Let's finish eating our meal, and then we can go into the living room and I'll tell you all about my horrendous day."

****

Pierce watched Taite walk past him. She stepped up on a treadmill not more than six feet across from him. He let the weights he'd lifted click back onto their resting place as he studied her. In confusion, he watched as she nonchalantly met his gaze. She smiled at him as if nothing had happened between them not more than an hour prior.

Strangely, his blood didn't sing as it had before. He guessed their violent encounter at the office had cured him of whatever had afflicted him. Standing, Pierce decided to finish his workout by swimming laps in the gym's pool. *Hell*, if the woman could act like nothing had happened between them, then so could he, although he didn't want to stay around and test the situation.

Diving into the heated pool, Pierce began his standard fifty laps, something he tried to incorporate within his workout at least twice a week. Someone else dove into the pool and began to pace their swimming strokes to his rhythm. Pierce didn't bother to acknowledge the individual. The person who swam along beside him suddenly stopped and with a light, tinkling laugh, began to tread water.

"I thought I could stay up with you."

Abruptly, Pierce stopped swimming. His feet touched the bottom of the pool as his surprise rippled through him. Curiously, he turned toward the woman who had spoken. She laughed as if suddenly nervous. "Hey, I just thought I'd try to strike up a conversation. You seemed interested in me earlier."

"I don't know what game you think you're playing at, Taite. But I want no part of it. I am sorry over what occurred between us earlier at the office. However, don't now act as if nothing happened. It won't fly with me." At his words, Taite looked queerly at him for a moment. She turned and treaded water to the pool steps. With another curious glance back in his direction, she left the poolside.

Shaking his head, Pierce considered that he was lucky to be rid of her. The woman must have some serious emotional problems.

****

Sprinting toward the elevator doors in his condominium, Pierce just managed to squeeze through them before they closed. *Shit, I'm freezing,* he thought. Going out into the night air with wet hair hadn't been a good idea. The Christmas displays and soft, holiday music broadcasted within the condominium lobby welcomed home all its owners who lived there.

"Oh...no..."

Turning at the anguish-filled words, Pierce only at that moment became aware of the lone woman who stood huddled against the far wall of the elevator. His blood began to sing in sexual awareness. "Shit!" he exclaimed. His awareness of Taite was back in full force. The tan cocker spaniel that sat quietly at her feet watched him. Pierce's anger, irrationally, rose higher.

Taite turned so she didn't face him, her face white.

"Listen, I'm sorry for that. But, lady, you need help."

"I am going to be sick. I am really going to be sick."

Pierce watched Taite clamp a slender hand over her mouth. Her eyes wide, she frantically motioned for him to move from in front of the elevator doors when they opened. Shoving past him, she ran full blast down the lit hallway and disappeared into her private condo.

Glancing down at the dog who still sat at his feet, Pierce sighed in irritation.

"I guess I better take you home, boy. On the other hand, I ought to leave you right here. I should just go away and forget about you and your crazy owner."

At the dog's whine, Pierce impatiently snatched up its leash and walked toward the condo its owner had disappeared into. When he reached Taite's door, he stood unable to move. The dog beside him whined as it looked up at him. It seemed that the mutt asked, *"Why are we standing out here when my mistress is inside?"*

"Well, hell, I don't exactly know what to do," Pierce irritably stated down at the dog and then he flinched with embarrassment. Quickly, he glanced up and around hoping no one had heard him talking to the animal.

Reaching out and giving a slight twist of his wrist, Pierce turned

Taite's doorknob. Her door swung inward, unlocked.

"Taite," Pierce softly called out as he stepped past her doorway and into her home. Tempted to turn and leave, now that he'd returned the forgotten dog, he paused. If the truth were known, he was actually worried about the woman who'd just fled from him. *Do I really want to get involved, though?* Pierce wondered as he glanced into her living room beyond the pristine, white-tiled entryway that he stood within. It was a nice room, her living room.

Taite Carpenter was apparently an avid reader. The large bookshelf against the far wall of her living room was chock full of books. There were also scattered pictures of who Pierce assumed must be family members. There were several pictures of her as well. *Seems a little odd,* he thought, someone having pictures of just themselves sitting around, usually there was always someone else in the photos when personal pictures were displayed in a home.

"Taite," Pierce called out again.

Suddenly, she came from the hallway straight across from him. She stopped short, and her eyes grew wide with fear as she stared at him. It was obvious that she hadn't realized he'd followed her into her home.

"Get out!" she hoarsely snapped. Her hand trembled as she pointed a finger toward the door behind him.

Pierce cautiously stretched out a hand trying to show that he wasn't a threat. "Listen, I'm not going to hurt you. I just brought your dog to you. You left him on the elevator. I am sorry for my behavior at the gym earlier, but lady, you talking to me and acting as if nothing happened between us this evening jarred me."

"It was Caite you talked to."

Straining to hear the low-voiced words, Pierce let his gaze follow Taite's arm as, with obvious impatience, she motioned to the pictures of herself on the bookshelf.

"My twin, you must have met my identical twin. I left the gym early tonight. I didn't work out. I most certainly didn't know you were there, nor would I have spoken to you if I did."

In astonishment, Pierce looked closely at the woman who stood before him and then at the pictures she pointed to. That explained the whole bizarre situation at the fitness center and why his blood was singing now in awareness, but not before. It hadn't been the same woman. The only observable difference in the twins that Pierce could determine were the clothes they had donned for the evening.

The twin I mistook her for had on a black workout suit. The one in front of him wore a black and white workout suit. Both women had identical high cheekbones and thick, copper-colored hair, and both were slender built, but with curved hips that let you know they were women.

Taite spoke, "I'm sorry for my actions today. I don't know what came over me. I...I...don't normally go around forcing myself on strange or married men."

Pierce laughed. Although her apology didn't warrant his laughter, he couldn't hold it back. It roared from him.

Taite glared at him as her anger and embarrassment obviously soared. He laughed harder. When her eyes filled with tears and spilled over, Pierce's laughter abruptly stopped. "Sorry. I shouldn't have laughed. This whole damn day has just been too bizarre."

"I am going to be sick again." Whirling, Taite took off. This time Pierce quickly followed her. When her heaving stopped, he pressed a wet hand towel to her face that he'd found and dampened at the sink. He flushed the stool.

"Please leave," she mumbled into the cloth she kept to her face.

He didn't move.

She jerked the cloth down and she glared at him. She waved her hand with a vague motion as if to shoo him away.

"If what happened between us is the cause for your stomach upset, I'm going to stay here until I know you're going to be okay," he stated.

Taite groaned with clear embarrassment as she turned to avoid his gaze. She rinsed her mouth and then spit and then set the cup she held aside. Slowly, she wiped at her mouth with a dry hand towel as if she deliberated what to say to him. Her eyes refused to meet his.

"It's not just what happened between us today, although that is horribly embarrassing in itself and enough to make me sick, but I have a tension headache, and I am out of my pills, and well...well...it's...it's just everything."

Her hand waved in the air again.

Pierce wondered how he could be attracted to a woman who'd just been sick in front of him. "If it will ease your embarrassment, from the first moment I saw you, I wondered what it would be like to kiss you."

****

At the husky, low-voiced comment, Taite jerked her gaze upward to meet the gaze of the man before her. A coffee-colored stare was returned. Hastily, she took a step back. She was alone in her bathroom with a stranger.

What, exactly, do I know about this man? she thought with renewed panic. The only thing she did know for certain was that his name was Pierce Holden and that he owned her prior boss's business and—and that when she looked at him, she lost all her common sense.

Nervously, Taite dropped her gaze. She fidgeted with the hand towel she still held. *Could it be used for protection against assault?*

"I don't even know you. Never, ever, have I done what I did today. I don't want you to think I'm the type that has casual sex."

"Neither do I," the man before her responded.

When Taite looked up at him, he added, "Have casual sex."

She slid her gaze away.

Suddenly, he stuck out a large hand making her jump, and Taite swung an anxious gaze back up to meet with his.

"Hello, Taite. I am a widower with a two-year-old child. I loved my wife and believed my life was over when she died. I still miss her."

Taite watched as the man before her shifted when she didn't reach out to shake his hand.

"When I saw you the first time in the lobby of this condominium, it was your hair color that drew my attention. I've always been a sucker for thick, luscious, coppery-colored hair."

With a grin given toward her, his gaze flitted over her hair before it came back to rest on her face. "I would be pleased if you would give me a chance to get to know the real you and you the real me, Taite."

Slowly, Taite laid her palm within his still extended hand. Her gaze searched his as his lean fingers clasped firmly around hers. A jolt of awareness hit her. *He wants to get to know the real me*, she thought in bemusement.

"I...I..." she stammered in bewilderment.

"Just say, yes. Yes, to us starting over."

"Yes."

"Good. I expect you for dinner tomorrow night around six at my home, condo number ten, third floor. I'll cook. If it will make you more comfortable, bring a friend."

Taite watched Pierce give her a wide, handsome smile. He then dropped the hand that he held and walked from her bathroom, and out her front door without a backward glance.

In confusion, Taite locked the front door behind him. She looked toward the closed guest bedroom door where Chad slept just beyond it. It didn't surprise Taite that he hadn't woken. Chad always took a sleep aid when in the city. What did surprise her, was that she just realized, everything that had been said between her and the man who'd left her home had been quietly stated. As Taite walked to her bedroom, her bewilderment as to what had just occurred made her head spin.

Sexy quietly followed at her heels, until Taite realized what he was about. Turning, she sternly ordered him back to his sleeping mat. Her pet knew he was absolutely not allowed to sleep with her, although he tried.

****

The next morning around midday, Taite called Emma and invited her to come over before Chad had to begin his trip back home. As before, the child Emma babysat wanted Taite to hold her as soon as she opened her door.

"Hello, sweetie," Taite cooed. She eased small fingers from her hair that were happily being twisted through the loose strands. Taite looked at Emma. "I've fixed us sandwiches for lunch, Emma. Go on into the kitchen. Chad is already in there setting the table for me."

Taite smiled at the cherub-faced child she held as she followed Emma. "I guess I'll just have to hold you in my lap, won't I, sweetie, since I don't have a chair for you."

Emma glanced over at Taite as she sat down across from her. Taite reached for a sandwich to cut it in half. She then gave one of the halves to the child she held.

"Lacy has taken quite a liking to you, Taite," Emma commented.

"She is adorable."

"When Chad called this morning, he told me that you got fired from your job yesterday."

Taite choked on her bite of sandwich at the unexpected statement from the woman she'd only met the night before.

Chad sputtered for a moment until Emma laid a blue-veined hand on his arm. She looked at Taite, and her eyes twinkled as if she knew an interesting story was to be heard. "He didn't give me the details, although as nosy as I am, I'm dying to hear what happened. He said something about you and a new boss ending up on an office floor."

Emma's laughter erupted as Taite retold how she and her new boss had landed up on his office floor with her straddled, hiked dress and all, on top of the man. Taite left out Pierce's response when she'd kissed him. She only stated that after she had forced her kiss on him, he'd told her she was fired.

"I've been invited to his home for dinner tonight."

Chad abruptly pushed his chair back from the table to gaze at Taite in surprise.

"How did you come to be invited to dinner?" Emma asked when her laughter subsided. She patted Chad on the knee as if to calm him.

Taite watched Chad look from her to Emma. He was obviously confused over the invite and unable to find any humor in the situation.

"I don't know if Chad has told you that I have an identical twin. And when I say identical, I mean exact. She works out with me at the local fitness center. When Chad called yesterday and told me that you were going to have to babysit later than you had thought, I called Caite and we met at the center. Well, lo and behold, who turns up? You guessed it."

Taite raised her arm to wave her hand in the air. "The new boss who'd just fired me and he mistook Caite for me."

Taite detailed their meeting in the elevator afterward and the subsequent happenings that followed.

"I don't see why this strikes you as funny, Emma," Chad retorted stiffly when Taite finished telling her story. "I don't like that this man came into her home last night after everything that happened between them, and I wasn't aware he was here until this moment. You haven't even told us his name, Taite."

"Pierce Holden," Taite responded, understanding Chad's concern. She herself didn't know this man who'd so abruptly disrupted her life. But she wanted to. Oh, yes, she most definitely wanted to. If you had asked her yesterday morning what was most important to her, her response would have been her job and only her job. Now she wasn't so sure.

Her skills at her chosen profession seemed to impress her father. He had smiled when she'd told him of the two sales she'd made that month. He'd also smiled over the fact that most of the earnings from those sales had quickly been put into her savings account, although he hadn't issued any comment, had just nodded his head, as if to say *good girl*.

With excitement, Emma swiveled toward Chad. "Pierce Holden—he's Lacy's father! Oh, Chad, you don't have to worry about him. He is a wonderful man."

Emma turned back toward Taite. "I'm sure he is already planning to give you your job back."

With obvious eagerness, she began to tell Taite and Chad all about the daddy whose little girl she cared for.

It seemed that Pierce's wife of two years had been killed in an automobile accident when Lacy was just a newborn. The baby had been at home when the accident had happened. His late wife's parents and his own were now both deceased. Pierce had inherited his parents' estate as well as his in-laws, both he and his wife the only children to elderly parents.

He was a semi-wealthy man who had a motherless child to raise and no one to turn to but Emma, the aunt of a childhood buddy. Apparently, he and his family had always lived in the state of Virginia and had real estate businesses across the state. Needing a change of scenery and feeling restless, he had decided to buy Taite's prior boss's business.

"He felt that he could build it up, saw potential in the flagging business," Emma stated with obvious pride in Pierce's ability to do just that.

Taite smiled at Emma's enthusiastic history-telling of the man she had attacked. The same man who'd fired her, and then followed her uninvited into her home, and who had asked her to meet him for dinner at his home that evening. He was a saint as far as Emma was concerned. Taite shifted and she pulled Lacy's roving fingers from her hair. Studying the little girl's face, she saw Pierce's eyes gazing back at her. Taite's heart did a funny little flip.

Pierce wasn't a saint. Taite knew that. He was someone though, that she would like to get to know better. For some reason he was able to break down the barrier toward others that she always kept erected. A barrier that protected her from emotional hurt.

Chapter 4

Nervously, Taite smoothed a hand down her dress front one more time before she reached out to push the doorbell to Pierce's condo. Chad had called and spoken to Pierce before he would let her keep the date. The men had talked for at least ten minutes before Chad hung up the phone. He didn't go into the details of what had been said on the other end, only that Pierce had seemed a likeable fellow.

Taite jerked her hand down from the doorbell when the door before her suddenly opened.

"Hello," she stammered.

"Hello."

Taite looked from the handsome man that smiled appreciatively at her to the child he held within his arms. The baby's cherub face split into a familiar grin as she held her arms out to Taite to be held.

"T. T.," the child squealed.

Taite looked to her father for his approval of her taking the child from his arms.

"Only if you want to," he stated quietly. "At two years old, she can walk. She just likes to be held."

Taite reached for the baby. Soft arms were wrapped about her neck as Lacy nuzzled against her when she followed Pierce into his living room. The innocence of the child eased Taite's uncomfortable need to apologize again for her behavior in the office.

"Come on into the kitchen. I'm just finishing up. I hope you like spaghetti. It's mine and Lacy's favorite meal," Pierce looked at her as he spoke.

"It's my favorite meal, too. Can I help make a salad or anything?"

"Everything's already done. Just take a seat. Put Lacy in her highchair."

Bending down, Taite eased the child from her arms and onto the seat of the highchair that'd been pushed up to the edge of the kitchen table. Smiling at the baby, she sat down beside her. She then watched as Pierce efficiently finished setting the table before he sat down across from her. He made a motion to fill her plate. Taite lifted it to him.

"So, my babysitter and this Chad fellow who grilled me over the phone are getting married," Pierce stated as he filled the plate and handed it back to her.

Nodding, Taite gave a slight laugh as she picked up her fork. "I'm sorry, but I am so nervous that I don't know what to say to you. After everything that occurred between us yesterday, it seems extremely odd that we are now sitting here trying to get to know each other."

Pierce met her gaze before he turned to begin to cut up a small scoop of spaghetti for his daughter. Taite watched with surprise when instead of leaving the meal on the plate and setting the plate before the child, he scraped the spaghetti onto the highchair's attached flat front. The child happily dug her small fingers into the pile of food.

In question, Taite looked up at the man across from her. Pierce smiled and shrugged his broad shoulders. "She likes it that way.

"Now," he stated as he reached across the table to grasp Taite's fingers. "Do you think I'm not nervous? We got off to a bad start, you and I, but I want to know you. Can we just agree to forget yesterday and start over?"

Taite nodded. Pierce let go of her hand and picked up his fork.

"I called Paul last night and asked him about you."

Taite laid her fork down. "And what did my boss say about me?"

"Prior boss."

"Okay, what did my prior boss say about me?"

"Nothing but good things, in fact, he sang your praises for half an hour, told me that if I didn't hire you back, I was a fool."

Taite swallowed as she felt her tears threaten. Was Pierce going to give her another chance? And why with that thought was her relief so great? Relief that she wouldn't have to inform her father she was without a job.

In confusion, Taite blinked as she stared down at her plate. At twenty-six years of age, why did pleasing her father still mean so much to her?

"What of it, Taite? Will you come back to work for me?"

Her emotions back under control, Taite looked up to meet Pierce's direct gaze. She smiled. "I would be pleased to come back and work for you. Thank you."

****

Taite smiled at Mickey when ten days later, he dropped a muscled shoulder against her office doorframe. A habit of his that was somehow endearing to her. Their Thursday evening workday was drawing to a close.

"Hey," she stated softly.

Mickey frowned at her.

"Your sister tells me that she's decided to go home for Christmas after all."

Nodding, Taite filed away the last of her paperwork. The days had flown by. Tomorrow was Friday—Christmas morning, and Pierce had agreed to let her keep her vacation plans that had been scheduled. Tomorrow morning, she would be heading home.

"Thought she was going to spend it with me," Mickey mumbled.

Mickey and Caite were constantly an on-again, off-again couple. Personally, Taite thought that Caite loved to keep Mickey guessing as to her feelings for him. Mickey was a needy individual. Taite knew she herself wouldn't have been able to stand his jealousy of any and all that she surrounded herself with. Caite, though, seemed to enjoy his jealous fits, even encouraged them.

Abruptly, Mickey straightened and then smiled that crooked smile that had attracted Taite to him the first time he and she had met. Raking his fingers though jet-black hair, he winked good-naturedly.

"It's time to go home. I guess I better give Caite her Christmas present tonight. Drive careful, Taite. I'll see you when you get back."

Smiling at Mickey's sudden shift of mood, Taite watched as he quickly shut down his computer. He gave her a jaunty wave before he left the building.

With Mickey's disappearance, Taite let her gaze drift across the empty office cubicles to where Pierce still sat behind his desk. The office building was empty now except for them two. She watched as he placed his phone on its base and then lifted his arms. Placing his hands behind his head, he leaned back in his chair deep in thought.

Suddenly shifting, he turned to meet her gaze. Taite's heart skipped a beat when he directed a slow smile her way. Had it only been Monday of the prior week that she and he had met and collided? They had spent every evening together since.

Taite was suspicious she'd let her feelings for Lacy's father develop way beyond what he wanted. Pierce, she knew, still deeply loved and missed his late wife. It seemed as if he looked at her as more of a friend. She was someone to bounce his questions off of in his concern as to whether he was raising Lacy right.

That first evening together had been jarring when she'd walked into his living room after their meal and came face-to-face with the picture of his beautiful wife. Warily, Taite had wondered if Pierce saw his wife in her somehow. Then she'd shaken off her concern. She and the woman in the picture might have the same color of hair, but they didn't look anything alike.

Sighing, Taite wondered what Pierce and Lacy were going to do over the holidays. With it being Thursday evening, tonight would be the last night she would have with them until she returned from her vacation. Watching Pierce, Taite straightened when he rose to walk toward her. Her breath caught at his long-legged loose stride. *Damn, he's gorgeous.*

Unable to move, Taite watched as he entered her office, and, with what seemed to be a determined stride, walked around to the back of her desk to stand next to her. He lowered his hand toward her.

In surprise at his action, Taite laid her palm within his extended one. Closing his fingers around hers, he firmly drew her up from her chair.

"I am going to kiss you," he murmured, surprising Taite even further.

When their lips connected, it felt right, as if she and this man were made for each other. He was her other half and with him, she was whole. When Pierce drew her closer to him at her sigh, Taite didn't resist. Instead, she reached up to wrap her arms around his neck letting her fingers trail through the hair at his nape as she'd longed to do all week. Dreamily, she glided back to earth when Pierce eased her from him.

"I've wanted to do that all day. No, I take that back. Not just today. I have wanted that for the past ten days," Pierce stated, his voice husky.

Tongue-tied, Taite could only inch closer to the warm body pressed against hers. Pierce's hands tightened on her hips at her movement.

"That was Emma on the phone. She wants to keep Lacy tonight. She says she's bought her a Christmas present and wants Lacy to open it. I told her that it would be okay with me." Pierce smiled at Taite. He reached up to play with a strand of her hair before he lightly tugged on it. "How would you like to go out on a real date with me? With no baby to watch tonight, we can go out and eat like real grownups."

"I would like that."

"Let's shut the office down and go home then. I'll come by at seven to pick you up. How does that sound? Is two hours enough?"

"More than enough," Taite replied. Pierce stepped back and with one last glance given toward her lips, he turned and left her office. Taite quickly shut down her computer. Excitedly she picked up her coat and purse. She gave Pierce a short wave as she left the office.

Chapter 5

With a certain shyness that she was unused to, Taite looked over the dinner table to the man who sat across from her. *Could I have actually fallen in love within just a few short days with this man?* she wondered in helpless confusion.

With a slight tremor to her fingers, Taite reached out to pick up her wine glass. She'd had her fair share of romances, but none of the men she'd been involved with had ever made her feel as she did now. What was it about this particular man that caused her heart to beat just a little faster every time he happened to glance her way? What was it about him that made her want to open up to him, to allow him access to her heart when no one else had been allowed to enter that private arena?

Pierce suddenly seemed arrested by whatever was behind her when their waitress walked away. Glancing over her shoulder, Taite came face to face with her twin.

"Taite! How unexpected. Mickey and I spotted you two when we started to leave."

Her sister smiled prettily at Pierce. The low-cut black dress that she wore looked good on her. Pierce sat back to place an arm over the back of the chair to the right of him. He glanced from her sister to her and then back to Caite.

He seems to be comparing us, Taite thought.

"Hello, Caite, Mickey," Pierce drawled in his quiet way.

Caite laughed, the sound light and sexy. Taite noticed that several men who sat close by swiveled to look her sister's way.

"Do you mind if we sit and visit, Pierce?" her sister asked. "When I spotted Taite, I told Mickey that I wanted to come over and see what time she was leaving for Daddy's tomorrow."

Pierce motioned for them to sit. Taite felt her muscles tighten when Caite automatically took the chair closest to Pierce. *What is Caite up to now?*

Not only had her sister suddenly decided that she wanted to come home for Christmas, it seemed she was also determined to flirt with Pierce, had in fact openly flirted with him the night before in Taite's home. Taite glanced at Mickey to gauge his reaction. His eyes were narrowed as he studied the two.

Laying a hand on Pierce's arm, Caite smiled charmingly up at him. "At work today, I started thinking about our mix-up at the gym and died laughing. My boss made me tell her what it was I found so funny. I had to tell her the entire story of what happened at your office the first time you and Taite met and then what happened at the gym between us. My boss thought the entire situation hilarious. She even told her boss the story."

Eyes twinkling, Caite gave Pierce a wide smile as if she and he shared a mutual amusement.

With rising anger, Taite glanced at Mickey again. Caite hadn't waited even a day to tell Mickey what had happened between her and Pierce. Mickey had promised her, though, that no one in the office would hear about the incident from him.

Pierce's smile was slightly off center when Taite's gaze met his. Taite wondered if he was attracted to her sister. His gaze held hers for a moment, before he frowned, breaking their eye contact. He looked at Caite.

"As I told you last night at your sister's, I would gladly be the first to tell others that Taite literally knocked me off my feet that first day in my office, but as you can see, it embarrasses her to be reminded of it. I believe, Caite, you said that you wanted to ask your sister what time she was leaving for your father's tomorrow?"

Turning fully toward Taite at Pierce's disapproval, Caite's hand slid from his arm.

"Mickey has decided to come home with me tomorrow and stay the weekend at the farm. So, I'll be riding up with him. I just wanted to let you know the change of plans and to make sure you would be at the farm when we arrive. You know how I need you as a buffer between me and the old man."

"I probably won't arrive until around noon." Taite's answer was short. Her anger at her sister seemed lost on Caite though, as she and Mickey stood.

"We will see you tomorrow afternoon then," Caite stated as she patted Taite on the shoulder. She smiled at Pierce before she turned away.

Taite studied her sister's backside. Caite, self-assured as usual, sashayed out of the restaurant, drawing all eyes of the male customers. With a small sigh, Taite brushed off her anger. Caite was Caite. She probably hadn't even realized that she was coming across as flirting with Pierce.

****

Pierce silently tipped his wine glass to his mouth as he watched the woman across from him. *What is it about her that affects me and yet an exact copy as the one leaving leaves me cold?* Who would have thought that the little spitfire across from him could have him—a man who'd just turned thirty and a widower to boot—panting as if a schoolboy in his first throes of a crush?

The long-time hurt of his wife's passing had faded these past two weeks, Pierce realized with a start. He even had the oddest sensation that his wife approved of Taite. That she wanted him to move on with his life. This budding relationship with Taite was right. It was right for him and for his daughter in every way.

Pierce laid his hand over Taite's, drawing her attention back to their table and away from her sister. When she raised shuttered brown eyes to his, he smiled. There seemed to be a long-standing tension between the two sisters. Taite hadn't said as much, but it was easy to pick up that the two weren't close. It seemed odd. He would have thought that identical twins would have had a special bond.

"What do you want to do after our meal? We could go check out what movies are showing."

Taite shrugged a slender shoulder. Her action drew his gaze to the tops of satiny breasts above the low-cut blouse she wore.

"Why don't we just go back to my place?" she stated. "I still need to pack, and I have a Christmas gift that I want to give to you for Lacy. Sorry, but it will have to be put together."

When Taite's smile suddenly stretched wide and her eyes glowed with mischievousness, Pierce felt a sharp jolt of desire.

"What's this? I thought I told you last night that I hated those types of gifts."

Taite's laughter pealed at his mock frown and grimace.

Several heads turned at the light sound. The men's gazes lingered on the woman who leaned mischievously against the table toward him.

"Too bad. When I came across her present during my lunch hour today, I just knew she had to have it."

Letting his mock frown fade, Pierce leaned back into his chair, and with a smile directed her way, he asked, "Do you want dessert? No. Then I'm ready to leave if you are?"

When Taite pushed back her chair, he stood.

With a hand to the small of her back, Pierce noted the elderly gentleman who sat alone. The gentleman gave him a thumbs-up, his eyes scanning down over Taite's cascading hair as they walked by. Pierce could well understand the man's admiring glance. Taite's hair was thick and lush and the color vibrant.

Tonight, he was going to push their relationship to the next level. He had made that decision earlier that evening. Life was too short to stand back and see where the chips might fall. He physically wanted Taite, and he damn well was going to let her know it.

****

When Pierce's thumb rubbed once again across the inside of her wrist as they stepped into the elevator, Taite glanced at him. Her hand lay within his much larger one. Taite didn't know when she and Pierce had clasped hands, but he'd definitely found a previously unknown erogenous zone on her person. Restlessly, she moved closer to him as his thumb slowly moved across the sensitized skin yet again. Mentally, Taite went over the contents in her nightstand. *Yes*, she thought, *yes, there are condoms in there.*

She wasn't fast and loose by any means, but in this day and age, it was wise to be safe, hence condoms. Would the man by her side understand? Or would he wonder about her standards?

Taite shifted slightly away from Pierce at her thoughts. He smiled down at her, and then pulled her back up against him. Breaking their clasped hands, he wrapped an arm around her shoulders. His fingers played with her hair.

Taite was unquestionably getting the vibe that Pierce wanted more from her than their usual chaste goodnight kiss. She was a willing partner to that vibe.

"Would you like to come in for a drink or a cup of coffee?" she asked when the second-floor light on the elevator panel flashed.

The elevator doors slid open.

Pierce didn't say anything.

"I think you know that I'm asking you in for more than a drink, don't you?" Taite stated quietly. She hoped she hadn't been wrong in the signals he was sending. Maybe she had read more into his actions than was meant.

Tilting her chin, Pierce bent forward to softly kiss her lips. A hand slid within her loose, unbuttoned coat to mold against the underside of a breast. Slowly, she was backed up against the elevator wall, and the ball of his thumb moved across her hardened nipple.

"If you weren't asking for more, then I was going to be one disappointed male," he huskily said.

When he captured her lips once again with his, Taite moaned in surrender. Wrapping her arms around his waist, she lost track of time and space. Her world was in the here and now.

Abruptly, Pierce pulled back. "You make me weak, Taite. Your condo...let's go."

When Taite opened the door to her home, Sexy bounded down the entryway toward her. Pierce stepped out from behind her and the dog abruptly slid to a stop to sit back on his haunches. His gaze shifted between the two of them.

It was the strangest sensation, but Taite felt as if Sexy looked at her in approval before he turned and went back toward the kitchen, where he slept.

In an undertone, Pierce graveled, "You have one smart dog there. Now," he stated as he leaned forward to help Taite remove her coat even as he slipped his own from his shoulders. "I don't want a drink, coffee or otherwise, but I do want you. Call me brash, uncouth, whatever, but, lady, I'm not waiting a moment longer."

Taite gulped at the straightforward comment and lost her grip on her coat. It fell to the floor along with Pierce's.

One moment she was standing in her home's entryway, and the next, Taite found herself lying naked across her bed. In startled surprise, she looked up at the man who hovered over her. How had he accomplished undressing her without her even being aware of it? *And he kept our mouths fused the whole time,* Taite acknowledged as she sighed with pleasure. She shivered in delicious abandonment when Pierce's bare skin touched hers as he climbed on top of the bed alongside her.

Gasping at the sensations that rippled through her, Taite eagerly reached to learn the texture of his body. When he groaned at her touch, she drew closer to him, her breathing ragged. Her hands were everywhere and she couldn't seem to stop their movement. With a sudden swiftness that surprised her, Pierce snatched up her wandering hands.

Holding them within his large grasp, he moved his mouth tenderly across one hardened nipple, then to the next one.

"Your touch is going to send me over the edge," he rasped when he met her bewildered gaze.

"Taite...ah...Taite," he stated softly as his eyes held hers. "What is this strange hold you have over me? Just a touch from you and I go wild."

"Let me touch you, Pierce. I want you to go wild. When I first met you in the elevator and you mentioned having a child, I felt almost devastated at the belief that you were married."

Taite felt Pierce tense for a moment before he relaxed against her again. With concern, Taite wondered if her mention of his marriage had caused his reaction. Her worry was forgotten when his mouth found hers again. He released his hold of her hands. She didn't lift them.

"Touch me, Taite," he whispered a moment later against her lips. "Touch me, please."

Eagerly, Taite slid her fingers across Pierce's broad back and then down his arms. His arm muscles rippled at her touch. His breath drew in sharply when she ducked her head to run her tongue across one of his nipples.

Abruptly, he jerked her upright, and roughly covered her mouth with his. He shifted to raise her hand to kiss the soft skin on the inside of her wrist. His touch at that sensitized area caused heat to leap through her body, melting her.

****

Pierce felt his hard-earned control slip at Taite's sharp cry of pleasure at his simple gesture of kissing the inside area of her wrist. Her second cry he captured within his mouth even as a responding growl vibrated through him. He slid smoothly into her warmth and then readily delved deeper when she lunged upward to meet his action. Dimly, he heard Taite huskily murmur that it seemed he had a strange hold over her, too. Goosebumps rose on Pierce's arms as he lost control at the same time, she cried out her pleasure.

Gradually, his intellect returned, and he became aware of the woman who lay quietly beneath him. Tenderly, Pierce kissed Taite's forehead and then lay down alongside her. He felt her reach for him, and he laced his fingers with hers.

"What is this rush of emotion that you and I have for each other?" he questioned. His breathing labored.

Taite rolled against him and loosened their clasped hands. Propping herself up on an elbow, she reached out with a slender forefinger to trace the outline of his eyebrows. She continued the motion down the side of his face to his chin. Her look was thoughtful and serious.

"I think that what I have is love at first sight."

Pierce watched as after her husky words, she seemed uncertain and shy at what she'd just stated. She directed a half smile toward him before she ducked her head to hide her gaze from his.

With a hand to her chin, he raised it so that their gazes locked. "I don't know about love, honey," he responded. "But I do know that my feelings for you have me spinning. I haven't been able to think straight since the first moment I laid eyes on you."

Her words low, she responded, "I've never believed in love at first sight. I can't believe that I even said that to you just now."

Pierce didn't reply as Taite watched him.

"Where do we go from here, Pierce?" she asked as if unable to stop herself. Her question held such a lost and confused note that Pierce felt his heart constrict in response. Kissing her forehead, he silently urged her to lie against his chest.

Running his fingers down through the silky strands of her hair, he thought about his rolling emotions for the woman in his arms. He had loved his wife. What he felt for Taite was different, more lustful. *Is it love?* he wondered. He didn't know.

"Let's just take it slow, sweetheart. And we will see where this thing between us leads, hmm…?" Curious when there was no response, Pierce rolled to his side, Taite still held within the circle of his arms.

She had fallen fast asleep unaware he'd even spoken or moved. Rising to his elbow, Pierce slowly looked his fill of perfectly arched eyebrows and full lips. Reaching out, he eased the tip of a finger down a soft cheek. Her skin was like porcelain. Perfect. Her lips parted slightly at his touch. She breathed in.

Groaning when he felt the distinct stir of desire again, Pierce lay back to close his eyes. His body tensed as the woman by his side slumbered on—unknowingly, she pressed close against him.

Chapter 6

Taite smiled the next morning and glanced in her rearview mirror to change car lanes as she recalled her and Pierce's conversation that morning. Sexy lay beside her in the front seat of her car dead to the world. The dog slept sound. He always did when riding in the car.

"Oh, I don't want to get up this morning," she'd told Pierce upon waking. She stretched out fully in her bed as he yawned.

He turned toward her at her exclamation. Taite thought he looked handsome all sleepy-eyed. He reached out to push her hair back from her face.

"Good morning, beautiful. Merry Christmas."

Taite grinned. She felt beautiful. "Good morning yourself," she responded.

Pierce leaned forward to plant a kiss square on her lips. Pulling back, he studied her, his expression suddenly serious. Raising her hand to his mouth, he kissed the center of her palm. "We need to talk."

Stiffening, Taite wondered if he was about to let her know the prior night had been a mistake on his part.

Noting her response, he quickly shook his head, understanding.

"No, baby, not that. But you do have my emotions all over the place, and I think yours are, too."

Taite nodded her head in agreement. He continued.

"You stated last night that you love me. I think that we should examine our emotions further before we rush into anything. Don't you agree?"

"I agree."

Pierce sighed as if he felt relief.

"Let's take it slow and see where this goes, okay?"

"Okay," Taite responded.

A few seconds of silence passed between them, and when Pierce didn't say anything else, Taite laid her hand against his cheek. She gazed with a solemn expression up at him. Her mouth twitched with a need to laugh.

"Well, I've examined my emotions, and I know now that I definitely love you."

Taite watched Pierce's eyes slightly widened before he roared with laughter. Shaking his head, he rolled from the bed to his feet.

"You better get dressed, honey, or your sister is going to be upset with you arriving late to your father's."

****

Coming out of her thoughts, Taite flipped on her car's left signal light. She accelerated the speed of her car and passed the slower vehicle in front of her. She had gotten a late start that morning, but was still making good time. She was an hour into her two-hour drive home, but with the traffic running smoothly, she should be able to make it home no later than one o'clock. It was an hour later than the straight up twelve noon time she'd planned on arriving. Her father wasn't ruffled when she'd called to inform him. He had stated he'd let the kitchen staff know to hold up their lunch plans until she arrived. He seemed in a good mood, had even shocked her when he'd said he was looking forward to everyone being home for Christmas that year.

Caite had been in a good mood that morning also. Taite had heard Mickey's deep laugher in the background when she and Caite spoke.

Shrugging at everyone's jovial attitudes, Taite let her thoughts return to Pierce and what they'd shared the night before and then again that morning.

He'd raised his eyebrows in mock horror later that morning when she'd informed him that she'd bought Lacy a My First Kitchen.

"And this thing needs assembly?" he'd groaned as she handed over to him the wrapped box that she held. He raised his eyebrows in feigned anger. At her happy laughter, he leaned forward and mumbled, "I'll get you for this."

His lips captured hers one last time with both of them laughing.

Pulling into the property entrance of her childhood home, Taite followed its circular drive toward the home. Steering her car to the front doors of the dwelling, she pulled the car to a stop and with a smile, she sat for a moment before she opened her car door to step from the vehicle.

Taking her suitcases from the trunk of the car, Taite paused for a moment to gaze up at the expansive three-story brick home that she'd spent her childhood in. The twelve-bedroom plantation-style house was nestled among thirteen acres of rolling fields. The hills around it peppered with large, sprawling trees.

In the summer the fields were a luscious green and the leaves on the surrounding trees full and glorious. A knee-high stone wall ran the length of the driveway separating it from the expanse of the yard and the surrounding property. The backyard contained formal gardens that her father took great pride in. Taite knew the gardens were currently dormant, but in the spring, they came alive, singing with color, her father's flowers in full show. The only live color outside the house that day was the evergreen shrubs that grew beneath the first-floor windows around the front entrance of the sprawling mansion. The two large, evergreen Christmas wreaths with their traditional red bows hung center point of the two glass front doors, added color also, Taite noted as she glanced up the steps of the expansive wraparound porch from where she stood below it at ground level.

Over the years, her father had steadily sold off the land he'd owned, only retaining this home and the thirteen acres that surrounded it. There were many outbuildings and a huge barn that she and Caite used to play and hide in on the remaining acres. That huge red barn was where she'd broken her arm at the age of nine. She and Caite had been playing hide-and-seek in it when Caite jumped from the loft above her and accidentally landed on her arm, snapping the bone into two pieces.

The ringing of her cell phone pulled Taite from her thoughts. "Hello," she said after she quickly withdrew it from her purse.

"Hey, sexy."

"Sexy? Did you want to talk to him?" Taite smiled with amusement when Sexy stopped sniffing the ground around him and turned to look at her, his tail wagged eagerly as if he expected to be talked to.

Pierce's low laughter came across the phone. "I just called to make sure that you made it to your father's safe and sound."

"I just arrived. And I'm all in one piece. Pierce…?" Taite paused.

"Taite…?"

Taite laughed at Pierce's teasing. Her name lilted out by him just as she had his.

"I was thinking. Why don't you and Lacy come down here for the weekend? There's plenty of room, and I am sure Dad won't mind. I would like for him to meet you. I mean, you're going to be alone anyway for the Christmas weekend and I, well, I…I…."

"You're madly in love with me, and you miss me already. I know. I know."

At Pierce's long-suffering tone, Taite snapped out her reply, although she was smiling, "I think I've just changed my mind about loving you."

Pierce's laughter rolled through the phone's earpiece. "Clear it with your dad. If he agrees, Lacy and I will see you tomorrow evening. I miss you, honey. Bye, now."

Taite stared at the silent phone that she held. With her smile lingering, she closed the instrument. This intense emotion she felt for Pierce was a heady, delicious feeling, and for once, she was going to take a chance. For once, she would allow her heart to lead instead of always holding back, always afraid of getting too involved. For once, she would trust someone.

Opening the large front doors and then stepping into the foyer of the quiet house, Taite inhaled deeply the scent coming from the bundles of red cedar that the household staff had scattered throughout the home.

The staff had also attached large, red velvet ribbons down along the length of the smooth handrail of the sprawling staircase that opened up into the foyer. The sight and scent of the decorations was a familiar one.

Cedar and cinnamon were the signal of the Christmas holidays and had been for as long as Taite could remember. A feeling of calm washed over her. She was home.

Looking up at a sound, Taite's gaze met her sister's and that of Mickey's. He and Caite walked side-by-side down the wide stairway toward her. Caite looked pretty in her red dress. It swirled around the calves of her legs as she stepped downward toward Taite. The high-heeled, pointy-toed, red shoes she sported made her long legs seem even longer than normal. Sexy. Eye-catching.

"So glad you finally made it, Taite," Mickey stated with a strained smile directed her way. He hurried to where she stood, leaving her sister stopped midway on the stairwell.

"Here, let me take your luggage, and Merry Christmas," he stated.

Taite grinned when Mickey boldly winked at her as he easily hefted both of her over-packed suitcases with no difficulty. He turned back toward an unsmiling Caite. Taite frowned as she walked up the stairway toward her sister.

"You and Dad already fighting?" she inquired of Caite when she reached her.

"It's not me. It's him! I asked him two days ago if it was okay for Mickey to come home with me, and he said fine. Then when I get here, he wants to know if this Mickey is the same Mickey that you dated last summer. He even asked this in front of Mickey. When I told him he was, he snorted and left the room, completely ignoring Mickey."

Taite moved her gaze to the man who stood beside her. He shrugged. She and Mickey had dated the prior year, that was, until he and Caite had met. Thankfully, she and Mickey's relationship hadn't developed any further than that of light kissing.

Caite had been out of the country on a two-month sabbatical at the time. *To find myself,* she had airily stated when she'd finally returned home. Caite's gaze had immediately locked onto Mickey's when he'd strolled from Taite's kitchen the night of her return. Taite had seen their attraction to one another and hadn't cared. She considered Mickey a good friend. No more, no less.

"I'll talk to Dad and let him know that I don't have any hard feelings with the relationship between you two."

Caite snorted before she turned to flounce away and to head back up the stairs. She yelled back down at Taite when Taite didn't follow her.

"You shouldn't have to tell him. I already told him!"

Mickey glanced toward Taite as they started up the staircase behind Caite's rapidly disappearing form.

"I'm sorry, Taite. I didn't realize that your dad knew of our dating. I don't think that I would have come home with Caite, if I had. You know I hadn't originally planned on being here anyway, but when Caite suddenly suggested it, I didn't want to refuse."

Taite clasped Mickey's corded wrist, her fingers unable to completely encircle it. She turned toward him. "Don't worry about it, Mickey. Dad is just funny about what he considers boundaries that people should maintain. My sister dating someone that I dated, to his mind, crossed that boundary."

Mickey abruptly stopped walking, and his action surprised Taite. She slid to a stop beside him. Setting the suitcases that he held down onto the thick carpeted hallway, he grasped her hand, his fingers wrapping around hers. "I didn't hurt you, did I, Taite, when I stopped seeing you and started dating Caite?"

Mickey's face was tight as if he'd just that moment realized that she might have been wounded by his desertion of her.

Taite affectionately patted the top of his strong hand and she smiled up at him. "You should know that after two full months of our dating, and the most that we ever did was kiss goodnight, that I wouldn't be pining away for you, don't you?"

Mickey's gaze searched hers for a moment before he smiled sheepishly. He picked up her suitcases again.

"Where is your room?" he asked.

Taite guided him down the hallway to the room that had been her childhood sanctuary. She opened its door. With one last searching glance toward her before he set her suitcases down, he flashed his endearing, crooked smile and then left the room.

Tossing her designer handbag onto the top of the bed, Taite kicked off her shoes. She curled her toes into the deep piled carpet under her feet.

Oh, it was so nice to be home.

The phone beside the bed shrilled. Taite picked it up. Silently, she listened and then set the phone back down to its resting place.

She had fifteen minutes before they would gather together for their meal.

****

Taite wordlessly handed Caite the steaming bowl of brown gravy that she held. Caite just as silently took it and then dipped some of the savory sauce onto the top of her whipped potatoes. She passed the bowl to Mickey.

Without a word said, Mickey in turn dipped the light brown sauce onto his potatoes, and then he carefully set the blue flowered, fine china bowl down onto the table before him.

For everyone to have been in such good moods this morning, they certainly are all sour pusses now, Taite thought, as she took a bite of her thinly, sliced turkey. *Well, I'm not going to let Caite or Father ruin my weekend,* she decided. Swallowing, she cleared her throat.

Her father gave her a questioning look. Taite smiled at him, although, a bit hesitantly. She wanted to ask him about having Pierce at the house for the weekend. One never knew how her father would react at having strangers in his home when he was already mad. He might just look pained and everything would be okay, or he could blow up and storm from the room.

"Dad, I want to invite someone here for the weekend. Would that be okay with you?"

"Depends," he harshly responded with a narrowed glance directed toward Caite. Caite slammed her fork down on top of the table as she returned their father's look with a narrowed glare of her own. Their father dismissed her to look back at Taite.

"I am assuming you want to invite a male friend, since Caite brought one home," he continued. "Is this person someone who Caite might decide she wants? She could decide to exchange Mickey boy for this new man."

"I knew I shouldn't have come home for the holidays! You mean old fart!" Caite yelled.

"Caite," Mickey stated beside her.

Caite swiveled toward him. "Don't you *Caite* me. He has always criticized me over everything I do. Taite, here, is his perfect little angel."

Lunging up from her chair, Caite pointed a finger at Taite as she glared at their father. "Well, let me tell you something. Your perfect little angel is fucking her boss. How do you like that, you old fashioned fart? He's someone she's only known for two weeks, and this so-called *friend* that she wants to invite home, is that boss. He fired her when he met her, but your little angel wormed her way into his bed and secured her job back."

In stunned shock, Taite stared at her sister. "I did not get my job back by going to bed with my boss!"

Whirling toward her, Caite baited, "Oh. Do tell, sis? Can you sit here, and honestly tell Dad that you and Pierce haven't slept together?"

Taite's face flamed. She jumped when her father abruptly stood to throw his napkin down onto the tabletop.

Suddenly, he clutched at his chest and his face lost all color. "Dad!" she screamed.

"My pills," he moaned. "My pills."

Neither Taite nor Caite moved. Taite was paralyzed with fear, unable to move. She helplessly watched as Caite sank back down onto her own chair, her eyes wide.

Mickey jumped up to run around the table to grab the pill box her father weakly tried to pull from his front pocket. Shaking out one of the white pills, Mickey placed it in the older man's mouth. Within just a few seconds, her father slowly sank back down onto the chair he'd just surged from. He looked closely at Taite and then at her sister.

Taite thought he looked tired and extremely old.

"Taite, I want you and your sister in my study in fifteen minutes." He stood after his sharp words, as did Taite.

Caite suddenly seemed unable to look at their father. She fidgeted with her cloth napkin, but she didn't rise.

"Did you hear me, girl?" their father questioned.

Mickey took his gaze from Caite to glance worriedly at Taite. He then looked toward their father. "Sir, if my being here is a problem, I will leave right now."

In the ensuing silence, Taite spoke up.

"Dad, please. I don't have any hurt feelings over Caite dating Mickey. Mickey and I are friends. It is all we ever would have been even if Mickey and Caite hadn't fallen for each other."

Mickey gave Taite a sharp look at her heartfelt declaration. The fingers of his right hand fisted for a moment before he laid his palm on her twin's shoulder drawing Caite's attention. "Caite, go with your father. I'll wait for you," he told her.

Their father stomped from the room.

Taite turned toward her sister. "I don't think it would be wise for you to ignore Father this time, Caite."

Her heart pounding, Taite entered her father's study. She took a seat on the couch positioned across from his desk. Her father hadn't sat down. He just stood within the dark paneled room, behind his desk, with his hands in his pockets. He turned to look at the picture of their mother that hung on the wall behind him.

Taite thought he grimaced, but the action was so fleeting, she decided she must have imagined it. *Does he still miss Mother after all these years?* she wondered.

Caite strutted into the study to plop down onto the dark brown cushioned leather chair positioned before the large bay windows of the room, their curtains pulled back to invite the outside world into the space. Taite noticed that snow had begun to fall in that outside world. The bare branches of the trees in the backyard already covered with the white flakes.

Crossing her legs, Caite glared at their father. Her elegantly clad foot swung in agitation at his continued silence. He watched her actions.

"Let me just say in my defense, Dad, that you hold Taite to a different standard than me. If I had dated Mickey and then Taite started to date him, I don't think you would have batted an eye."

Their father silently walked forward to shut the study door with a firm click. Walking back to his desk to stand in front of it, his gaze met Caite's.

"I wouldn't have batted an eye, girl, because I know Taite would have made sure you had no feelings for the man. However, that is not why I wanted you both in here. You've lied and abused your sister, and you have gone too far this time, Caite."

Abruptly, Caite sat up straighter. "I did not lie about Taite. She is fucking her boss."

Taite hissed in anger as she shifted toward Caite. "I am not going to sit here and listen to your foul mouth. Personally, I really don't know what Mickey sees in you. Maybe you should be the one to leave this house instead of him!"

Their father's hand slammed down onto his desk. Afterward, his fingers clenched into a fist.

Taite watched as he visibly, forced his muscles to relax. Flattening his palm out, he looked at her sister.

"I don't give a damn if Taite is fucking her boss, as you have so crudely put it. Hell, girl, you both are twenty-six years old. Don't you think I know what goes on out in the world. What I do care about is that you perpetrated a lie when you went on your so-called sabbatical this past summer."

Caite's face blanched and her lips tightened, thinning.

"You wouldn't have given me the money to go," she snarled, her eyes hard.

Taite in confusion glanced from Caite to their father.

"What has Caite done?" she inquired.

Their father ignored her question as his gaze firmly held her sister's glare.

"So, Chad knew and gave me the money anyway, but then ran to you with the tale. Typical," Caite snipped.

Their father continued to stare at Caite as if in a quandary. Caite didn't seem embarrassed by the action he was talking about, only mad at being found out. She did finally drop her gaze from his.

Their father walked around the desk to lower himself onto the chair Taite had known since childhood. The chair, its fine cracks and worn leather like an old friend, seemed to surround him, protecting him. Taking a deep breath, he slowly released it. He then looked at her.

"Your sister impersonated you. She went to Chad as you and told him a wild tale of how she—*you*—needed five thousand to repair your car, but was afraid to ask me for the money. Being Chad, he gave your sister the money and then kept quiet about it. By accident, I just happened to see the noted transaction on his desk late this morning after I spoke with you."

With a gasp, Taite whirled toward her sister.

Her sister rolled her eyes at her. "Oh, shut up with your righteous condemnation. I plan on paying your precious Chad back. It was just easier to let him believe that I was you than for me to face him as myself."

"Did you believe that Chad wouldn't know you from Taite? Hell, girl, he breathed life into your sister at her birth," their father rasped.

Caite turned toward him, and her eyes flashed, her anger obvious. "What about you, Dad? Would you have known me from Taite? Maybe I should have come to you and pretended to be my dear sister. I don't think you would have been any the wiser, would you?"

At Caite's hateful comment, their father's fingers tightened over the arms of his chair.

Caite leaned forward toward him. Her face set in tight lines. "Oh wait, I forget. I couldn't ask you for money even as Taite, could I? You aren't loaning us money, anymore, are you? Some stupid rule you now have about us standing on our own two feet. Our own two feet, Dad, when you are loaded?"

Breathing in, their father, with seemingly leaden arms, pulled out papers from a drawer of the desk he sat behind. Laying the papers that he held down onto the top of the desk, he smoothed a hand over the ruffled pieces. The two women he'd raised as an only parent didn't say a word as they watched him. Looking up, he met both their gazes.

"My lawyer, although surprised by my call this morning, immediately delivered this legal document when I contacted him. I have here a change to my will."

When Caite issued a curse, he ignored it, refusing to be drawn. "Caite, since you seem so determined to get your hands on my money, I from this day forth bequeath you ten million to do with as you wish."

Caite straightened, her eyes becoming so wide that the whites glowed. Then a huge grin split across her face. Taite, watching her twin, knew that she'd expected their father to write her out of his will. He had threatened it numerous times. As Taite continued to watch Caite, her insides twisted with disbelief and with some sadness. Gaining access to her inheritance apparently was what her sister had wanted all along. Taite had always believed that Caite's rash behavior had been because she tried to push their father into expressing his love for her.

Looking down at her hands as he continued to speak, Taite felt her eyes mist. Not once had their father ever expressed the words, "I love you," to either her or her sister. Oh, he had taken care of them as they had grown from childhood to adulthood, she would concede him that much. *He must care for us*, she thought as she studied her hands. *But what flaw in his character prevented him from saying those three little words that meant so much to children?*

Sighing, Taite admitted with a curl of hurt that those words meant a lot to a person even once you reached maturity.

At least she now had met someone who she felt loved her and wouldn't be afraid to tell her so, once he adjusted to it. At her thought of Pierce, Taite's insides warmed. She missed him already. How could someone whom she hadn't even known three weeks ago come to mean so much to her, and so fast? Her feelings for Pierce bewildered her.

Are my emotions too strong, maybe even unhealthy? she wondered.

Looking up at the sudden silence within the room, Taite felt startled. Had she heard correctly? Her sister's mouth was twisted with anger. Caite half stood and then slumped back into her chair. She stared at Taite.

Taite jerked her gaze from Caite to their father. "I'm sorry, Dad. I...I... was lost in thought. What did you say?"

He frowned. "I said, I am bequeathing you twenty million, plus this house and the surrounding property. I want you to have the house and property, Taite. You've always expressed how much this home means to you. I know you will take care of it. It has been in my family for five generations. I would like for it to continue to stay in the family. The extra ten million is for expenses in keeping the house and the property up. I know that your sister would immediately want to sell everything off if I gave it to her. My one stipulation is that I continue to live here and have full power over all concerns with the house and property until my death."

"I have no problem with that, Dad," Taite whispered.

"Then it is resolved. After the holidays, I will have both your inheritances transferred to you. All the legalities will be taken care of."

Caite stood and without a word said, left the room. The study door she slammed shut behind her.

"Dad, do you think it was wise to leave the house and property to just me. Wouldn't it have been fairer to Caite if it had been left to the both of us equally?"

Taite's father sighed, the sound heavy. He placed the papers that he held back into the safe in his desk. "It would have been a constant battle if I'd left the house and property to the both of you. You know that, Taite. And Caite doesn't deserve my property. Not after I have bailed her out from one scrape after another. I thought when she sold two of my thoroughbred horses without my knowledge last summer, and forged my name on the transfer of sale paperwork, that that would be the last of her escapades. She promised it was. But what did she do? Not a month later, she cons money out of my oldest friend. And she has always stated that she hates the country anyway.

"She has always declared to any and all who would listen that she couldn't wait to move to the city and shake the dirt from her heels. That was her favorite saying, even as a child."

At Taite's continued concern, her father waved his hand in the air at her dismissing it.

"Don't worry about your sister, Taite. She's smart enough to realize, once she gets over her hurt feelings, that the maintenance of this property and this home would be a headache for her. Caite will realize she wasn't shortchanged after all, but that you were."

At her father's half smile directed her way, Taite tilted her lips into a returning grin, her worries leaving her. With a laugh, she replied, "You're right, Dad. Caite would have cursed us all once she realized the responsibility of this old house. She is probably even now recognizing that she's the winner out of the two of us today."

Taite rose to leave the room. "I love you, Dad."

At her father's curt nod, Taite with an accepting sadness smiled at his failure to voice his love for her in return. He remained unaware of her response. His head already bent to some paper on his desk. Before she left the room, he surprised her by saying, "Call your man and tell him to come on up to the farm."

Taite heard happy laughter from beyond her sister's bedroom door as she approached it. With raised eyebrows, Taite lightly knocked on the door. It hadn't taken Caite long to lose her anger, it seemed.

Caite opened the door. She motioned for Taite to come in the room and then told whoever was on her cell phone bye and disconnected. She placed the phone in her purse.

In confusion, Taite watched her. Who had her sister called so fast? Mickey was here in the house. Taite would have thought Caite would've ran to him with her news.

Caite flung her thick hair back over her shoulders as she plopped down on her king-sized bed, a huge smile plastered on her face. She dramatically raised her arms to spread them wide seemly pleased with life in general.

"We're rich, sis. Rich!"

Taite walked on into the room.

"You lost your anger quick enough, I'm glad to see."

With a casual shrug of her shoulder, Caite responded, "I realized that I don't want this house or this land Dad loves so much. And you'll have to deal with him for years to come since he wants to continue to have control of the property, something I'm glad I won't have to do."

Taite responded with hesitation, unsure if Caite really was happy with what had occurred or pretended the emotion. "I'm sorry that Dad didn't make you part owner, Caite. Although, I do think he was correct in his decision, you've always said that you couldn't wait to shake the dirt from your heels and move to the city."

Caite let out a happy laugh, and with an agile move, she jumped from the bed. "I meant it, too. Sorry about my comments earlier in regards to Pierce. Just my jealousy rearing its ugly head, I guess."

With a quick motion, she hugged Taite and then drew back to put distance between them. "You've always been Dad's favorite though, you know."

"I don't believe I'm Dad's favorite, Caite. You two just don't hit it off. Never have. And you know me. I always try to stay in the background and avoid the fireworks, which is why Dad and I never seem to disagree."

Caite's gaze met Taite's.

"No hard feelings from either of us then? And I want to stay for the Christmas weekend. Mickey included of course. Dad never said he couldn't stay. One big happy family, how about that, do you think you and I can accomplish that feat?"

With a nod of surprise toward her sister, Taite turned to leave the room. "I'm going to go call Pierce and tell him to come on up. I love you, sis."

"Yeah, yeah. Doesn't everyone," Caite stated with an exaggerated grimace. She waved a hand and dismissed Taite. She turned toward the suitcase she had yet to unpack.

When Taite hesitated to leave, Caite looked back up and she laughed. "Go!" she said with a grin. "Go call Pierce. I know you are dying to."

With a laugh of agreement, Taite left the room. It seemed her sister was actually, genuinely, happy with how things had turned out.

Chapter 7

Taite couldn't stop her excited jump the next evening when the house doorbell chimes sounded. Glancing at her watch, she realized that Pierce had arrived precisely at five p.m., just as he'd stated he would do. At the sudden silence in the room when she quickly stood, Taite flushed. Emma grinned broadly at her, as did Chad, before they glanced at each other as if in understanding.

Caite and Mickey's whispered argument halted. They watched her expectantly, as did her father.

"If you're going to answer the door, you better hurry before the butler gets there first," her father stated dryly. It seemed that her feelings for Pierce were apparent for all to see. Taite quickly exited the spacious living room where they'd all gathered as they waited for the last two guests to arrive. Dinner would now be served and gifts opened.

"I'll get the door," she told her dad's newest butler when she caught up with him. With a nod, he halted to let her pass him by. Her father seemed to hire a new butler every other year. *No. No problems*, he would always tell her when a new man showed up and the other one left. This new man's name was Jim. He seemed a nice enough fellow.

Slowing her pace, Taite took a deep breath. Wiping her damp palms down over her hips and then smoothing the fabric that covered them, she slowly approached the door. Good grief, she was nervous. She didn't understand how one person could make her feel so out of control. *Yes, I do*, Taite quickly admitted as she halted to take another deep breath before opening the door. She knew that Pierce made her nervous because he held her heart in the palm of his hand. It frightened her how fast he'd become so important to her. The intense feelings he evoked didn't make any sense.

Anxiously, Taite glanced at her reflection in the large ornate mirror that hung in the foyer. It seemed to pick up the hollows of her cheeks. Quickly scanning the rest of her mirror image, Taite straightened the collar of her crisp, white shirt, and then adjusted the wide belt angled at her hips which matched her black wool slacks and black, high heeled shoes.

With one last critical glance in the mirror, Taite reached out and opened the front door to the home. Her gaze took in that of the man who stood before her. He was dressed casually in jeans and a dark brown leather jacket. The dark brown of his silk shirt accented the coffee color of his eyes.

****

Pierce sat Lacy down beside his leg onto the porch, his gaze locked with Taite's. Lacy had wanted down. Dimly, Pierce heard and was aware of the child squealing in delight as she reached to pet Taite's dog, who'd bounded up the steps when Taite opened the door to them. Sexy squatted beside his daughter as Lacy grabbed a handful of the dog's hair and cooed about the pretty baby.

"Hi, beautiful," Pierce murmured. Reaching out, Pierce brushed his knuckles across a satin cheek. With a jolt, he felt as if he had come home, and in that same second, he felt fear. His emotion for Taite made him vulnerable. As open to hurt as when he had lost his wife.

Quickly withdrawing his hand, Pierce looked down at his daughter. The action gave him time to collect his senses.

"Lacy, are you ready to go inside?" he questioned.

His daughter lifted her arms to Taite.

"T. T. hold."

Bending, Taite picked her up.

"Hello, Lacy," she stated softly. Her gaze caught his, an uncertainty held within their beautiful depths.

"Did you have trouble?" she quietly asked. She stepped back and made a motion for him to come into the hallway of the home. Pierce knew his smile was tight as he knocked the dusting of snow from his shoulders. "No. I arrived on time, didn't I?"

"Yes, exactly on time. Everyone is waiting in the family room, if you'll just follow me."

At Taite's hesitant tone, Pierce reached out to clasp her elbow and he halted her retreat. "I missed you."

"I...I...you, too."

"Me, too," Lacy piped up.

In surprise, Pierce and Taite looked at the child and then they burst out with laughter. They were still smiling when they entered the room where the others waited.

"What's so funny?" Caite questioned.

"Nothing," Taite replied. She turned to the elderly gentleman who lowered the newspaper he was reading. The man met Pierce's gaze.

"Dad, I would like you to meet Pierce Holden. Pierce, this is my father. Blake Carpenter."

Taite's father stood at her introduction.

Pierce walked across the room to stretch his hand out to him.

"I understand that you purchased the real estate business that Taite works for," her father stated, giving his hand a firm shake. He then motioned across the room.

"Sit there, Pierce, on the couch. We have a few minutes to visit before our dinner will be served."

Lacy squealed with delight when Taite set her down to the polished hardwood floor and immediately darted to the Christmas tree, her eyes huge. The tree was enormous. It had to be at least twelve feet tall. Wrapped gifts lay beneath it.

Pierce was glad that he had had the foresight to bring gifts. Taite hadn't said anything about opening gifts the day after Christmas. However, he'd wondered since Chad and Emma weren't to be there until Saturday as well.

He sat down beside Taite and leaned back on the couch. He watched his daughter. She didn't touch anything, just clapped her hands in delight.

Emma smiled tenderly across the room at him. "That is what gift giving is about, isn't it, Pierce? It's for the children. Look at little Lacy's excitement."

****

Taite picked up the expensive high-quality scarf Pierce had given to her for Christmas and wrapped the supple cloth about her neck.

She sat down on the side of her bed lost in reflective thought. He had brought gifts for everyone, which had surprised her.

He must have gone shopping first thing that morning before driving down, the busiest shopping day after Thanksgiving, and if he was like most men, he had hated the crowd and the shopping. She hadn't thought to let him know that they would be opening gifts that evening. When she apologized, he'd told her that he had brought gifts, so no worry.

After their late dinner, everyone gathered back in the great room to exchange presents. She gave Pierce an antique paperweight for his desk at the office. He seemed to like it as he looked it over, thanking her. She'd bought the paperweight the last time she had come home, when she stopped at an antique store to just browse. The paperweight had drawn her, and it seemed to fit Pierce.

Lacy squealed with happiness when Taite began to hand her the gifts that Emma and Chad had brought for her. Taite was glad that she'd had the prudence to call Emma with a request to run to the mall and pick up the gifts for the child before they left the city that morning.

The muffled ringtone of Taite's cell phone drew her from her thoughts. Reaching for her handbag, she pulled the slender instrument from it and then glanced to see who could be calling her. In surprise, Taite quickly responded. "Pierce?"

She removed the scarf from around her neck.

"Hey, sexy, I'm looking out my bedroom window, and I can see a huge, red barn. The backyard lights, plus the snow has made everything very visible out there. I was wondering—would you like to venture out? I need to stretch my legs, and I would like to visit that large barn."

"What about Lacy?"

"Guess who just came by and took her."

Taite laughed. "Emma."

"Yep, said she didn't want to sleep in that big ole bed she had been assigned to by herself."

"Meet me in the hallway. Five minutes?"

When Pierce agreed, Taite slipped her snow boots on. Quickly she checked her makeup. After brushing her teeth, she hastily ran a comb through her hair and then picked up the scarf Pierce had gifted her. Pulling on her coat, she was ready to go.

A little breathless, Taite opened her door and almost plowed into Pierce. *I need to tell him about my inheritance*, she suddenly thought. *Would it change things between them?*

"Woah, there," he stated. A deep sound of laughter was issued as he steadied her.

Taite's gaze collided with Mickey's, when he stepped from Caite's bedroom. He went on into his room after giving them a sharp glance. His face was set, a thundercloud.

With a mental shrug, Taite dismissed him and her sister. They were fighting again as usual.

Looking up at Pierce, she smiled. "I'm ready."

Wrapping an arm about her shoulders, Pierce returned her smile. "Lead the way then, pretty lady."

****

"So, you and Caite played in here as kids?" Pierce looked around the barn. He took in the square bales of hay stacked to the back of the barn and the sacks of feed neatly lined up. Reaching out, he petted the nose of the horse that had walked up to the opening of his stall, to where Taite and he now stood. He glanced up at the loft that spanned across the space above them.

Taite gave a quick look around the inside of the barn, following his line of interest. The large barn as always was very neat and clean. Nothing was allowed to be out of place in it.

The familiar scents that were stamped in her childhood memories were a combination of horse manure, hay, and the smell of sweet feed fed to the horses daily. It had been ages since she'd been in the barn, yet the old scents caused memories to bloom. This old barn was where she and Caite had played out their fantasies of a daddy and a mommy who loved them.

"Come on," she stated as she walked over to the heavy wooden ladder that led up to the barn loft. With a laugh, Taite bounded up the steep steps and then turned to watch Pierce follow at a more careful pace. With an arched eyebrow, he stepped up the last step of the ladder and then onto the floor of the loft.

"This is where Caite jumped from and landed on your arm, breaking it?" he inquired as he looked down to where they had just stood. "It's a wonder she didn't break her fool neck."

Walking over to stand at the very edge of the loft, Taite gazed down at the tops of stacked hay bales that stretched out from underneath the loft. She felt Pierce grab hold of the back of her coat. Laughing, Taite let him pull her from the edge as he took several steps backward.

"I wouldn't have fallen. I'm very balanced," she reassured him. "When Caite jumped that day, the barn was stacked completely full of hay, so she didn't really have very far to fall. I'd just jumped, but I didn't get out of the way fast enough before she followed me down."

Pierce pulled her farther away from the edge of the loft and into the circle of his arms.

"I'm going to kiss you," he said softly as he snaked his arms in between her coat front to draw her in close to him.

Feeling her heart give a funny little lurch when their bodies connected, Taite wrapped her arms about his waist. His aftershave had a slightly woodsy scent to it. She thought it smelled wonderful. It was uniquely him.

Slowly, he lowered his head to capture her lips with his. Taite sighed and tightened her arms. When he moved his lips down to the side of her neck, she felt her knees give way.

"Pierce, I...I..." Taite couldn't complete her thought, her need to tell him what had transpired the day before, concerning her inheritance, forgotten. Her desire heavy, she gave way to the sensations that flooded through her at his touch.

****

Pierce kissed the silky skin at the base of Taite's throat, and he felt the lurch of her pulse against his mouth. He couldn't get enough of this woman. His need for her was insatiable. Had it only been a morning ago that he'd held her in his arms? It felt a lifetime. Lifting his head, Pierce met Taite's heavy lidded gaze. "Can we?"

Understanding his question, she gave a slight nod of her head. Her consent given.

"No one will be coming down here?"

"Not at eleven o'clock at night," she replied a little breathlessly.

Taking hold of her hand, Pierce guided her to the very back of the loft where they were hidden, in case someone did happen to walk into the barn. Grasping hold of her heavy coat, he slipped it from her shoulders to spread it out on the wooden floor.

Shrugging off his leather jacket, he let it drop to his feet. He began to pull his shirt from the waistband of his pants and watched as Taite moved to unbuttoned her shirt. When he glimpsed her nipples through the white, delicate, lacy bra she wore, he reached for her. His hands were unsteady as he helped her to finish her undressing. He shucked the rest of his clothes.

Easing them both to their knees, he laid Taite back onto her coat. He gazed his fill of her. She didn't issue a word as he moved his palm lightly over the bared skin of her stomach.

Reaching up, she passed her palms over his arms and then down to his fingers.

"Taite, ah, Taite," he breathed, loving the feel of her and loving her touch of him.

Bending forward, Pierce kissed her deep. He buried his face against her neck. Her thick mane of hair, its texture like silk, brushed against his face. The soft lavender scent of her shampoo filled his nostrils. Lost to his emotions, Pierce quickly entered the warmth of the woman beneath him.

She gasped softly at that entrance. Then there was silence.

Pierce couldn't get enough of her. She consumed him emotionally and physically.

Wanting to guard his feelings, he attempted to pull back, to control his devouring of the woman below him. He hadn't meant to have a quick coupling, and yet that was what it was turning out to be. With a hoarse groan, he gave in to her power letting go of his self-control. His world was her world. She was his and he was hers. No longer would he be alone.

When Taite stiffened and held on to him tightly, Pierce felt his release. Afterward, they lay in silence only their breathing heard.

Pierce became conscious of the cold seeping into his bones. His breathing now calm he lay on top of Taite for several more seconds before he rose, relieving her of his heavy weight.

"You were a quiet lover tonight." Pierce reached for the jacket he'd dropped earlier and placed it over Taite's bare form. He pulled her snow boots back on over her feet. Wordlessly, she lifted his jacket to position part of it over his shoulders when he lay back down beside her. She curled toward him to snuggle up against his chest.

"Are you cold?" she asked softly.

"A little. I was afraid you might be too."

After several moments of continued silence, Pierce shifted, and he looked down at the woman he held in his arms. "What's wrong, sweetheart? Why so quiet?"

Taite shrugged a bare shoulder. "This wood floor is too cold and hard for us to lay here. Let's get dressed and go back to the house."

Sitting up, she silently removed her snow boots and then rose to begin to pull on the slacks she'd worn and her blouse. She pulled her boots back on her sock covered feet. Her eyes failed to meet his.

Pierce frowned. Reaching out, he grasped her arm to force her to look at him. "Talk to me, honey. If you didn't want this to happen, you should have told me when I asked."

Taite averted her gaze from his again. Were his emotions all one-sided? Why had she asked him to come down to her family home if she was now going to turn the cold shoulder to him?

Grabbing his clothes, Pierce dressed. Not only did he feel Taite's mental withdrawal but he was beginning to shiver from the cold night air.

He watched as Taite quickly donned her coat. She went to the wide doors at the end of the loft to swing them open. Cold wind blasted through the space and swirled icy fingers around them.

Pierce swiftly walked to where she stood intent on yanking the doors back closed. He grabbed a tight hold to the back of her coat when she stepped to the edge of the opening to gaze out into the night sky. His heart leaped in his throat at the long drop to the ground. Farm equipment was parked up against the barn. If she fell, that equipment would impale her.

"What the hell do you think you are doing?"

****

With shock, Taite came out of her thoughts to focus on the intensely angry man beside her. She'd been lost in memory. Memory of her and Caite's childhood. Pierce's fingers bit into her arm.

"I didn't mean to frighten you, Pierce. I'm sorry."

He dropped his hand from her arm as he took several angry steps away from her, back to the center of the loft floor.

With concern, Taite followed him.

"I told you earlier that I am very balanced, Pierce. Caite and I used to crawl all over this barn. We even walked those rafters up there." Pierce glanced to where she pointed. A look of disbelief flashed before his gaze caught hers again.

"And your father was aware of your activities in this barn?"

Taite shook her head. "No…I don't believe he was. But as long as we stayed out of his hair, he didn't ever ask what we were up to. It was the staff's responsibility to take care of us."

Taking hold of Pierce's hand, Taite laced her fingers with his. "I need to talk to you about something, and I can't help but wonder if it will change how you see me. My feelings haven't changed for you, though. I still love you. Just as I told you I did."

Taite watched Pierce. His gaze was thoughtful as he studied her. She had wanted to discuss her sudden wealth with him before they'd made love, but once he began to kiss her, she'd lost all coherent thought and had surrendered to his lovemaking. Even now her skin tingled where his fingers touched hers. *Am I wealthier than him?*

Taite couldn't help her thought. Her father always said you couldn't trust people when it came to money. Sometimes that was all a person could see. Pierce pulled her close to him as he studied her, and Taite felt that electric shock of desire rising once again for the man who stood so still beside her. She shook off her thoughts. What worried her about her wealth was that Pierce was a proud man, maybe it would change the dynamics between them if she were the wealthier of the two of them.

"I was beginning to wonder, sweetheart, what had come over you with your quiet lovemaking, and your silence afterwards. What is this something that seems so important to you?"

Pierce ran his fingers down through her hair his gaze questioning.

"I come from a wealthy family."

With an arched eyebrow, he returned her gaze. His eyes began to reflect laughter within their depths as he lightly pulled on a strand of her hair. "Honey, I figured that bit of news out all by myself. First, you own a condo at a young age. Twenty-six, your employee file showed."

Taite nodded. He continued, "Once I glimpsed your family home, I realized that your father must be extremely well-off. But what has any of that to do with you and me?"

Taite sighed. "Yesterday, Dad gave Caite and me our inheritance. What I am trying to tell you is that I personally am very wealthy."

Pierce frowned. "So? I am not a pauper, Taite. Why is this so important?

Are you afraid I might see only your money when I look at you?"

Pierce's frown deepened at her silence, and Taite looked away.

"I see," he stated. Dropping her hand, he took several steps back from her, his jaw clenched. Taite realized that she had insulted Pierce terribly. She hadn't intended to. This money thing weighed heavy on her.

"Yes, I did," she teased, trying to break his mood. She flung out her arms and gave a forced laugh. "I was afraid that you would want to become my kept man. My gigolo who would spend my millions! Baby, buy me that red car. Sweetheart, I need some new leather pants."

There was truth to her words, although Taite didn't want to admit to it. It seemed so ugly, her thoughts.

Taite died into genuine peals of laughter when Pierce's mouth literally fell open.

"Hell," he growled. His face turned a bright shade of red.

Running to him, Taite leaped into his arms, and he held tightly on to her as she laid her palms against his cheeks. Her love for him swelled.

"I wasn't sure how you would react, Pierce. One way or the other. I know you are not a pauper, but I also know that you're a very proud man. I was worried it would bother you if I had more money than you. Emma told me how you refused to accept your parents' financial help when you went to college. And even though your father owned the real estate business you went to work for, you started at the bottom."

"Tell you what, honey," Pierce responded as his gaze held hers. "I am not even going to ask how much money you have. You just keep your money, and I'll keep mine. How does that sound?"

Taite smiled happily at the man who held her. She kissed him.

"Leather pants?" he asked with a sick look as he let her slide down the length of him.

"Yes, and tight ones," Taite stated, a happy giggle issued when her feet touched the loft floor.

"I think that it's time for us to return to our respective bedrooms," Pierce dryly responded, although laughter now lurked within the depths of his gaze.

With a happy laugh, Taite went down the loft ladder first. When her feet hit the floor, she stood and watched Pierce follow at a more cautious pace. *No skipping any steps for him*, she thought with silent laughter at his caution.

His hand reached for hers when his feet finally touched the floor of the barn. It was then that Taite heard the sound of a creature in pain. She turned toward the horse stall where the sound came from. Walking to the stall, Taite opened it, curious as to what wild animal could have gotten into the empty space. A silent scream rose and then escaped as she rushed to Sexy's side.

Her pet was curled up in the far corner of the empty stall. Falling to her knees, Taite lifted Sexy's limp head to her lap.

"Oh…you poor baby…, you poor baby," she cooed.

Pierce knelt beside her.

"What could have gotten hold of him?" he asked. He reached out a hand to stroke her pet. Sexy let loose a low growl, his teeth bared. Pierce jerked his hand back. "It appears he only wants your touch, Taite."

Taite's tears ran freely as her gaze met Pierce's. "There is no animal, tame or wild, that I know of on the farm that would have torn Sexy up like he is."

Taite looked back down at her pet. A deep gash ran the length of his left side and another the same side of his face. Blood freely flowed from both wounds. His hair was slick with it.

"He had to have gotten into something, sweetheart," Pierce responded softly. "Those wounds are deep. Maybe he got caught in between some type of farm equipment and the wounds are from his trying to get out of his own trap."

Nodding, Taite agreed with Pierce's theory.

"I'm going to take him back to the house and call the vet. I never should have let him run free. He is a housedog after all. And if Father gets upset over my taking him to my bedroom, I will leave in the morning and take Sexy home."

Collecting a horse blanket, Taite gently wrapped her pet up in it and then carefully lifted him. He whimpered at the movement, but then lay quiet and still within her arms.

The house was silent when Taite and Pierce entered it. Glancing at the hallway clock, Taite knew that everyone must be asleep. It was well past midnight. On quiet feet, she and Pierce climbed the stairway to the upper floor and entered her bedroom.

Laying Sexy down onto the carpeted floor beside her bed, Taite reached for the phone book. Her pet whimpered with his pain.

"Will the vet come out here this late at night?"

"I am rich, remember. I can pay him whatever it takes!" After her sharp words, Taite immediately regretted them. She met Pierce's surprised look.

"I'm sorry. I shouldn't have said that. The vet is a family friend. I'm sure he will be willing to come, even though it's a holiday weekend."

Pierce nodded. Turning he sat down on the side of her bed. It seemed he was willing to wait with her until the vet arrived. Taite smiled wanly in his direction when she finally got off the phone.

"Bill says he'll be here within the hour. You don't have to stay with me, Pierce. It's almost one a.m."

Reaching out, he softly touched her cheek. "Go take a shower and change those clothes. Your slacks are ruined."

Taite looked down at her blood-covered pants and then back up at the man who held her heart. "I'm glad you're here," she stated softly.

****

Taite reached out to take Lacy from Emma's arms when Emma walked into her bedroom the next morning.

Her father and Chad walked in directly behind Emma. All looked at the dog that lay asleep beside her bed.

Her father spoke quiet. "It looks as if Bill did a good job sewing him up. Pierce just informed us as to what happened when he came down for breakfast. He said that Bill was puzzled at the wounds the dog received."

Her father looked up at Taite, his gaze questioning.

"Pierce stated that Bill said the wounds didn't look as if Sexy had gotten caught in any farm machinery or mauled by an animal. The cuts didn't have any jagged edges, both were smooth cuts?"

Taite gave a nod.

"He must have got caught in something, though, Dad. I'm just glad that I found him last night when I did. Bill says that he will recover nicely. I blame myself for what happened. Sexy is a house pet and not used to being outside. I never should have left him to roam the countryside. Do you mind, Dad, that I have my dog with me in my room?"

Her father looked startled for a moment at her question. He gruffly said, "Come down and eat your breakfast with everyone else.

"And of course, your dog can stay in your room," he added before he exited the bedroom.

Chapter 8

Pierce looked up from his desk and smiled wide when Taite walked into the office building the following Thursday evening, just before closing time. Returning his welcoming smile with her own happy one, she adjusted Lacy where she had her positioned on her hip. She and Pierce had talked on the phone daily since he and Lacy had left the farm for the city the prior Sunday evening, and she'd missed him terribly. It had only made her love him more when he asked, each time they spoke, how Sexy was healing from his wounds. Every day, her pet had gotten stronger and stronger, until now he bounced around as if he'd never been injured.

Giving a kiss to Lacy's soft round cheek when they entered Pierce's office, Taite handed the child over to her daddy when he stood and reached out for her.

"This is nice. When Emma called and said you had picked Lacy up and were coming to see me, I was surprised. I didn't think you were returning home until Saturday evening."

Pierce looped an arm around Taite's neck and pulled her toward him. "I missed you."

At his husky words, Taite leaned into his toned body. "I missed you, too, which is why I came home early. I also missed our little missy here."

Reaching out, Taite ruffled Lacy's curly, black hair. The child gave her a dimpled smile back. She looked so much like her father that Taite's heart melted.

"Did we have a busy schedule this past week?" Taite inquired turning back toward Pierce.

Pierce sat down to settle his daughter on his lap. Taite noticed that the paperweight she'd given him for Christmas had a place of honor on the corner of his desk. The bronze sculpture of the woman with her arms lifted gracefully in the air, as if in a ballet dance, was elegant looking. It had found its rightful home.

"Not too busy," Pierce replied in response to her question. He reached to pull his pen from Lacy's grasp that she'd managed to secure.

"Only two customers this week, but it is the holidays. People are not going to want to buy a home during the Christmas holidays or before the New Year. I expect January to pick up. Speaking of the New Year, what are you doing tonight to celebrate? Want to come over to my place and bring in the New Year with Lacy and me?"

"I would love to," Taite responded. "Dad wasn't keen on watching the New Year come in. He said he'd rather go to bed at his usual time, and that there was no reason for me to stay with an old fuddy-duddy and miss out on the celebration because of his disinterest in the thing."

Taite stood when Pierce did.

"You should invite your sister and Mickey to celebrate with us," he said as he sat Lacy on the floor to play. Taite looked at him in surprise at his invite of the two. Her sister and Pierce hadn't talked much between them while he was at the farm. Taite had assumed that Pierce didn't care for Caite and her continual baiting of Mickey. Twice during the two days they were all there, Mickey had stormed from the room where they all sat and visited after Caite in an undertone had said something to him.

"Are you sure that you want my sister and Mickey with us tonight?" she asked as Pierce reached for his coat.

He looked toward her and Taite continued, "They might spoil the celebration for us."

He shrugged on his coat. "Mickey is a good employee, and I would like to get to know him better out of the office. Just invite him if you want."

"I can't very well invite Mickey without inviting Caite."

Leaning forward, Pierce placed his mouth over hers. His thorough kiss made her knees weaken. Lacy pulled on Taite's pant leg, drawing her back into the room and aware that she and Pierce stood in the middle of his office.

"Invite your sister then. The decision is up to you," Pierce stated as he released her. He drew his thumb across her bottom lip, his look thoughtful. "You're good for me, Taite. Good for Lacy, too, isn't that right, darling?"

Pierce looked down at his daughter. Bending, he picked her up when she lifted her arms to him. Lacy's head bobbed eagerly as if she were in total agreement with her daddy.

Taite laughed. "Come on you two. I have some shopping to do before tonight gets here if we're to give a party."

****

Pierce watched Taite as she buzzed around his kitchen. She smiled absentmindedly at him when she noticed he'd stopped making the dip she'd ordered him to put together and now just watched her.

As he continued to eye her, with a self-conscious gesture that captivated him, she swiped at her cheeks and then hesitantly glanced down at the dress she wore. "Have I got something on my face or dress?"

Reaching out, Pierce secured a hold of her arm to pull her to him. "Mind if I steal a kiss?"

"We only have a few minutes before everyone will begin to show up."

Pierce shifted his gaze to Taite's lips at her harried response to his question. Unable to stop his action, he bent his head and captured her soft mouth with his. He loved the taste of her. Loved the way she felt in his arms. It was as if she'd always belonged there, as if she had been made just for him. His feelings for Taite were different than they had been for his wife. He had loved his wife deeply, and they had been happy during their brief marriage, but somehow, this woman stirred him in ways he couldn't remember his wife doing. Had it been so long since his wife's death that his memory played tricks?

Pulling back, Pierce gazed at Taite's bemused expression for a moment. He pulled her tight against him again.

"How did our party grow from just two guests to six?" he asked.

Reaching up, he smoothed a stray hair away from Taite's face, and he let his fingers trail across her soft cheek as he did so. She sighed.

"When I called to invite Mickey and Caite, Chad called as I hung up the phone and wanted to know what I was doing tonight. He is coming up to be with Emma for the weekend. I didn't think you would mind if they came over. And then Emma called and said that her nephew was footloose, as was his girlfriend."

Pierce smiled at Taite's worried frown.

"I don't mind, honey."

He watched as her frown eased. Leaning forward he planned to steal another kiss from her.

The doorbell chimed.

"And here are our first arrivals," she breathlessly stated.

With one last hurried kiss, Pierce turned to head for his front door. He glanced back toward Taite to find her standing exactly where he'd left her. When their gazes connected, she abruptly turned, but not before he caught her bewildered smile directed his way.

****

Taite sat down beside Pierce. She handed the fresh plate of appetizers that she held in her hand across the table to Mickey. She and Mickey were card partners. They'd won the last four hands easily. Taite smiled wide at her friend when he dropped an eyelid, very slowly, at her and then dove into the prepared food she handed him.

At Mickey's wink, Caite threw her cards down onto the tabletop. "We might as well give it up. Mickey and my sister are going to win this hand, too."

Caite's sudden action and sour tone made Taite look at her sharply. She noticed that Pierce watched her sister with an arrested expression. Taite hoped that Caite didn't ruin the night by beginning a fight with Mickey or herself. When Lacy crawled up onto her lap, Taite was glad for the diversion of the child. Lacy curled her arms around her neck, and her eyelids drooped.

Pierce leaned forward, his gaze now on his daughter.

"Time for this child to go to bed," he said as he reached for Lacy.

Lacy wrapped her arms tighter about Taite's neck and snuggled deeper against her. She refused to let loose her hold.

"I think Lacy wants Taite to put her to bed, Pierce," Emma said. She watched Taite and Lacy with a smile.

"I believe you're right, Emma," Pierce responded.

Taite slid her chair back. "I'll put Lacy to bed if you'll turn on the TV, Pierce. When I get back, we can all watch the New Year coming in. I can't believe this baby lasted as long as she did. Another thirty minutes and the little sweetheart would've made it to the New Year."

Quietly, singing some little ditty that she couldn't remember all the words to, Taite watched Lacy quickly fall into a deep slumber. Leaning forward, she kissed the rounded cheek of the baby now oblivious to the world around her. With one last check that the child was adequately covered, she stood.

"Will you marry me, Taite?"

Jerking around at Pierce's question, Taite stared at him. She hadn't realized that he had come into the child's bedroom. Had she heard him correctly?

"I...I..."

Walking to her with measured steps, Pierce pulled her into his arms his face solemn. "I'm asking again. Will you marry me, Taite? Will you make me one of the happiest men to celebrate this coming New Year?"

With a joyous laugh, Taite threw her arms around Pierce's strong neck. "Oh, yes! Yes, I'll marry you."

With a soft laugh, Pierce gave her a tight hug. "I want us to get married as soon as possible."

Drawing back, Taite looked at him in surprise.

"As soon as possible?"

"Two weeks too soon?"

"I don't need a huge wedding, Pierce, but two weeks? I don't even have an engagement ring."

"We can pick out an engagement ring next week. What if we get married at your father's? Just a small intimate ceremony with your sister, Mickey, Emma, Chad and your father, and Chad's two sisters?" When Pierce reached up to stroke Taite's cheek, his expression was tense as if he was afraid she would refuse his request. Taite melted against him.

"I need you, Taite," he whispered. "Lacy needs you. Please tell me your answer is yes."

Straightening, Taite reached to touch her fingertips to his lips. He kissed them tenderly as he watched her. Taite smiled. Happiness warmed her heart. "Let's go tell the others that within two weeks we will be husband and wife."

Holding her hand, Pierce and Taite walked back into his living room. Drawing Taite close to his side, Pierce placed an arm around her, his hand at her waist, and he cleared his throat. "Everyone, Taite and I have an announcement to make."

Emma jumped to her feet from where she sat beside Chad. "You two are getting married!"

"Emma," Chad scolded. He watched Taite. Taite nodded at him, unable to keep her wide grin from spreading. She looked at Pierce who smiled back at her. "And Pierce wants us to get married in two weeks' time," she informed.

"Well, sis, it seems that congratulations are in order."

Gracefully, Caite stood. She and Pierce's eyes met for a second before she gave Taite a tight hug. Caite turned and gazed, it seemed, almost gleefully at Mickey. "Mickey, aren't you going to congratulate the happy couple?"

For a moment, Mickey didn't move, but then he quickly stood and he smiled at Taite before his gaze connected with Pierce's. "Take good care of her, boss. She's priceless."

"Yes, she is, Mickey. She most definitely is."

At Pierce's response, the cheering of the crowd on the TV showed that the New Year had slid in.

Taite laughed as she grabbed hold of her fiancé to wrap her arms tightly about his waist. For once she would believe in herself. She would take the chance that someone could love her.

Chapter 9

"I, Janise Taite Carpenter, take you, Pierce Jay Holden, to be my husband, to have and to hold from this day forward, for better or for worse, for richer, for poorer, in sickness and in health, to love and to cherish; from this day forward until death do us part."

Her wedding vows barely audible, and her emotions strong with the love that overflowed from her, Taite could only whisper her vows to the man who stood so handsomely before her. Everything over the past two weeks had happened so fast that things were beginning to blur.

Suddenly, the wedding ceremony was over and everyone in the room issued congratulations to her and to Pierce.

When her father approached, Taite smiled happily at him. Pierce and Chad now talked quietly together in one corner of the family room. They seemed to hit it off and had from the first moment they'd met.

"Would you like another piece of cake, Dad?" Taite asked him when he approached her. He wasn't smiling.

"No, Taite. I do, however, want to talk to you about the changes you made to your will."

"Dad," Taite whispered. She looked worriedly over to where Pierce stood. He raised his cup of punch to her and smiled broadly at her. He dropped his gaze as he glanced back toward Chad to respond to something Chad said to him.

"Let's not talk about this here, Dad. I wanted to make those changes. Pierce doesn't even realize that he is to inherit half my estate if something should happen to me."

Taite didn't know why it was so important to her to name Pierce in her will. There was just something inside her that had pushed her to do it. It was almost as if the action was her proof that he really loved her and not her money.

"I still don't think that it's right, Taite. Why couldn't you wait until you two had been married for some time? Why the rush to change your will? Did he ask you to?" Her father's gaze narrowed sharply.

"No!" Taite gasped. She hadn't realized that her father would be so suspicious of Pierce when she'd wanted her will changed. Stepping closer to her father, Taite spoke in an undertone, "Pierce has said that he doesn't even want to know how much I'm worth. He doesn't care. Besides, he isn't poor. And it is *me* he married, not my money. He loves me for me alone."

Her father's suspicious gaze glanced off Pierce before he swung it back to her again. "I hope you're right, girl. There are people out in the world who never think that they have enough. You would be easy pickings, Taite. You're too trusting. I hope that you haven't let Caite know she is to inherit the rest of your estate. That girl would be chomping at the bit for something to happen to you."

Hurt curled within Taite at her father's cruelty. Caite might seem to always be in one scrape or the other, but most of her escapades were an attempt to get their father's attention. Taite was sure of it.

"I am not naïve, Father. I know there are untrustworthy people in the world. You always made sure Caite and I both were made aware of it. However, I trust Pierce. The only reason I'm not going to tell him just yet, of what I've done, is that I'm afraid it won't please him."

At her father's snort of disbelief, Taite turned from him. She fiddled with the silver ladle that lay in the punch bowl. Lifting the ladle, she slowly refilled her cup.

"Can't you just be happy for me, Dad? I...I...thought that you liked Pierce?" Taite could feel the pressure build behind her eyes. Fighting the sensation, she was determined that her father would not make her cry. His cynicism could just be too much at times. For the first time in her life that Taite could remember, her father reached out and voluntarily touched her. In shock, she looked down at his lean fingers that lay against hers.

"I like your husband, Taite, but my trust of him will take a lot longer.

Don't love or trust too much, girl. It will only cause hurt in the end."

With those graveled words, he walked away. In dismay, Taite watched her father stroll to where his best friend and Pierce stood together, talking.

"Congratulations, gorgeous. I have to tell you—my heart is officially broken into tiny pieces by it not being me you married today." Mickey dramatically laid his palm over his heart placement, his face an expression of sorrow.

Pulled from her assessment of her father, Taite tried to smile at Mickey and his joke. She must not have pulled it off because he frowned and stepped closer to her. "Are you okay, honey?"

Shaking off her melancholy, Taite managed to give Mickey a wide smile. "Now, why wouldn't I be okay? I just married the man I love, didn't I?"

Feeling arms snake around her waist, Taite inclined back against a toned body and she looked up at Pierce. He smiled back down at her.

"I hope that you just married the man you love," he told her before he leaned down to kiss the side of her neck. Glancing back up at Mickey, he smiled wide. He seemed extremely pleased with life. "Can Taite and I get out of here now?"

Mickey nodded. "I brought your car around a couple of minutes ago."

"Tell Emma that we'll be back tomorrow night to pick up Lacy." At Mickey's nod, Pierce grabbed hold of Taite's hand and swiftly walked them from the room. With a laugh, Taite attempted to stay up with him as she trotted along beside him.

"Wait, Pierce," she finally gasped.

"Why are we leaving in such a hurry? You act like someone might stop us. Shouldn't we tell everyone goodbye?"

Pierce gave a growl, but he slowed his pace.

"Two weeks, Taite. It has been two weeks since we've been together."

Quickly pulling the front door of the home open when they reached it, Taite darted to the waiting car.

"What are you waiting for then? Let's go home," she gaily called out when Pierce didn't move just watched her from the doorway of the home.

At his sudden movement her way, Taite slammed her car door closed. Laughter abounded when he slid in beside her and reached for her.

He stopped laughing to just look at her. His hands at her waist.

Taite sobered as she returned his serious look.

"I love you, Pierce."

Turning, he silently started the car. He reached to pull her across the seat of the car, so that she sat beside him. The car accelerated gaining speed as they left the mansion and the others behind.

****

Pierce watched Taite wiggle and work to remove her wedding gown. She looked even more beautiful that day than usual, something he hadn't thought possible. She glowed with youth and vitality. His breath had caught that morning when she'd walked into the family room where he and the others waited for her. Boldly, she'd met his eager stare with one of her own and seemed to see only him. He'd felt proud when she hadn't missed a step at Lacy suddenly running to her wanting to be picked up.

She had gracefully reached down to lift her up, and then kept her within her arms throughout the wedding ceremony. Taite was a precious gift, a renewal to his and Lacy's life, a new beginning for them. Reaching out, Pierce gently brushed his wife's fingers away from the side of her dress and from the row of tiny, white buttons that ran its length.

"Beautiful, but completely impractical," he stated as he worked the buttons loose.

Taite reached to undo his tie and then the buttons on his shirt. Pierce felt a quiver start deep within him when her fingers touched his bare skin as she removed his clothing. He stepped out from his pants at her urging for him to let her have them.

"I love the dark hair on your chest, and the way it tapers down into a *V* to there," she whispered.

At her touch—to *there*, Pierce's flesh tightened. He helped her to step out and away from the wedding dress.

His breathing became labored as she continued to touch and caress him. She appeared completely focused as to where her fingertips connected with his skin. Grabbing her hand, Pierce led her to their bed. She crawled onto it on her knees and then turned so that she faced him. He stretched out beside her on the mattress

"I love your shapely legs and derriere," he said as he settled.

"You do?" She seemed pleased.

Pierce ran his hands up over her bent legs and then cupped her rump. He looked up and met her gaze. "Oh, yes," he whispered. "I do. And I love your beautiful, copper-colored hair and your gorgeous, dark brown eyes. I even love your fingertips. Especially when you run them over my skin as you always do."

"Like this?"

With a groan, Pierce reached out and pulled her to him so that she sprawled over the top of him. He buried his fingers deep within her hair, and tilting her face upward toward his, he brushed his lips across hers. His touch of her ignited a fire in them both it seemed.

Chapter 10

Taite's smile was a visible expression of how she felt inside as she walked along the concrete sidewalk toward the office building where her new husband waited for her. *My husband is perfect,* she thought, as her smile grew wider. She waved toward a local resident of the town across the opposite side of the street that she recognized. The woman gave a jaunty lift of her own hand in response.

Taite shivered not only from the cool air, but at the blissful thoughts which continued to circulate through her. She'd had two months of total bliss. *Absolute total happiness.* Pierce promised that by the same time next year, when their first-year anniversary came around, he and she would get to go on that honeymoon they hadn't been able to take. Taite understood. With her husband having just recently purchased the real estate business, he couldn't very well take off and leave it now. It would flounder while they were gone.

When he suggested that she should take some time off from work and plan on finding them a larger home than the condo's they both owned, Taite jumped at the opportunity. Her time from work would give her a chance to develop a tighter bond with Lacy, who she adored, and who she'd reluctantly left with Emma that day. *I really don't need to work,* Taite mused, although she did want to go back to the office as soon as she found a home for her new family and all were settled into it and into a family routine. She needed to have that mental stimulation of work. And the first house that she'd toured that day, only one week after taking her stretch from work, was perfect for her new family.

It was a stately, two-story brick home with a glorious view of the Blue Ridge Mountains from its kitchen windows. She wanted Pierce to tour it with her before she agreed to its purchase and price, although he'd told her he would be happy with whatever she chose. Pulling open the door to her husband's business, it startled Taite to see her sister sitting in his office. Caite, as usual, was dressed in a pretty outfit. It made her hair shine.

There was another man in the office as well, someone Taite didn't recognize. Pierce's door was shut and all three in the office were laughing over something that had apparently been said.

Pierce looked up and noticed her. With a smile, he made a motion toward her indicating that he would be a moment.

With a nod of understanding, Taite turned to go visit with Mickey.

He glanced up at her when she walked into his office.

"Hello there. This is a nice surprise. I haven't gotten to see you in awhile. How've you been?"

Taite sat down across from her friend. The chair—one of two always positioned before their desks for their clients—was comfortable. Leaning back, Taite crossed her legs. Looking down, she dusted a piece of lint from her black-colored jean-covered leg. She noted that Mickey couldn't seem to keep his gaze from drifting past her to her husband's office.

"I'm fine. I just finished touring a home which I think will be perfect for my new family."

Mickey jumped from his chair and with stiff strides he walked to shut his office door. Just as abruptly as he'd lunged up, he slumped down beside her in the empty chair alongside the one that she was seated in. He reached for her hand as if she was a lifeline, and he squeezed her fingers tight within his. Taite sat up straighter. *Now what*, she wondered.

"Taite, I don't trust Pierce."

Irritation rose swiftly in Taite at Mickey's theatrics. A desire to defend her husband followed just as quickly.

"You are talking about my husband, Mickey. Be careful."

"And you're my friend, Taite. Caite may not be you, but she is all I have."

"What a strange thing for you to say."

With confusion, Taite studied Mickey. He always had a flair for the dramatic, and this seemed to be one of those days for it.

"I think Caite and your husband are having an affair."

"How dare you say such a thing!"

Throwing Mickey's hand from hers, Taite stood, ready to storm from his office. She glared with hurt and anger at her friend.

Mickey jumped up to seek her gaze with his own. "Did you know that your sister has been coming in here quite often? To buy a home she says. I don't believe her. Why didn't she come to me? She and Pierce are always in his office secretly talking. She tells me when she finds a house, she'll discuss its purchase with me then."

Taite felt surprise this wasn't the first time her sister had been to see her husband. He hadn't made any mention of Caite's prior visits to the office.

Her anger leaving her as swiftly as it had rose, Taite reached out to lay a hand in sympathy on Mickey's arm.

"Listen, Mickey, your imagination is playing tricks on you. Pierce and my sister are *not* having an affair. If Caite told you that she wants to buy a home, I'm sure that's what she's doing. You know how much money she and I inherited. She can afford it. Caite never did like her condo. You know that. Who's the man sitting beside her?" Taite turned to look toward her husband's office.

"He's a client," Mickey replied as they both gazed through the glass partitions toward the gentleman. As if embarrassed, Mickey turned away from them and then he mumbled, "We have his home listed."

Leaning toward her friend, Taite kissed his tightly clenched jawline. Tenderly, she laid a hand against his smooth cheek and she met his wounded gaze with hers.

"See," she said softly. "Caite says she wants to buy a home, and who is she talking to? Someone who is selling. Mickey, darling, you can't allow jealously to tear you apart where my sister is concerned."

Mickey's door opened, and Taite dropped her hand back to her side. Turning, she smiled at Pierce. He didn't smile back but looked from her to Mickey. Stepping to the side of the open doorway, he let her sister enter the room.

"Well, well, here is the blushing bride. Mickey, doesn't my sister look radiant? Marriage agrees with her, wouldn't you say?"

Looking from her sister to Mickey, and then to her husband, Taite could feel the undercurrents that seemed to be circulating around the room. Why was Caite talking to Mickey as if he should be jealous of her and Pierce's happiness? Taite furrowed her brow. Unless...Mickey had asked Caite to marry him, and she'd refused. It would be just like her sister to rub Mickey's nose in it, too, Taite realized with renewed sympathy for him.

"Taite, come into my office."

Turning at her husband's quiet order, Taite placed her hand on Mickey's shoulder and gave it a quick squeeze in sympathy for him. She looked at her sister. "Call me, Caite. We haven't gotten to talk in a while."

At her sister's nod of agreement, Taite followed her husband.

"I found us a home. I want you to look at it, though, before I tell the people we are interested," she informed when they entered his office.

Pierce didn't respond as he shut his office door behind her. Reaching out, he flipped the blinds closed to his window.

When he faced toward her, Taite was surprised that he seemed angry, furiously so. She raised her brow in question. He watched her but didn't say anything.

"What's wrong?" she finally asked.

"I don't want to look up and ever see you groping that man again, do you hear me?"

In shock, Taite took a step back and then plopped down onto the couch behind her when the back of her legs hit its edge. Pierce leaned in closer. His eyes hard.

"Why have you never mentioned that you and Mickey dated last year, before he started dating your sister?"

Taite, unable to speak, watched her husband straighten when she remained silent. He walked to the front of his desk, and he lifted the paperweight that she'd given him. His posture was stiff as he studied it, and his hands tightened around the bronze figure as if he wished to snap it in two.

"Who told you that we dated?"

"It doesn't make a difference who told me. Why didn't you?" Pierce lifted his anger filled gaze to hers as he set the paperweight back to its resting place.

Taite lunged up from the couch, her own anger finally overtaking her shock. "Do you want a list of all the men in my life before you? I didn't mention that I once dated Mickey because it's irrelevant."

"If it's so irrelevant to you, then why is it that every time I turn around you or Mickey has your hands on each other?"

"I refuse to listen to this stupidity."

Pierce quickly stepped from his desk to grasp her upper arm when she turned to leave the office.

"Stay away from the man, Taite."

With bewilderment, Taite looked at her newly acquired husband. She didn't know this person. This…this…angry stranger wasn't the man that she had married.

"I'm going home."

When her husband failed to respond but let his hand drop from her arm, Taite picked up her purse. Jerking open the office door, she marched from the room. At Mickey's salute as she passed his office, Taite gave a stiff tilt of her head in response and hurried past him.

****

With sharp disgust felt at the obscene behavior he'd just displayed, Pierce watched Taite sweep past Mickey's office and then on out the front door of the office building and from his sight. Wearily, he ran a hand through his hair.

Turning, he shut his office door and then slumped down onto the couch. He felt stupid, just as she had called him.

His anger had overtaken him when he'd happened to glimpse his new wife leaning over to kiss Mickey's cheek and then to caress it as she said something to him. The scene between the two had seemed tender, loverlike, as they gazed into each other's eyes. His temper had flared with it and irrationally, he'd acted on that jealous emotion. He should have waited, asked her about Mickey and their past relationship, when they were home and alone. Hell, he knew Taite loved him even if she might at one time have had feelings for the man who now dated her sister.

Caite let it slip, just that day, that Taite and Mickey had dated before she'd started dating the man. If she hadn't acted so funny when he'd questioned her about it, he wouldn't have thought anything about their history.

Sighing, Pierce stood and walked to sit in the chair behind his desk. He shuffled the paperwork on his desk not seeing the legal words written. He would need to make a humble apology to his wife, and to help smooth the way, a new bracelet brought home with him that evening might help to relieve her anger toward him.

Chapter 11

"Coke, please." Paying the young cashier before her, Taite picked up her drink and walked to an empty table. Glancing around the mall, she sipped at the drink she held as she sat down. Feeling the spurt of fresh tears, Taite squashed the reaction. *It is just a silly misunderstanding that will be cleared up once I force myself to go home,* she determinedly told herself.

"Oh, jeez," she quietly moaned when the cause of her troubles rounded the mall corner and noticed her. With quick strides, Mickey walked to her. Pulling out a metal chair, he straddled its seat.

"Fancy seeing you here. Buy anything special?"

With a halfhearted motion toward her bags, Taite couldn't meet Mickey's gaze. "Just some stuff from Bath and Body Works. I was getting ready to leave."

"Where's hubby?"

"Home, I assume."

Leaning forward, Mickey searched Taite's face. "You've been crying." His gaze softened. Suddenly, he stiffened, and he stood quickly.

"Come with me," he stated.

Curiously, Taite looked around the mall.

Mickey grabbed her bags and took off. Taite hastened after him.

"What in the world is wrong with you, Mickey? Give me my bags."

Coming to a sudden halt, Mickey grabbed her chin, and he forced her to look toward the jewelry store she favored. Dropping his hand from her face, he motioned toward the couple who stood side by side, their heads bent over something.

"I wondered when I saw her and him both pull out from work at the same time what was up. What did I tell you, Taite? Do you believe me now?"

"You followed her?"

"Damn right I did."

Taite sighed. "There's an explanation for this, Mickey. I'm not going to jump to any conclusions without first hearing my husband's side of why he and Caite are in that store together. Come on, let's go in."

When Taite took a step toward the couple, Mickey jerked her back to him. He hissed in her ear, "You can confront your husband if you want, Taite. However, I don't want Caite to know that I've seen her. What I don't understand is why you can't see what is going on here? Caite doesn't have boundaries. You know that, Taite. She didn't care that you and I were a couple before she came back into the country. Her actively pursuing me was what made me break up with you."

"Our nonexistent sexual attraction to each other is what made you breakup with me," Taite responded drily.

At Mickey's pained look, she threw her hands up in the air. "Fine, I will talk to Pierce about why he and Caite are in the jewelry store, later, when he gets home. I won't let him know that you were with me. I would hate to spoil the drama for you."

Mickey shot a narrowed look at the couple still engrossed with what the jeweler held out to them.

"Good," he stated, giving Taite's arm a tight squeeze. He turned fully toward her.

"I'll walk you to your car. You call me when Pierce tells you his side of the story. And Taite, don't be fooled by some elaborate explanation that he comes up with. I feel it in my gut that something isn't right."

With a slanted look given to the man by her side, Taite gravely agreed to Mickey's request, although she couldn't stop her small grin that quivered. *Mickey should've tried his hand at acting*, she thought with an inward laugh. The people in that field seemed to love the exaggeration of their lives. The way he loved drama, he would have fit in perfectly. Taite had no worries about Pierce having an affair with her sister. He loved her.

She was confident of that.

Her cell phone rang just as she slid into her car. Giving a wave goodbye to Mickey, Taite reached for it. Starting her car, she glanced to see who was calling.

It surprised her to see her dad's name reflected. He hardly ever called. "Dad?"

"Taite, I want you to come and see me tomorrow. There is something I need to talk to you about."

"Is everything okay?"

"I've had him investigated."

"What? Who? Wait! Have you had Pierce investigated? I should hang up on you."

"Listen, Taite. There are some things that you need to be made aware of."

"Good grief, Dad. If it's not Mickey, it is you."

"Mickey? What has he been saying about Pierce?"

"Nothing of importance. His imagination running away with him is all."

"Come see me tomorrow, Taite. Don't let Pierce know of my investigation. Not until you see me."

"Dad, I—"

"Come see me, Taite."

Her phone suddenly went dead, and Taite looked at it in amazement. Her dad had just hung up on her.

****

Pierce smiled with puzzlement as Taite practically jumped a foot into the air when he walked into the living room where she stood beside Lacy, and the toys his daughter had scattered over the living room. The bracelet that he'd wanted to give to her in apology for his actions that day was still at the jewelers. After purchasing the piece, he'd requested a special engraving to be placed on the inside of the clasp. To his irritation the engraver had been out. No one else in the store, he was told, had the required skills to engrave a simple endearment it seemed. Tomorrow evening was the earliest he could pick up the gift if he wanted it engraved.

Taite hastily lowered her eyes from his when his gaze met hers. Walking to her, Pierce leaned down to kiss the soft skin at her nape.

"Should I apologize again?" he questioned softly when he drew back from her. Pierce frowned when Taite took a quick, sideways step away from him. She rubbed at the spot where he'd kissed her as if it irritated her.

"Why were you so late in getting home?" she asked.

His frown deepening, Pierce watched her fiddle with the toy that she held. It was the third time since he'd gotten home, she'd voiced that same question. He had arrived home later than planned, so he wasn't surprised when she'd asked him the first time. He'd responded that a client stopped by unexpectedly detaining him. He hadn't told her he'd gone back to the office to pick up some paperwork he'd forgotten, after leaving the jewelry store, and that the customer called then wanting to drop by.

Taite kept her eyes on the toy that she held not looking at him. With sudden determination, she knelt and began to grab at each of Lacy's toys scattered out around their feet.

"I told you when you asked earlier, sweetheart. A client who wanted to list his home came in at the last moment. I was held up talking to him. Why the third degree ever since I walked through the door?"

Throwing the toys she held into his daughter's toy storage-box, Taite lifted her head. For a moment, she stared at him almost as if she wanted to say something to him.

Dropping her gaze, she stood instead.

Pierce reached out to grasp hold of her hand. Gently, he pulled her toward him. "I'm sorry, honey. What else can I say with what happened between us at the office, except that?"

Taite didn't attempt to pull away from him, although she stiffened. Her fingers finally wrapped tightly around his, and she met his gaze.

"I need to go see my father tomorrow."

"That's fine, sweetheart." Pierce let loose her hand when she gave it a tug. He watched as she bent and picked up Lacy and then turned to leave the room.

"I love you," he said before she left.

Taite paused. She didn't turn around.

"I love you, too," she whispered.

Turning on the television, Pierce watched the news as he waited for her to return. When an hour passed and she still hadn't come back into the living room, he stood, and flipped off the noise maker. Walking by his daughter's bedroom, he stopped to glance in on her. Sexy was curled up at the foot of her bed.

The mutt didn't lift his head, but his eyes watched him.

Lacy lay in a tight ball in the center of her bed, sound asleep. The innocence of the sight caused Pierce to curve his mouth into a smile before he turned away.

Taking a quick shower, he toweled dried his hair, and then walked into the master bedroom where Taite was already in bed. Sliding between the sheets beside her, he reached out to her. The light scent of her freshly washed and dried hair was an achingly and endearing essence of her. Pierce felt Taite stiffened at his touch. Rising on his elbow, he looked down at her.

Lifting a silky strand of hair, he wound it around his fingers to give it a slight tug. "Hey, I thought you were coming back into the living room. What happened?"

Met with silence, Pierce leaned forward.

"I will say it again, I'm sorry, Taite. You and Mickey are just friends. I know this. I give you a promise; I won't let my jealousy get the best of me again where you two are concerned. The next time I'm jealous, I'll just drag you off to bed to make sure you know who it is who loves you."

At his attempted joke, Taite sniffed.

Loosening his hand from her hair, Pierce placed a finger under her chin to gently force her face upward. He feathered his lips across hers. At his intimate touch, Taite cringed backwards. She twisted her face from his.

"I have a headache, Pierce."

At the age-old excuse, Pierce stiffened. He had apologized not once, but four times now. Turning Taite so that she faced him completely, Pierce was intent on their talking. He then noticed the whiteness of her face, and it gave him pause.

"Is it bad?"

"A…a…migraine." When her tears began to slip down the sides of her face, he tenderly bent and kissed her forehead. Reaching past her to the lamp on their nightstand, Pierce switched it off.

"Go to sleep, baby."

Taite rolled against him to bury her face in his chest. Pierce wrapped his arms around her and held her tightly to him. He would have to remember in the future to watch how he spoke to his wife when he was angered. He hadn't realized that a simple fight would upset her so.

Chapter 12

Blowing her nose, Taite threw the dirty tissue she held onto the pile of others on her front car seat. Passing the vehicle in front of her with an acceleration of speed from her own, she felt the spurt of weak tears again. It seemed she cried at the drop of a hat these days.

With an angry exclamation, Taite squashed her need to have another good howl. Her husband had out and out lied to her, not once, but several times, and what made her even angrier was with her knowing he lied, she'd still not challenged him on it, informing him of what she'd seen at the mall. She had given him another chance that morning to tell her the truth of his late arrival home.

On a casual note, she'd informed him she'd gone to the mall the evening before and had thought that she'd seen his car in the parking lot when she'd left. She'd watched Pierce closely as he shook his head in denial at her question. With a sweet half-smile, he'd responded that he would have a gift to give her that night for his harsh words of the evening before.

Tenderly, he pulled her to him to kiss her good-bye. When he softly said how much he loved her and missed having her at work with him, she had melted.

Grabbing another tissue, Taite wiped at her nose. *I'm weak*, she thought with bitterness. Weak and so desperate to believe in her husband that she would swallow whatever he told her, even knowing he lied, and not challenge him on it.

She would have spilled everything to him that morning if he hadn't been running late for an appointment with a client. She'd almost told him that she'd definitely seen him and her sister together at the mall. She wanted him to have a chance to change his story. She wanted to tell him her father had him investigated. She would have, too, if Mickey hadn't kept texting her, telling her to keep their secret until she talked to her father.

With a sniff, Taite turned her car down her father's long driveway. Reaching its end, she parked and killed the car engine. Checking her face in the car's rear-view mirror, Taite stepped from the car onto the pebbled driveway. *What could Father have unearthed from Pierce's background that is so important for me to know?* she wondered as she looked up at the three-story house.

Emma believed that Pierce walked on water and always gushed about what a good man she had married. Could she and Emma both be so wrong in their belief of Pierce and his goodness? With a helpless shake of her head, Taite sighed deep. No matter that Pierce hadn't admitted to his and Caite being at the jewelry store together the evening before, she still couldn't believe that he and her sister were having an affair as Mickey alleged. When she returned home that evening, she'd demand that he tell her why they were together the evening before. She had let her insecurities scare her into remaining silent.

"Come on, Sexy. It's time to go in and see what conflict awaits us now."

Obediently, Sexy hopped out from the car, his tail wagging.

"No, Sexy, you come with me," Taite stated sharply when her pet started to trot off. As she glanced around the large expanse of yard and the trees that dotted the rolling landscape, Taite felt a sudden unease. Shivering, she bounded up the steps to the front door of the mansion.

****

Leaning back into the chair situated across from her father's desk, Taite's insides twisted and her nausea rose. Swallowing hard, she kept her gaze lowered. "Is this investigator a reliable source?"

"He was recommended by an acquaintance and one who has personally used the man himself."

Taite couldn't stop her smoothing motion of her hand over the document that she held, as if by her motion, she could erase the words printed on the paper. The pictures she'd been given were scattered on the floor at her feet. Her throat hurt.

"I saw him in the mall yesterday with Caite. They didn't know I was anywhere around." Taite looked up to meet her father's gaze.

"I don't know what to do," she managed to say past the obstruction in her throat as her father watched her.

His lips tightened.

"Divorce the man," he ordered.

Taite's heart slammed into her chest at his harsh directive. Her father's steel grey gaze held hers. As if in a vacuum, Taite noted the worn chair that he sat in. When she thought of her father, it was always this picture that she envisioned. Him—alone—in that old leather chair. Was this how her life was to turn out, also? An embittered old woman just as he was a cynical old man? One who always looked at others with suspicion and distrust?

Could her husband be one of those people who preyed on the wealthy as her father always warned her and Caite about? *Poor little rich girls,* one of the housemaids used to be fond of sneering to her and Caite when no one was around to overhear. *Had Pierce known all along about her father's wealth? Was that why he had bought the condo in the same building as where she lived? And Caite, how can my sister, my own flesh and blood, do this to me?*

With an inward, shrinking back at her rioting thoughts and swirling pain, Taite wanted to scream and to tear madly at the paper she held. If her husband had married her for her money, he was certainly messing things up by becoming involved with her sister when she was the wealthier of the two. *Am I clutching at straws to disbelieve what is before me?*

Taite had never thought of her husband as being particularly dense. In fact, the opposite was true. He was a very clever and smart man, too smart to be caught up in this type of scheme. And he loved her, didn't he?

Unsure if she were doing the right thing, but with the same steely determination her father displayed, Taite folded the paper report that she held, and she pushed it back into the manila envelope it had come from.

The time for me of running from life's hurts is over, she decided with a sudden, firm decision made. She would confront her fears head on. Her sister and her husband both needed to be given the benefit of doubt before she did anything. She needed to trust and not to act in a rash manner.

Taite raised her gaze to her father's. "I want to talk to my husband, Dad. Then I'm going to show him this report and the pictures, and I'm going to tell him what I saw for myself at the mall."

Taite straightened her shoulders. "I need to hear what he has to say in his defense on all counts before I act."

Her father's brows snapped together. "I was afraid that would be your response. He is using you, girl. Don't let this game go any further."

He leaned forward.

"The evening of your wedding, I found that the paperwork on my desk had been shuffled around. The copy of your changed will shoved between the middle of the pile. I'm certain that I placed it at the bottom of my paperwork. I had planned to put everything inside my safe that morning, but got called away and forgot about it, until later."

Taite felt her body begin to shake. She fought to get its trembling under control. "Maybe you moved the paperwork and just didn't realize it, Daddy."

"I know how I had my paperwork filed, girl," he retorted sharply. "And the staff knows not to touch anything on my desk."

Taite pressed her lips together to still their quivering as her father stared at her.

"Pierce didn't come into your office, Daddy. I am positive of it."

Several seconds of charged silence sliced between them.

"Change your will, Taite. At least until we get everything resolved."

With her despair choking her, Taite nodded as she agreed to her father's demand. "First thing in the morning, I'll go to the lawyer's office and have everything changed back. But it will only be that way, until I know my husband is not the man that this report portrays. How could I love him if he were?"

His face twisting with bitterness, Taite watched her father's expression become shuttered. "Love can blind you to faults that will bring you to your knees, Taite."

"Dad?"

Her father gave a shrug and then shook his head as if he cleared away memories. "Nothing, Taite. I just wish you wouldn't return to that man. I can see, though, that you are determined to have a full accounting from him. Have it your way then."

At her father's dismissive gesture, Taite stood. In confusion, she watched him for a moment. She wondered what, exactly, it was in his lifetime that had embittered him so. He never talked about his childhood or even his adulthood. It was as if he had no past.

"I love you, Dad. I know that you only want what's best for me, but I need to talk to my husband before I make a decision."

With a cough, her father reached for a pen. He didn't look up.

****

"Hello."

"How did the visit go with your father?"

At the velvet sound of her husband's voice, Taite's throat tightened.

"Babe, you there?"

"I'm here. I…I'm just watching the traffic around me. Let me pull over." Looking behind her, Taite maneuvered her car over into the other lane and then into the truck stop/rest area to the right of the highway.

"I'm on my way home," she stated after she parked her car. Her hands shook so badly that she almost dropped her cell phone.

"We need to talk, Pierce."

"Where are you, honey? Are you almost home?"

"I'm halfway there. I stopped to get gas at a truck stop. After I fill up, I plan on driving straight home."

"I'll be home by the time you get here. We'll talk then. I love you, sweetheart."

"I love you, too," Taite whispered as the phone she held went dead. Wiping at the tears that flowed freely down her cheeks, Taite sat quietly for a moment as she stared out her car windshield. The report from her father's private investigator was wrong. It had to be. Pictures could lie, couldn't they?

Paying for her gas, Taite walked to her car and slid into the seat beside Sexy. With exasperation, she slung her car door back open again upon noticing that a flyer had been placed under her windshield wiper. Taite hated it when people put announcements on the windshield. It was a pet peeve of hers.

"Why didn't you scare them away, Sexy?" she asked as she set a foot back out of the car onto the black asphalt and then leaned up and forward to grasp hold of the flyer. Jerking the piece of paper out from under her windshield wiper, Taite started to wad it up as she sat back down when the handwritten words on it caught her attention.

Scanning the parking lot, she read the scrawled words again. Only five words and they had an ominous ring.

This is just the beginning.

Jerking her foot into her car, Taite slammed the car door shut, and locked the doors. *Just the beginning? The beginning of what?* She swiveled to scan the vehicles parked around her. All were empty.

Exiting the gas station, Taite inspected every automobile and every person within when she drove by. She accelerated her car's speed at her return to the main highway. She hadn't recognized anyone. And no one appeared to pay any attention to her. No car followed behind her either.

Reaching her hand out, Taite petted at the top of Sexy's silky head. "This is the beginning of what, Sexy? Who left that note for me?"

At Sexy's whine, Taite shivered. "Strange," she whispered.

Pushing her cell phone button to dial Pierce, Taite listened as his voice mail came on. She cancelled the call. She shouldn't be driving and trying to call him anyway. The sun was already beginning to go down, and it was past time for Pierce to have picked Lacy up from Emma's. He'd probably gone home first and then had forgotten his cell phone when he went to collect the baby.

Laying her phone aside between her and Sexy, Taite glanced in the car's rear-view mirror. Traffic was light that evening. She'd been the only car on the road for about a mile now. Relaxing, she looked at Sexy, and she laughed.

"I'm seeing boogie men everywhere, aren't I, Sexy?" Her dog whined. Taite reached out to pet him, reassuring him that she was okay.

Boom!

Taite screamed as her head slammed backwards onto her headrest. She fought to keep her car from careening off the road. Giving a quick glance in her rearview mirror, all she could see was the grille of a truck. Taite pushed her foot down hard on her car's accelerator. Her hands tightened on the steering wheel when the truck behind her picked up speed also. It caught up to her again in no time.

Boom! The back of Taite's head crashed into her car's head rest again. This time, the car lifted into the air as if it were in slow motion. Taite heard her own screaming. Everything seemed unreal. Her car hit the embankment on the side of the road. The contact jarred.

Dizzily, unable to close her eyes, Taite watched through the car windshield as earth connected with sky and sky to earth before her car came to an abrupt and rocking halt from its roll. Groaning, she tried to unbuckle her seatbelt.

Blackness pulled at her, sucking her down into a dark abyss. Taite fought it. She hurt all over. She blinked. She couldn't see.

Sexy?

Blindly, Taite groped along the top of the seat of the car. Encountering her pet's hair, she curled her fingers tightly into the soft strands of comfort. With a whimper of pain, Taite gave up the fight for consciousness and let the swirling shade take her.

"Can you hear me? Can you hear me, angel?"

Taite felt someone's touch. The voice—it came from a distant place. It had a soothing, calming quality. Taite tried to lift her eyelids. They refused to cooperate even though she struggled with them.

"Sweet angel, I'm going to slowly raise you, okay?"

Taite tried to nod, but then she cried out when her arm was lifted.

"I'm sorry, angel. Just listen to my voice and try not to pay attention to being moved, okay."

"Okay."

"My name is Gabriel. What's yours?"

"T...Taite."

"Beautiful name. Married?"

"Yes."

"Lucky man. Children?"

"One. You...?"

At Taite's hazy question, the man named Gabriel fell silent. When a few moments passed and Taite could no longer feel his presence, she cried out with fear.

"Shh...I'm here. I have many children. We are at the hospital now. I have to leave you, angel."

"No...No...Stay. Please stay." Taite felt a hand caress her cheek and the touch calmed her. She wished she could see her hero's face.

"You will survive this, angel," he told her. "I'll come and visit with you soon. But I must go now."

Taite tried to reach out to grasp hold of the man who had rescued her. He was gone as suddenly as he'd appeared, as if he'd never been.

Chapter 13

"It has been three days now, and she keeps calling for someone by the name of Gabriel. Do any of you know this person? The person's presence might help to calm her."

Taite groggily woke at the question being asked. She felt the negative responses by people who she sensed were crowded around her bed. She knew without being able to see that her father and Chad stood over her.

"Dad?" she rasped through a dry throat. She couldn't open her eyes. She remembered hearing someone remark they were swelled shut. She felt a light touch to her hand as the blackness wanted to claim her again. Then Gabriel stood beside her. Taite didn't know how she knew it was him, but she did.

"You came back," she whispered.

"Yes, I told you I would."

"I don't think. I don't think that I—"

"Shh. Yes, you can."

"I lost my baby. A baby that I didn't even know I was carrying."

Fingers reached to smooth away the tears that flowed down Taite's cheeks. "You are loved, angel."

With those words, Taite felt her hero move away. She reached out, but knew she would encounter air. Unconsciousness wanted to claim her again. She didn't fight its call, and its blackness soothed her once again.

****

Pierce watched as his wife's tears left wet tracks down the sides of her face. Her slender hand moved as if she searched for something. He felt her dad stiffen beside him when he grasped her fingers and pulled them to his mouth. He needed, had to touch her.

He had died a thousand deaths when Emma, her face devoid of color, had told him that she'd just received a call that Taite had had an accident and was in the emergency room. For a moment, he hadn't been able to move or to even breathe as memories of his first wife's death swamped him.

Not again... was all his numb mind could think.

Gazing at Taite, Pierce felt his love for her well-up inside of him. Swallowing hard, he fought back his tears as he scanned her injured face. Both her eyes were swollen shut, and her face and body heavily bruised, but no broken bones, thank God. No broken bones, but she'd been tossed and jerked around enough that it had caused the loss of their baby. Sexy hadn't survived the crash either.

Taite's father shifted again. In irritation, Pierce looked up at him and then glanced away. Blake and Chad both acted fiercely protective of Taite, as if he, himself, might harm her in some way. Their actions left him puzzled, even angry.

Pierce glanced toward Mickey and Caite who stood against the hospital room wall. Neither had said a word upon entering his wife's room. They stood silently beside each other as they gazed across the small space toward the bed where Taite lay. Caite raised her eyes and her gaze locked with his. Taite's nurse walking back into the room pulled Pierce's attention from her. In a quiet voice, the nurse informed the group that her patient needed to rest. Having so many in the room seemed to agitate her patient, she stated with a frown.

Pierce looked down at his wife. Leaning close to her ear, he whispered, "I love you, sweetheart."

At his quiet words, Taite cried out. His presence seemed to upset her. It clutched at Pierce's heart. The nurse's frown grew deeper as she looked from him to her patient. Pierce knew the woman wondered what it was he'd said. Even Blake and Chad took a step forward. Pierce glared at both men. *What in the hell is going on here?* He watched Blake glance at Chad.

Pierce sensed that some silent message passed between the two elderly gentlemen.

****

"I don't want to see him and that is final, Emma."

Taite kept her eyelids lowered and her gaze locked on her fingers she'd laced together. Emma had come alone that day to the hospital to visit. Taite's tenth day of recovery since her admittance into the medical center. The first question that had popped out of Emma's mouth was *why* Taite had given instructions that her husband was not to be allowed to visit her. Taite had also given the same instructions with regards to Caite.

"I just don't understand it, Taite. This is killing Pierce. Chad and your dad have refused to answer any of his questions or mine. Both say it is up to you to decide if you want to discuss it with him or me."

"And I don't want to discuss it, Emma." Taite raised her multi-colored eyelids to meet her friend's questioning look. Emma frowned at her. Taite sighed.

"I made a mistake when I married Pierce."

Emma sat down in the hospital chair. She looked at Taite with obvious bewilderment. Taite chose to ignore her confusion. Emma settled back into the chair with a soft sigh. Apparently, she decided her argument for Pierce was going nowhere.

"Did Dad have Sexy buried on the farm as I requested?"

Emma nodded her head. Taite with her fingertips smoothed at the wrinkled blanket that lay draped over her legs. Her eyes teared at the thought of her beloved pet. "The doctor said that I can get out of here tomorrow. I've made the decision that I'm going home to stay with Dad for a while. Let Pierce know, Emma, so he won't try to come here to see me tomorrow."

At Emma's sound of distress, Taite shook her head. She didn't want any argument.

Sighing deeply, Emma quieted, understanding her silent command,

and then she asked, "Have you heard back from the sheriff?"

"He came to see me this morning. Since I couldn't identify what type of truck rear-ended me and there were no witnesses, he said he was coming up empty-handed."

"I don't understand why someone would purposefully do what was done to you. I just can't wrap my mind around the cruelty of it. And that note left on your windshield. The whole thing is bizarre." Emma's brow creased.

Taite felt her insides twist. She had her suspicions as to why she was deliberately run off the road. As soon as she'd been able, she had asked her dad to bring her lawyer to her so that she could change her will. She'd begged her father not to tell the sheriff or to approach Pierce and Caite with what she and he both suspected was true.

Her father finally agreed to her request, although with loud and angry objections issued. Taite couldn't stomach for the whole world to know how she had been duped, and she told her father so. But, if Pierce or her sister thought they would inherit one penny of her money at her death, they were going to be in for a shock.

That note, left on her windshield hadn't made sense at the time just as Emma said, but it did now. It was filed away with the rest of the evidence against her husband and her sister if she should ever need it.

Taite hoped after she was released from the hospital that she would be able to forget how naïve she had been about her husband. She would rather Pierce and her sister to never realize she knew what they'd been about. It helped her pride, somehow, for them to think she had thrown them aside unaware of their plan.

Mickey stuck his head around her hospital door. "Hey, beautiful, how are you this morning?"

At Mickey's cheerful profile, Taite's spirits lifted.

"Hi, Mickey."

Emma abruptly rose when Mickey sauntered on into the room. She kissed Taite's bruised cheek. "I have to leave, Taite. However, I'll come with Chad to visit you this weekend at your dad's."

Taite smiled tentatively up at Emma. She sincerely hoped she hadn't hurt her feelings by refusing to talk with her about Pierce.

"Bye, Emma. Thank you for coming to see me. Kiss Lacy for me, will you?"

With a probing look toward Mickey, Emma left the room.

At Emma's departure, Taite felt her composure falter. "Why, Mickey? Why couldn't my husband have been happy with me?"

The hospital bed dipped as Mickey sat down beside her. "I would have been happy with you."

At his grave statement, Taite, with surprise, raised her gaze to meet his. He watched her intently for a moment and then waggled his eyebrows at her.

With a sniff, Taite lowered her gaze. As usual, Mickey was trying to joke his way out of an emotional scene. Lying back on the hospital pillows, Taite slapped at his hand in irritation when he tried to clasp hold of hers.

He straightened to look at her. "I'm not seeing Caite anymore."

Taite gave a harsh laugh. It felt as if her heart were breaking in half. "Well, I'm not seeing either of them. The accident put everything in perspective for me."

Mickey leaned forward, his face intent. "Do you really think they tried to kill you? That is hard to believe, Taite. I mean, Caite is your sister after all."

"A sister I've never been able to feel close to. She always has this sneering defensive wall around her."

"Yeah, the same protective wall as you, Taite, although you're not so 'in your face' with it as Caite."

Realizing that Mickey's statement was true, Taite plucked with the tips of her fingers at the blanket over her legs.

"And no wonder," she finally mumbled with hurt felt deep within. She looked up at Mickey.

"Look where it got me when I finally did trust and give my heart to someone."

Mickey leaned close. He brushed his lips across hers. In stunned surprise, Taite was unable to move.

"I could be the one for you," he whispered against her lips. He deepened the kiss when she didn't pull back from him.

"Get your damn hands off my wife!"

Mickey lunged up from the bed to whirl toward Pierce. Mickey's shirt collar was bunched within a hard fist, and he was slammed against the hospital wall.

With a grunt, he seemed to wilt, his expression that of a caged animal. Guarded. Watching.

"Stop it!" Taite screamed.

"I'll kill the son-of-bitch if I ever see him near you again." Pierce bit out the words, each one pronounced. His eyes were flint when they met Taite's.

"Let him go, Pierce. Now. Please."

Pierce flung Mickey from him. A nurse hurried into the room. Mickey straightened. The nurse looked from him to Pierce as if wondering which one of the men might make the first move.

Pierce pointed a finger toward Mickey. "I want him gone, and I'm going to talk to my wife. If you want a fight, you just try and stop me."

The male nurse flexed his muscles as he looked to Taite. "Do you want to talk to your husband?"

"You better agree to talk to me, Taite, or all hell is going to break loose in this hospital."

At Pierce's low-growled words, Taite swiveled her gaze from the poised nurse to her husband. When her gaze clashed with Pierce's, she realized he meant exactly what he said. Embarrassed, she looked back at the nurse. "I'll talk to him."

"Taite, don't—"

Before anyone could react, Pierce snatched hold of Mickey to pitch him through the open doorway and out into the hallway of the hospital.

"Shut up, you damn pretty boy," he snarled.

Kicking the door shut on Mickey's staggering frame and the exiting nurse, Pierce didn't immediately turn around to face Taite.

Taite warily watched him. Her heart raced.

She curled her fingers over the lowered bed rails. Her husband placed his open palms against the hospital room doorframe and then took several deep breaths.

When he finally turned, Taite could almost believe the hurt and bewildered expression that he directed her way.

Almost, she silently scorned to herself before she tightened her lips and dropped her gaze from his searching one.

"I suppose I can thank Emma for that ugly scene," she snapped finding her voice. She brought her hands to her lap.

With two long strides, Pierce stood beside her. Taite twitched nervously. His anger was back, it seemed. Her finger hovered over the room's call button.

"Since Emma is the only one who will talk to me, yes, you can thank her. I was waiting just down the hall. Look at me, Taite."

When Pierce reached out a large hand to grasp hold of her chin, Taite shrank from his touch. Her eyes met his for a moment before she quickly averted her gaze. He dropped his hand from her.

"I don't understand this, sweetheart. Why have you refused to see me? This surely can't be because of my jealous display over Mickey in the office, can it? Look at me, damn it."

Taite jerked her gaze back up to connect with her husband's. He roughly combed his fingers through his hair, strands of it stood up with his action. Taite noted that lines fanned out from the sides of his eyes as if he hadn't slept in a while.

"What is happening between you and me, Taite? Tell me, because I'm at a loss here?"

"I made a mistake."

Slowly, Pierce lowered his arm back to his side. "You made a mistake?"

"I shouldn't have married you, and I want a divorce." Taite looked squarely at her husband with a set jaw. She watched and waited for him to beg. She knew he would. He wouldn't want a divorce. He and Caite wanted her money after all, didn't they? They believed her too gullible to realize what they were about.

Pierce took a step back, and blankly, he stared at her as if confused and not knowing what to say.

"I think, that maybe, I'm the one who shouldn't have married you, Taite," he finally said.

Incensed by Pierce's hurt tone, Taite sat up straighter on the bed. "That's right, you shouldn't have married me. You and my sister deserve each other."

"What does that mean?"

Taite watched as her husband seemed truly baffled. She hardened her heart. "Figure it out. You're so damn smart. Or better yet, why don't you ask Caite?"

"Since your sister is out of the country, I'm asking you," he practically yelled back.

That was the first that Taite had heard of Caite being out of the country, but since she'd refused to hear her sister's name spoken, she supposed she shouldn't be surprised no one had told her.

Taite felt her composure slip. *How can I still love him?* Covering her face with her hands, she hunched her shoulders.

"Please leave," she brokenly whispered. *They thought to use me.*

When Taite felt Pierce's hand on the small of her back, she tensed, and a sob shuddered through her.

Jerking her head up, she glared at him. "I want a husband who isn't a liar. A husband who really loves me and doesn't just spout the words. A husband who grieves over our unborn child."

His eyes widening, Pierce lifted his hand from her. Wordlessly, he exited the room.

Taite's tears freely flowed as she stared at the softly closing hospital door.

Chapter 14

The next evening when her hospital door opened, Taite looked up from arranging her clothes in her small suitcase. Surprise rippled through her.

"Mickey? What are you doing here? I go home today. I thought I told you that when you called this morning."

"You did, sweetheart. However, I talked your dad into letting me take you home. He seemed relieved that he wouldn't have to drive back into the city."

Mickey walked up to Taite, and gently, he lifted her chin. His thumb caressed her lips.

"I have to say that that mottled shade of green around your eyes is quite becoming."

He smiled teasingly at her. His blue eyes sparkled attractively.

Taite felt her tears spurt again. She was an uncontrollable fountain, it seemed.

Abruptly she sat on the side of the hospital bed and pulled back from his touch. She couldn't help but think that it should be her husband who stood teasing her.

Brushing the wetness from her cheeks, Taite glanced miserably at a now silent Mickey.

"You shouldn't waste your tears on him, Taite." With a grim look, he stared at her when she didn't answer.

"Shit!" he exclaimed when Taite teared up again.

He went and flopped down in the hospital chair positioned in the corner of the small room. Crossing his legs at the knees, he watched her.

"He fired me this morning."

Taite wasn't surprised by her husband's actions. She wiped at her face, her tears drying. "I expected as much. Didn't you? He did catch you kissing me after all. I know you want me to feel sorry for you, but I can't, Mickey. I guess I should, but I can't."

At Mickey's fierce frown, Taite relented. "I'm sorry. I don't mean to be so uncaring."

Unhappy at her friend's hurt, she continued, "Don't you be mad at me, Mickey. Please. My husband and sister just tried to off me, and you want sympathy from me for getting fired?"

Mickey didn't respond. After a moment though and still frowning, he leaned forward to place his elbows on his knees.

He held her gaze. "We know that your husband doesn't actually want you for you, Taite, so why should it make him so mad to see me kissing you? Your only attraction to him is your money, we both know that."

Taite gasped in outrage at her friend's cruelty. "You…you…"

Swiftly standing, Mickey walked to her. "I kissed you for you, Taite. Can you say the same about your husband?"

With a feeling of unease, Taite stared at the unknown face of her friend. He reached for her. She stepped back and swallowed the lump in her throat. Abruptly, Mickey's hard expression softened. He waggled his eyebrows at her, just as he always did when emotions ran too high.

Blinking in confusion, Taite wondered if perhaps she'd imagined that harsh expression. She now looked at everyone with suspicion.

His thumbs caressed the skin on the underside of her arms. Taite pulled back from that touch. Mickey let his hands drop to his sides. He crossed the room, his back to her.

"You are so much like Caite, so much. I'm sorry, I spoke so harsh."

Huskily, Taite responded, "I'm sorry that Pierce fired you. It wasn't fair."

"Still friends?" Turning toward her again, Mickey brushed at the front of his coat with a nervous gesture. The action endeared him to Taite. She walked to her friend and stood on tiptoe to kiss Mickey's cheek.

"Friends," she stated with a smile.

Mickey squeezed her to him for a moment. With a lopsided grin, he stepped back.

"Well then, let's take you home, sweet thing."

****

Pierce watched his wife leave the hospital with Mickey. His hands gripped the steering wheel that he slouched behind in his car. They hadn't noticed him. What his wife saw in that pompous ass, he couldn't fathom. The man had had such a cocky, self-assured attitude when he'd walked into the office that morning that Pierce's teeth had actually snapped together.

If it hadn't been for Mickey's insolence, he might not have sacked him. Pierce was man enough to admit it was his own feelings of jealousy that resulted in the scene at the hospital the night before, but that didn't mean he had to sit back and take Mickey's sneering attitude.

If it wasn't for Taite and the hurt she would feel, he'd give in to his temptation to stomp Mickey's butt into the ground.

Lifting his hand to rake his fingers through his hair, Pierce wondered wryly, if he shouldn't cave to that desire anyway. Taite seemed to hate him as it was. What would one more wrong amount to? At least with that insult, he would know the why of it.

He'd called her early that morning to let her know he'd like to drive her to her father's, if that was where she wanted to go. It would save Blake the long drive into the city, he'd explained, and give them a chance to talk on the way, to mend this misunderstanding and share their loss of the baby. He had been dumbfounded the evening before when she'd accused him of not caring about the loss of the baby.

Met with cold silence on the other end of the phone line, Pierce couldn't help but express that he wished she would come home with him so they could work out whatever was wrong.

"I love you," he said, regardless of her continued silence.

The click of the receiver was the only response he had gotten. It was Emma who later that day urged him to personally drive to the hospital to try and get Taite to see him.

"Don't let her go home to her father without you two talking," she warned. With a sigh, Pierce started his car. Today, apparently, wasn't the day for communicating, same as yesterday.

"You didn't get to talk to her, did you?" Emma's expression showed her sorrow at his failure when Pierce shook his head as he entered her home. "I am so sorry, Pierce," she stated.

"Not your fault, Emma. Where's Lacy?"

"She's taking a nap. Why don't you go in to your office today, Pierce? I know that it needs your attention, and I can keep Lacy the rest of the day. I don't mind."

"It's Saturday, Emma. I can't ask that of you. Besides, you've kept Lacy late all week and even several nights these past two weeks. I don't want to abuse your generosity."

Emma snorted. "Generosity? I love that child. I keep her because I want to."

"The office does need my attention. But I can take Lacy with me, if you'll just gather up some of her toys for me."

Emma patted his arm, and with determination, she turned him toward her front door. "That child would want to take all of her toys. And you, mister, can get more work done without having to keep one eye constantly on what she's up to."

Bending down, Pierce kissed Emma's lined cheek. "What would I do without you, Emma? I'd be lost if it wasn't for your support and loyalty. Come live with me."

In amusement, Pierce watched Emma's face turn a pretty shade of red at his teasing.

"I'm taken," she stated with a young girl's twittering laugh.

"My loss for it," Pierce replied with a smile of fondness given. As he left the apartment, Emma was still issuing her young girl's laughter.

When Pierce entered his office an hour later, it seemed too quiet without the background noise of the others that were usually there. Walking to Mickey's desk, he looked it over. It surprised Pierce that Mickey was professional enough to have placed all his files into a folder and then to have laid that folder on top of the center of his desk to be easily found.

Flipping through the man's neatly arranged paperwork, Pierce frowned. The man was good at the business of selling homes, that was painfully obvious. Besides Taite, Mickey had been one of his top sellers. Pierce dropped the folder back onto the top of the desk beside three perfectly lined up pens. Turning, he walked to his office.

Chapter 15

Taite gave a slight smile at her dad when he walked into the sitting area where she'd been taking it easy and reading.

"Mickey coming down again today?" he asked.

With a nod, Taite laid aside her book. "Doesn't he come and see me every other day? I don't know how I'd have survived without his friendship, Dad. He works so hard to make me laugh every time he visits."

"I think he'd like more than friendship from you, Taite."

With surprise, Taite stared at her father. "Oh, I don't think so, Dad."

She would admit that Mickey had made overtones of interest toward her when she was in the hospital, a peculiarity she'd brushed off as his way of trying to cheer her up. It was his unique way of letting her know she was of value. Not once, during the past two weeks since he'd brought her home from the hospital, had he indicated any type of interest in her besides that of friendship.

They had fallen back into their easy camaraderie with each other. Just as they'd shared before she and Pierce were married, and as they'd enjoyed the summer they had first met.

"At least I know Mickey isn't after my money if he is interested in me," Taite tried to joke when her father remained silent. Her throat tightened as the joke went flat.

For a moment, Taite fought her tears.

"There is that," her father finally drawled. "I do like the fact he comes from old money, and he wants to make his own way in the world. His father and I went to the same college. I realized that when Mickey was down here for Christmas. His father and I were even in some of the same classes. I remembered him when Mickey mentioned who his parents were.

Did you ever meet his parents?"

"Yes. Mickey invited me to their home one weekend when we were semi-dating. Nice people. They doted on him when we were there."

The phone beside Taite rang, and she reached to pick it up. "Hello."

Silence.

"Hello?" she repeated.

With a shrug, Taite hung up the phone. "Wrong number, I guess. You should get caller ID," she added when her father looked at her in question.

He turned when the butler knocked and then walked into the room. "What is it, Jim?"

Jim glanced toward Taite for a moment. "Mr. Holden is at the door, sir. He states that he wishes to speak with his wife."

"You can tell Mr. Holden his wife is not here," Taite managed to choke out. Her heart had jumped to the base of her throat at the mention of her husband's name.

Even knowing what Pierce attempted, Taite realized she longed to see him, and she knew—wrong as it was—she still loved him. She'd wished many times, over the past few weeks that Pierce would show up and demand to talk to her. *Not because I still love him*, she'd firmly told herself, but because she wanted to show him that she didn't miss him.

She had even practiced what she would say should he appear. She'd been confident she'd be able to verbally cut him down, make him think she'd been the one to play him for the fool. She'd believed she would be able to convince him that she never loved him. Had even thought it herself. Now she knew better.

Is Caite back in the country? Taite suddenly wondered. Had her sister and her husband decided that the stakes were too high to continue with their deceit? Had Pierce come to tell her that once the waiting period to file for a divorce was over, he would file? Or did he and Caite think to give her some breathing room, and then try to play their game once again?

"Mr. Holden stated if you should attempt to say you aren't home, he knows better. He said to tell you he just called on the phone and you answered."

Taite glanced at the instrument that had rung just a few moments prior.

With a slap of his large palm to the top of his desk, her father stood. "I will tell the man myself that Taite doesn't want to see him."

"Wait."

With an arrested expression, Taite's father turned toward her.

"I...I...want to hear what he has to say, Dad. Alone."

"Young lady, I can't believe what I am hearing."

"I'm not going to let Pierce talk me into going back with him."

"I should hope not, girl. If you're so set on this meeting, then you need to tell Pierce you want a divorce. And be firm about it," her father growled.

"I will, Dad. I promise."

"Jim and I will stay close. You call out if he threatens you in any way."

"Thanks, Dad. I will."

"I don't think this is a good idea. Not one bit," her father mumbled.

Giving a sharp gesture, he indicated for his butler to fetch her husband. With one last glance at her, her father followed the somber-faced butler out the door.

****

Pierce's insides jumped when the butler opened the front door of the mansion once again. The man hadn't let him past the door of the home when he'd answered it prior. He apparently had been informed not to, by the look on his face, when he'd responded to the doorbell summons and realized who stood before him. Had Taite agreed to see him, after all? If she hadn't, could he turn and leave, act civilized, even though he wanted to tear into someone just at the thought of her imagined refusal to see him.

"This way, sir."

Sharp relief washed throughout Pierce at a chance given to clear his and Taite's discord. He followed his father-in-law's butler into the home and then down its long foyer.

The man who plodded before him remained stodgily silent as he led him to the closed door of Blake's home office.

The butler knocked and then opened the door at the soft summons given. Pierce caught a glimpse of Taite. She nodded her head at the butler's silent regard directed her way. Her father was nowhere in sight. When the man turned and indicated for him to enter the room, Pierce swallowed. Silently, the butler turned and walked away.

Pierce stepped into the study.

He felt weak in the legs. Closing the door behind him, he watched Taite slowly rise from where she sat on the couch. Hungry for the sight of her, Pierce ran his gaze down over her length. The jeans she wore accented her waist and hips. She'd lost weight since he'd last seen her, he realized. The sharp, crisp whiteness of her blouse made her hair seem to blaze with color. He wanted to tell her how much he missed her, how he loved her and wanted her back with him. He couldn't speak. His throat was closed so tight with longing that no words would pass through. Pierce fought down the urge to cross the room and drag her into his arms, bury his face into her hair, absorb the scent of her perfume once more.

****

Nervously shifting her feet, Taite watched her husband scan her form from the top of her head to her toes a second time. Glancing down at her black stocking-covered feet, she wished she hadn't taken her shoes off when she'd earlier curled up on the couch to read. Somehow, being barefoot before the man who tried to kill her made her feel vulnerable, unable to defend herself. Quickly sitting back down, Taite reached for her shoes.

"What do I owe for the pleasure of this visit?" she demanded as she fumbled with her loafers. One dropped twice from her hand before she managed slip it on. She watched Pierce seem to come out of a trance.

"What?"

Standing, Taite squared her shoulders. Shoes on, she felt secure. She stiffened when Pierce walked toward her. His forward move seemed resolute. Quickly, she backed up but then forced herself to halt her retreat.

If he tried anything, all she had to do was scream and help would come running. With a haughty toss of her hair to position it behind her shoulders, Taite inhaled and then she exhaled. "I asked why you were here."

Pierce stopped a short distance from her. "I wanted to see my wife. It's been two weeks now since you were released from the hospital. Is it too much to ask to have an audience with you? I've missed you, Taite. I've searched for an explanation as to what went wrong between us, and for the life of me, Taite, I can't think of anything that should make you act as you are toward me. I believe I deserve to know what went wrong between us, don't you?"

"You were fun for awhile."

"I was *fun*?"

Taite felt her heart give a funny little flip flop when her husband actually seemed to lose his color, his expression disconcerted. *Could I be wrong*? she wondered as doubt surfaced. Was everything a mistake on her part? Had she let her father and her own insecurities lead her down a wrong path? Silence reigned in the room as they stared at each other. Taite came out of her trance when Pierce's cell phone shrilled within the quiet space of the room. He ignored it as he brought his hand up as if compelled to touch her. Taite jerked backwards from his reach.

"Answer your phone, Pierce. It might be about Lacy."

Her husband didn't drop his gaze from her as he removed the phone from his shirt pocket. "Pierce here," he stated. He frowned. "I am talking to Taite now. She is doing better. Listen, Caite, we will have to talk later. Yes, I'll tell her."

Bile rose in Taite's throat when Pierce casually slipped his cell phone back into his shirt pocket. *Is he so confident in his and my sister's scheming that he doesn't feel the need to hide who he's talking to?* Her gaze searched his as he took both her hands within his. She was unable to pull back or to even move. His action baffled her. He stepped closer. He seemed so emotionally hurt and bewildered. *Is it a well-planned act on his part? Had it been choreographed between him and Caite?* Taite felt her mind recoil with her uncertainty. He seemed so true. But she'd seen the proof of his deceit. Had the verification of pictures and papers on it.

"I love you, Taite. Give me a chance, sweetheart. Talk to me. Tell me what this is that is going on here between us. Let's work out whatever went wrong. If it's the jealous anger that I displayed over Mickey, twice now, that has you so upset, I'm sorry. We can work through that can't we?"

At her husband's quiet, pleading words, Taite felt her insides quiver. He sounded so sincere and seemed so unhappy. She wanted to believe everything had a plausible explanation. Taite stiffened. She was weak. Hadn't her father expressed more than once, that love could blind you to others faults? Bring you to your knees, he said. Defeat you and break you emotionally.

"What did Caite want you to tell me?" she asked. She pulled her fingers from his grasp.

Pierce looked down at his hands and then around at the study. It seemed he now couldn't meet her gaze.

"She says to tell you she loves you, and she hopes that we work things out between us."

"No."

"No?" Pierce seemed shocked at her firm resolve.

With sheer terror that the man who stood before her would be able to see through her charade and know she loved him still, Taite gave a smile. She hoped it was a fair representation of slight embarrassment and rueful regret. Her lips trembled with her effort. She laid a hand on his arm, determined to give a perfect performance to the bitter end. Wasn't that what he and Caite were doing? Playing with her emotions, acting out their parts?

"As I told you in the hospital, I made a mistake, Pierce."

With a careless and deliberate sham of a shrug given, Taite issued a forced laugh. A laugh she hoped sounded bubbly and somehow contrite. It sounded hollow to her, flat. She'd never been good at false emotion, pretending what she didn't feel. Pierce didn't move. He watched her.

"Even before my accident, I was coming home to tell you that I wanted to back out of our marriage. The marriage just wasn't for me, Pierce. I realized my mistake a few weeks into it. I told Dad it was my one and only rich girl folly. No hard feelings, please."

When Taite started to remove her hand from Pierce's arm, he grabbed hold of it.

"No hard feelings?" he growled. His anger fairly cracked through the air.

He jerked her against him.

"Were your loving actions toward my daughter fake also? Should I have no hard feelings in regard to that? She's asked for her T. T."

Taite felt her tears welling. She wasn't going to be able to hold up her pretense. He seemed so hurt by her words and it killed her that Lacy asked after her. She loved the little one. Loved her as if she were her own. Taite wanted to show Pierce the pictures and the report that her dad had given her. She wanted to demand that he explain them to her. She wanted to scream that yes, she loved him and Lacy, and missed them both. She loved him still, even knowing of his deceit. It sickened her, her weakness.

"Don't you dare cry your crocodile tears with me, bitch."

Slinging her fist upward, Taite viciously punched her husband's face.

Pierce jerked backward.

His expression displayed his shock at her violence. His cheek wore the dark imprint of her knuckles. Quickly he twisted her hair around his palm and held her fast when she started to pull away. His mouth, he ground down onto hers until she moaned with the pain.

He pulled back from her, satisfied with her final acceptance of his dominance.

"No hard feelings," he bit down at her before he whirled to stalk across the room to its exit doorway.

"Pierce, I..." Taite couldn't continue. She felt her legs start to buckle beneath her.

Pierce paused in his step. He didn't turn around.

"Leave it, Taite. You made yourself plain enough. I'm just a rich girl's folly. My daughter's feelings and attachment to you a byproduct of it, but of no consequence to you."

Horrified at his belief of her shallow personality and the violence that she herself had incited between them, Taite watched the man she hopelessly and unconditionally loved walk from the room and out of her life.

Chapter 16

Laying the flowers that she held in her hand onto the top of Sexy's grave, Taite sat down on the ground beside where her beloved pet was buried. *The day turned out to be a nice summer day*, she thought, as she contemplated the green rolling landscape around her.

Her father worked in his beloved flowerbeds and bored at the house, she decided to take in some fresh air. She hibernated in her father's home, rarely venturing outside it. She decided in the predawn morning, that it was time to let herself heal psychologically, and she could only do that if she deliberately worked on it.

She hadn't looked forward to the Friday morning.

With a sigh, Taite leaned back onto her elbows as she studied the peaceful landscape around her. She needed to start the process of looking for another job. Needed to interact with others. Her daily routine of doing nothing was starting to wear on her nerves. Since she had left the hospital six months prior, her life had been quiet except for that one violent encounter with Pierce.

There had been no sign of her sister and no word from her husband since. Her only visitor to the farm was Mickey.

Every day, after their sixth month separation period passed, Taite had expected to find divorce papers in the mail. And, every day when none was forthcoming, she'd felt a queer sense of relief.

Her father asked when she was going to do what needed done and file the paperwork herself. She couldn't. Not just yet.

"Taite."

Looking up at her father's call, Taite lazily raised her hand so he could see where she reclined. As she observed his slow amble toward her, she realized her father was old and feeble.

"Taite, remember we are supposed to go to Chad's tonight. Emma has cooked a special meal in celebration of their one-month wedding anniversary."

Taite swallowed, and the action stuck in her throat. "Dad, I don't think that I feel up to going. What if Pierce is there? He was invited to their wedding after all. I will call Emma with my apologies."

Taite's dad sat down beside her, his movement slow. Arthritis held him in its grip.

"Emma has promised that Pierce won't be there, Taite. In fact, she and Chad had their first argument over it. Chad sided with me and my demand not to have to encounter the man at my friend's own home. Emma swears on the Bible that Pierce couldn't have done what we suspect him of. That woman is blind to his faults, and I told Chad, as much."

Glancing at her father, Taite frowned. "I hope Emma doesn't ever confront Pierce with it, Dad. I know she promised to keep silent when you told her our suspicions, but what if she does spill the beans? What could happen then?"

Taite studied her father. *Could Caite and Pierce panic and come after me again? Not for my money this time, but for my silence? Maybe I should go to the authorities with my story. What if they find someone else to scheme against, as Dad said they might?* Taite shivered at her thoughts as the warm air around her suddenly seemed to hold a chill.

"I'm not going, if you aren't," her father stated. He looked around the landscape as if he searched its outcropping, he'd noticed her shiver.

"No, Dad, you go. I'll be all right. I'm just scaring myself with our talk." Taite watched her father glance around the farm again as if still hesitant.

"Nothing has occurred since Caite left the country or since I told Pierce that I wanted a divorce. Go, Dad. I'll be safe," she urged.

"It will be late before I can make it back."

Taite stood. When her father rose behind her, she didn't dare turn to help him. It would anger him if she did, so instead she affectionately hugged him once he was upright beside her. She felt him stiffen before he raised his hand to hesitantly pat at her back.

"I love you, Dad. Did you know that?"

"Yes," her father replied, and instead of turning away as he usually did, he quietly studied her features.

"Dad?"

Slowly, as if he fought his action, her father lifted his hand to lightly touch her face. "Are you really okay, Taite?"

Tears that she couldn't control sprang to Taite's eyes at his question.

"I'm okay, Dad."

With a slight nod, he turned and left her.

Sitting back down beside Sexy's grave, Taite watched her father. *What happened to him in his life experience that had embittered him so?* she wondered. He kept his emotions and any personal background information so restricted from others, that Taite realized she didn't know the man she called 'Father'.

"Oh, Sexy, what is to become of me?" she asked. "Am I going to turn into my father? Am I going to ramble around in that big, old house the rest of my days and become embittered with life?"

With a sigh, Taite lay back, and she watched the sky and its slowly moving clouds above her. Shortly, she rose and walked to her rambling home to bid her father goodbye.

Closing the door on Blake as he left the mansion an hour later, Taite locked the large front doors and then turned to walk to her father's study. Against his argument, she'd dismissed all the household staff for the evening, even his butler. She wanted a night to herself.

Settling in her father's chair in his study, Taite ran her hands over the large chair's crinkled leather. Laying her head back against the chair's headrest, she sighed. Somehow the spot comforted her. It felt a safe place. She lightly dozed as she relaxed in her father's favorite place to recline, always away from the activity within the house and its hired staff.

When the doorbell chimes woke her moments later, Taite rose, and she gave a half smile toward the book lined walls around her. She hurried toward the front entrance of the home. Her father must have decided to come back and ask her one more time to go with him. He would be happy to realize that she'd locked the doors behind him as he'd ordered her to do.

"Dad, I..." Taite's voice trailed off into silence upon opening the door before her. Her gaze met that of her husband's. Quickly, she glanced behind him to search for her father.

****

"I saw your father drive away."

After his statement, Pierce's insides knotted at the flash of fear that crossed his wife's face. A fear of him that he could well understand with the way he'd treated her during their last encounter. She took a hesitant step back.

"The household staff is here with me."

"If you say so, Taite."

"What do you want?" she demanded.

Raising his hand, Pierce showed her the brown envelope he held. "I decided to drive down and hand this to you personally."

Pierce ached to touch his wife's soft cheek. He wanted to tell her how lonely he was without her. How sorry he was for their violent interaction the last time they spoke.

With trembling fingers, she reached out to pull the envelope from his hold. Unable to stop his action, Pierce grasped her hand. She froze, her eyes widening.

"How did I go wrong, Taite?"

Pierce watched his wife's eyes fill with tears. He swallowed the hard lump that rose in his throat at the sight. He dropped his hold of her hand.

"Before you set me free, Taite—I want you to know that I love you. I hate being without you and I don't want this divorce."

At the silent and stiff posture of his wife, Pierce turned. He was aware that she continued to watch him as he walked to his car. She didn't whirl and slam the house door shut behind her as he expected, but instead, continued to stand motionless on that large porch and scrutinize him as he drove away.

Looking in his rearview mirror, Pierce caught one last glimpse of her before she turned. Shifting gears, he realized his wife would always be in his memories and in his dreams, if not his life.

He reached for his phone.

Chapter 17

Carrying the brown envelope before her as if it were a live thing that could bite, Taite sank back down onto her father's chair. Tentatively, she placed the envelope onto the top of the desk before her. The phone beside her rang. Absentmindedly, she reached and picked it up.

"Hello. Hello," she repeated into the silence which greeted her. With a chill going over her, Taite placed the phone back on its base. It immediately rang again.

"Hello."

No response.

With a sudden shiver taking hold of her at the deafening silence coming from the other end of the receiver, Taite quickly slammed down the phone.

"Pierce!" she screamed. "Don't you dare do this to me!"

The phone rang again.

Frozen, Taite stared at it.

It continued its ominous ringing. When the resonating sound stopped, the sudden silence within the room mobilized her.

Jumping up, Taite ran to make sure that all the doors were locked. Running into the empty kitchen, she slid to a frightened stop. The kitchen door was wide open. It hadn't been before. She was certain.

Hastily backing from the room, Taite sprinted towards the front doors of the house and toward her car in the driveway.

Jerking open the front door, she froze in mid-step. Her husband stood between his car and hers. He'd parked the vehicle along beside hers. He placed his hand on the hood of her car as if he dared her to come forward.

His gaze met hers. With a determined look he moved toward her. Taite whirled and then in confusion she whirled about again. Her heart slammed against her ribs. She couldn't go back into the home. Someone was in there. *Caite?* She sprinted toward the large barn where she and her sister had always played as children, toward the comfort and safety known there as a child. She heard Pierce take after her. He called out to her.

Reaching the barn, Taite quickly slung back its broad doors and without a backward glance, hurried into its darkened interior. Scrambling up the wooden ladder toward the top of the barn's loft, Taite kicked out at hands that clamped hold of her ankles. She screamed when with a jerk of those ankles, she tumbled backwards unable to stop her fall through the air.

She didn't hit the hard barn floor as expected, but landed in her husband's arms. She clawed at his face. Abruptly dropped, she sat at his feet stunned and unable to run.

****

"Oh, Gabriel, where are you when I need you?" Pierce heard his wife quietly sob out. She threw her arms over her head as if she thought he planned to beat her or worse.

Squatting beside her, Pierce reached out to touch her arm.

"Taite, honey?"

"You are not in my will! Not in my will."

In confusion, Pierce stood. Wiping at the blood that dripped from his face, he bent to determinedly scoop her up into his arms. She shook with her fear, but didn't fight him as she had previously, as he expected she might. With long strides and with Taite held tight against him, Pierce walked toward her home and then into her father's study. Sitting Taite down onto the couch, he straightened.

"Don't hurt me," she whimpered as she drew herself up into a tight ball as far away from him as she could. She kept her face turned from his.

Squatting beside the couch, Pierce's heart squeezed tight within his chest. Her actions baffled him.

"Taite, I am not going to hurt you. Please believe me, honey."

Taite sobbed in earnest. Pierce longed to gather her into his arms. Instead, he stroked her back and let her cry.

Finally, she grew quiet.

"Why did you run, Taite? What had you so terrified?"

At her silence, Pierce lifted his hand from her.

Hesitantly, she raised her head to meet his gaze. Her eyes searched his intently. Pierce could tell she was afraid of what he still might do. Warily, she watched his every move when he shifted to a more comfortable position.

As he studied her, her behavior confused him. It didn't make sense. Pierce's mind began to click as she watched him, and the puzzling pieces of her behavior since her car accident fell into place and the result stunned him. "You named me in your will to inherit if something should happen to you, didn't you?"

"Y…yes…"

"When you were run off the road, you jumped to the conclusion that I must have done it? You believed, I tried to kill you for your money? Just now, you thought I had come back to finish the failed job. Oh, baby."

Pierce scrutinized his wife as she stared at him.

"I love you, honey. How could you believe that I would ever hurt you? I love you with my very being. The thought of your wealth has never crossed my mind. I don't want it. I want you."

****

Taite felt Pierce's shock and pain as if it were her own. She knew in that instant, deep within her soul that she had badly wronged him. The love she'd fought daily washed through her for the man who looked so wounded and lost.

Sliding from the couch to the floor beside her husband, Taite laid her palm against his cheek. "It…it…wasn't just the car incident, Pierce. There were other things that pointed to your guilt. Things that I didn't want to believe."

Pressing the palm of his hand over hers, he raised her hand to his mouth. His voice husky, he asked her, "Why didn't you come to me, sweetheart? Accuse me openly. Why didn't you confront me if this is what you believed? Why didn't your father?"

"I had planned to, but then so many things happened and…and…I…." Taite dropped her gaze from Pierce's unable to meet her husband's direct stare.

"I love you, baby," he huskily told her.

With a half sob, Taite scooted onto his lap to wrap her arms about his neck. "I love you, too. You were never my folly, Pierce. Never."

Clasping his arms around her, he pulled her up against him. Holding her tight to him, he kissed her neck and then her jawline. Turning her face upward toward his, he kissed her deeply on the mouth. His hands continued to caress her arms even when he pulled back from her. It was as if he couldn't stop his touch of her.

"It all started with Mickey and what he said about you," Taite told him and she watched him.

Spewing some strong curse words that Taite wouldn't want to repeat, he ground out in response, although his touch remained gentle, "And what did your friend say to cause you to turn from me?"

"That day in your office when you were so mad at me, that was when it all started."

Pierce's brow furrowed and Taite swallowed in hesitation. "Mickey told me he suspected you and Caite were having an affair."

At the shocked look on her husband's face, all of Taite's reservations flew from the room.

"Oh, Pierce," she whispered. "Please forgive me. I didn't believe him at first, but so many things happened immediately after that made you seem guilty of that and more."

His facial expression growing unyielding, Pierce listened quietly as Taite explained how she and Mickey had seen her sister and him together in the mall's jewelry store; and how right after seeing him and Caite, her father called and told her that he'd had him investigated.

"The investigator's pictures taken of you and my sister together were so damning, Pierce, and then there was the investigator's report of your bitter legal fight with your wife's family members for her inheritance after her death. Yet, even after all I was shown—I still told Dad I wanted to confront you with it all."

Taite looked directly at her husband. "I wanted to give you a chance to explain everything away, Pierce. But th…then…on my way home that day, after you had asked where I was, I was run off the road and left for dead. And there was a threatening note left on my windshield before that. It's all filed in with the accident report." Taite anxiously studied her husband's tightly drawn expression.

"Let me see the pictures, the report, and the note."

At the terse request, Taite stood, and Pierce rose to walk behind her to her father's desk. Withdrawing the package from her father's safe, Taite handed it over to him. She watched as Pierce leaned back, his hip against the edge of the desk. With his frown still in place, he undid the flap of the envelope to pull out its contents.

He looked over the note that had been left on her windshield, and then slowly flipped through the pictures of him and Caite. Last, he read the report that the investigator had compiled on him.

Abruptly, throwing the report and the rest of what he held onto the desk behind him, he grasped her arm to pull her to him. Settling her between his legs, he kissed her forehead. "It does look damning, doesn't it, honey?"

Taite nodded.

"First thing first. The record of Caite's calls to my cell phone. Just as it shows with that first call, it started during the Christmas weekend I came down here. Caite called me when you were all here: her, you and Mickey, the evening before I arrived. She informed me that she'd come into a boatload of money and that she wanted to start looking for a new home as soon as the holidays were over.

"I was surprised she called me when you and Mickey were here with her, and you both could have answered any questions that she had on the subject. When I asked her about it, she said that you and she couldn't get along and you'd told her to go through me, that you didn't want to be involved with any of it. I asked about Mickey helping her, and she stated that she didn't want to listen to Mickey insert his opinion on what she should buy."

Taite realized it was Pierce who her sister had called right after they'd learned of their inheritance. He was the one Caite was talking to that she'd wondered about. *She couldn't wait to spend her newfound money*, Taite thought without surprise at her action.

"I didn't know anything about Caite wanting to buy a home, Pierce. But if she had asked me about it, I can't say that I wouldn't have told her exactly what she said."

Pierce ran his fingers down through her hair and cupped her face within his comforting hands. His gaze directly met hers.

"Those pictures taken by the investigator of your sister and me were all when we were looking at homes that your sister was interested in."

Dropping his hands from her face, Pierce reached to pick up one of the pictures scattered over the desk.

Taite leaned forward to see which one he held.

"This one was taken when we'd gotten lunch together after touring those houses and Caite unexpectedly stumbled and fell toward me."

He frowned as he looked over the snapshot of her sister cradled within his arms. In the picture, Caite merrily laughed up at him. It looked an intimate scene.

Pierce glanced up at Taite. "I scolded her the day this picture was taken, after I caught her when she'd stumbled and almost fell. I told her to stop wearing such ridiculous high heels if she couldn't keep her balance."

With apparent disgust, Pierce threw the snapped picture back onto the pile with the others. His gaze caught Taite's again. "Do you believe me, honey? On face value, those pictures show one story and yet, here I am telling you another."

Leaning into her husband, Taite snaked her arms around his trim waist. "I believe that I made a grave error not just with you, but with my sister as well. But what about the report of the fight you had for your wife's inheritance? I don't understand that, and I don't understand my accident or the cryptic note left on my windshield. What had me so frightened earlier, after you left, was that I got three phone calls, one right after the other, and no one would say anything. Then when I went to lock up the house, I found the kitchen door wide open. That was when I ran to my car intent on leaving, and I found you in my driveway."

Pierce gazed down at her.

Reaching up, he lightly caressed her cheek. "Couldn't the staff have left the kitchen door open, honey? And with your heightened senses, maybe, you just imagined the phone calls were sinister?"

"Maybe," Taite replied wondering if what Pierce stated was true.

"But what about the note left on my windshield and then being run off the road? I didn't imagine those things."

Pierce kissed her forehead. "I don't know, sweetheart. The sheriff said that he didn't have any leads. It could have been someone that you unknowingly cut off in traffic and that person had road rage from it."

The door to the study exploded open and it startled them both. Pierce yanked Taite to him.

Taite's father, his face beet red, stomped into the room. He seemed to melt when he saw her wrapped within her husband's arms and she wasn't struggling to be let loose. Pierce's arms tightened around her when she did start to pull away.

"Sir," he issued, stiltedly.

Her father glared at Pierce. "Get away from my desk!"

When Pierce and she moved as one, his look sharpened. Slumping down onto his chair, once they'd walked a distance away from it, he directed his angry gaze on her.

"I can see this man has somehow managed to convince you of his innocence."

"I realize now that I made a horrible mistake, Dad." Taite smiled at Pierce, and from where they sat beside each other on the couch, he raised his arm to fold it securely around her shoulders. He gave her arm a reassuring squeeze.

"Why are you home so early?" Taite asked softly, turning back toward her father.

Her father, his eyebrows lowered, studied Pierce. He leaned back into his chair. His fingers drummed on the top of his desk.

"Emma let the cat out of the bag that she'd called him and told him you would be here tonight, alone. She thought that he would have time to drive down and talk to you before I could get home. Which it seems he somehow managed to do, doesn't it?"

Pierce met Taite's look when she glanced inquiringly at him. With a shrug he gave her a slow, sexy smile.

"I had already come by and delivered our divorce papers to you and was on my way home when I received her call—begging me to try and talk to you. So, I called my babysitter, and she said she could keep Lacy all night if I needed her to. I was hoping I would need her to," Pierce told Taite in an undertone as he watched her.

"Get a damn room."

"Dad!" With shock, Taite came out of her trance. She looked to her father.

Her father scowled heavily at Pierce. "This is Taite's home, and I can tell she wants you to stay. I can't stop that. But let me make myself perfectly clear, boy."

He leaned forward.

"Anything happens to her and I will personally go to the police and file charges against you. It will be in all the news media. I'll make sure of it. Chad will make sure of it."

Abruptly looking toward Taite herself, her father harshly asked, "Did you inform your husband he's no longer in your will?"

Feeling Pierce's muscles tightly bunch, Taite tensed herself. Her husband quickly stood. Taite jumped up to stand beside him, and grabbing Pierce's arm, she silently pleaded with him to let her father's insult go. Taite felt Pierce's arm muscle relax as he returned her pleading look with his own guarded one. Turning, he addressed his father-in-law.

"I don't want Taite's money, never did. It's your daughter I want, sir."

"Well, we shall see the truth about that, won't we?" Taite's father replied as he gave Taite a hard look.

When Pierce firmly clasped Taite's elbow urging her from the room, Taite knew she and Pierce were being measured, and they both came up short as far as her father was concerned. Her father was convinced that she had made a colossal mistake.

Chapter 18

Pierce walked up to lean a broad shoulder against the bathroom doorframe, and Taite smiled at him from where she lounged. She hadn't heard him come into the bedroom. With ankles crossed, he nonchalantly looked about the room as he noted her bathroom decor. With raised eyebrows, he studied the pink wall behind her. His gaze traveled from the wall to her bare shoulders and then on down to the tops of her breasts where they stopped there, the rest of her covered in bath bubbles.

Taite leaned back onto the sloped end of her tub and let her gaze travel up the painted wall behind her.

"It is called peony pink, with a bit of raspberry color in it. The raspberry is supposed to keep the color from being sickeningly sweet. Did I achieve it?"

"It looks good. Very feminine. That garden tub—I think it's large enough for me to join you."

"Please do."

Pierce abruptly straightened. His crossed arms dropping.

With a lazy grin given toward her, he began to yank his shirttail out from where it was tucked in at the top of his jean's waistband.

"Where did you go anyway?" Taite asked as she watched him. She'd been surprised when on their way up the stairway to her bedroom, he'd suddenly stopped and told her to go on up that he needed to fetch something from his car and would be up right behind her.

Her husband sucked in a loud hiss of breath when he eased down into the water on the opposite end of the bathtub from her. Stretching out his long legs on each side of her hips, he blew the rising bubbles and steam from his face.

"Hot enough?" he questioned with a half-smile. "Damn."

Scooting forward, Taite kissed his shoulder. Grasping hold of his arm, she began to lather the scented soap bar that she held over it. She ran the bar of soap down over his long fingers and then tracked it back up his arm. He watched her as she rinsed his hand and arm. Taite wiggled her fingers at him for his other arm to be held out to her.

"You didn't answer me. Where did you go?" she said as she repeated her action.

"I told you. There was something I wanted to get from my car."

Taite looked inquiringly up at her husband when he didn't state what that something was. Meeting his smiling gaze, she forgot the vague answer as he took the soap from her and began to return the favor of washing her. He reached for her leg. Taite had never thought that having her leg washed could be so provocative, so intimate. He switched his administration to her other leg and foot. Taite's gaze met Pierce's as he gently massaged her toes. His fingers trailed up past her ankle a second time and then to a bent knee.

Suddenly, he lowered her foot back to the water and his gaze dropped from hers as he briskly sat aside the soap he held. He seemed unsure of himself.

"I grieved for our lost child."

"I did, too," Taite whispered. She twisted, between her fingers, the washcloth that she held. Scooting forward, she dropped the cloth to embrace her husband, to hug him tightly to her. He moved his lips across her cheek and Taite shivered with need.

"I would like to try for another child," she told him drawing back from him.

"Three or four brothers or sisters for Lacy, I think would do nicely. I do love our Lacy; I hope you know." Lightly tapping the tip of Pierce's nose and leaving behind soap suds at her action, Taite met her husband's intense, coffee-colored gaze. She hoped that he didn't want to discuss the issue of their lost child any further. It hurt too much.

Staying silent, he finished his washing and then rinsed off. Standing, he reached for the close by towel and stepped from the tub. After drying, he motioned for Taite to stand up. When she did as he indicated, he lifted her from the tub and kissed her mouth.

"I love you, sweetheart," he said before he set her to the floor for her to stand on her own two feet.

"There are still a lot of unanswered questions between us that I need to clear up for you," he added before he turned to grasp and hand her the large towel she'd laid out for herself. When they walked into the bedroom, Taite flipped the bedcovers back and then slipped between snow white silky sheets.

Silently she waited for her husband to join her.

Dropping his towel from his waist, he exposed his nudity to her hungry gaze before he climbed onto the bed beside her. When he lay back, he propped his arms behind his head. After several moments of silence between them and with a deep breath drawn, he lowered his arms to clasp her hand within his. He raised it to his mouth to kiss the back of it.

"When my wife was killed, Taite, her elderly parents became completely immersed within their grief. Kelly was their only child, and they doted on her. They'd tried for years to have children and when Kelly's mother, out of the blue, got pregnant with her, they felt she was a gift from heaven."

Pierce smiled softly, seeming to become lost to his memories.

Taite felt a sharp sense of loneliness as she watched her husband. She shifted. He'd loved his first wife deeply.

Looking at her at her movement but not really seeing her, still caught up in the past, Pierce continued with his story, his eyes now hollow.

"Kelly's parents lost it with her death, Taite. And when I say lost it, I mean they became so disoriented that they had zero, rational thought. There were two female relatives on Kelly's dad's side who homed in on that grief-stricken confusion and lost ability to know right from wrong. These two women convinced my wife's parents that Kelly wanted these relatives to have her inheritance when her parents passed away.

"I contested my in-laws changed will when I found out what had been done, after they died.

"They'd changed their will, leaving out their only grandchild to Kelly's inheritance and giving all that they had to those two relatives.

"My in-laws died from grief only hours apart from each other: exactly, six months to the day after their daughter. They loved their grandchild, Taite, but lost the ability to think clearly at the death of their only child."

Pierce took a breath and his jaw tightened as he gazed at Taite. "So yes, just as your father's investigator reported, I did fight their will, and I won, and it was a bitter, public battle. My in-laws' property and money were my wife's inheritance and, with her death, Lacy's.

"If Kelly's parents had known what was happening, they would have wanted me to fight. I moved Lacy and me from our hometown to protect Lacy, before she became old enough to understand all the gossip that was spread about me by those two women. I've never encountered such a vicious and planned attack to destroy a person's reputation as those two women did to me. They even had their church members calling me to upbraid me on my selfish, money hungry mindset. 'Those two women were good women' those church members told me. 'How could I fight for that inheritance when I wasn't poor,' they demanded of me."

Pierce fell silent as his eyes became focused on the far wall of the room. He spoke with a choked and obvious sorrow, "All the money from my in-laws' estate is kept in a trust fund for our daughter, as my wife would have wanted me to do. When Lacy is old enough to take control of it, she can do whatever she wants with it. She can give its entirety away for all I care."

Taite felt her throat close tight as she watched the emotion that played across her husband's face. She knew he was remembering Kelly and their life together.

"You loved your wife profoundly, didn't you, Pierce?" she blurted out unable to stop herself.

Fidgeting with the sheet that covered them both, Taite hurriedly continued, wanting to voice her envious emotion before she lost the nerve to do so, "I can't help but feel jealous of this unknown woman who holds your heart. I know it's unseemly. But I...I...just can't seem to control it."

Taite met her husband's startled look.

Her insecurity swamping her, she wondered if he found her lacking when he compared her with his first wife.

With a look of incredible tenderness, Pierce turned fully toward her. Silently, he gazed at her for a moment, before he reached out a forefinger to gently trace her eyebrows and then her lips.

"So beautiful," he stated on a soft note as his gaze followed his finger's route.

"Ah, Taite," he said as he met her gaze again. "Yes, I loved Kelly. I loved her with all my heart. But what I feel for you is different, so different."

He took a deep breath almost as if he was afraid to open up to her, but he continued. "You are an integral part of me, sweetheart. Intertwined with my very soul. I wondered each morning when we were apart if I could survive yet another day without you."

Taite's eyes began to tear and she couldn't stop her reaction. Her husband's declaration rang with truthfulness.

"Don't cry, baby. Don't cry," he groaned as he leaned forward to kiss away her sorrow which traced its path down her cheeks.

Taite felt her muscles relax at his light touch, and a warm, enveloping tenderness toward him spread through her. "I'm sorry, Pierce. So sorry for what I put you through. Please believe me when I say that I love you with all that I am."

Gathering her to his chest, Pierce rolled onto his back. Taite lowered her head to position her ear over her husband's beating heart. The rhythmic sound of it comforted her. It was a sound she had missed these past many months.

"I feel jealous, too, of someone in your life that I don't know." She heard him huskily state. Pierce stopped his reassuring touch when Taite in question raised her head to meet his gaze. He smoothed her hair back from her face.

"I'm deeply jealous of this Gabriel person you keep calling out for.

You cried for him in the hospital, and again today when you believed I was out to harm you. Who is he, Taite?"

Taite laid her palms against her husband's face and she smiled in reassurance at him. "Gabriel is my unknown hero, Pierce. He was someone whom I never did get to see, but he talked me through my physical hurt after my car crash, and his voice guided me back to myself and pulled me from the darkness that threatened to consume me.

"He came to the hospital—just when I felt emotionally that I wanted to give up, that I couldn't continue. Although I didn't see him, I felt and heard him. Later when I asked the nurses and the ambulance drivers about him, they said that they didn't know of any Gabriel."

Giving a small shrug, Taite dropped her gaze from her husband's. She had come to accept that what she experienced to be true even if there was apparently no substance to it.

"The ambulance workers' report stated I was alone when they arrived at the accident scene. They said I was slumped against my car, and had crawled out my window on my own and was sitting, waiting for help to arrive."

Taite met Pierce's direct gaze again. "But I know that my hero helped me from my car and that he rode with me all the way to the hospital. He held my hand the entire time, Pierce. And he kept me focused on him by talking to me, instead of on the pain I was suffering.

"He is real—my hero. I know he is," Taite quietly said when Pierce didn't respond, just studied her. Why did no one seem to believe what she'd experienced?

"Let me be your hero, Taite."

At the emotionally charged words, Taite lifted her gaze back up to encounter her husband's. She was surprised to find his returning gaze dark and solemn. He brought her arm up to his mouth to kiss the inside of her wrist. "Run to me, honey. Run to me when the world is too harsh to face. Let me be the one you trust."

Taite felt her insides melt. She raised her arms to encircle her husband's neck, and he pulled her upward so that she sprawled completely over him.

He took full possession of her mouth.

Taite's breath caught in her disappointment when, too quickly, Pierce eased his mouth from hers. But then she gasped and arched with enjoyment when her husband flipped her to her back and that same gorgeous mouth of his moved down the length of her neck, to a breast.

Cupping her breasts' fullness within his large palms, he gave due attention to both. Rising, he kissed the sides of her mouth.

"I love you," she breathed and he smiled.

Unable to keep her hands still, Taite ran them up and down Pierce's muscled back. She loved the texture of his skin. Loved the sight of him. With a low, rumbling growl given, he positioned her for his possession. His breathing became heavy and labored as he settled into her warmth.

"Ah, baby, baby," he breathed.

At his slow and precise movement, Taite became lost to the heady sensations he evoked. With her love overflowing for him, she returned each touch he gave for an equally tender touch of her own.

Chapter 19

"Do you think your father will ever accept that I'm not after your money?"

Lying beside her husband, Taite gave a shrug as she smoothed a palm over Pierce's hair-covered chest. His chest hairs were dark and slightly rough. She loved the look and feel of them.

Propping her chin upon the chest she adored, Taite smiled happily up at her husband. Both she and Pierce were reluctant, it seemed, to give in to the coming morning. Neither of them wanted to have to face her father and his sarcasm.

Abruptly Taite's bare bottom was given a sharp slap, and she let out a howl of mock outrage. She rolled to her side as she rubbed at the offended area.

Slinging back the bedcovers, Pierce swung his feet to the floor and he stood. He smiled down at her when she didn't move. "Come on, beautiful. We need to get going. I have to pick up Lacy this morning, and your father, well, he will eventually come to realize that I love you and not your money."

Lazily, Taite rolled to her back, and she raised her hand to her husband to let him pull her upright to stand beside him.

"You can use the shower while I take my bath," she told him before she started to turn away.

She felt excited. *I'm going home.*

Pierce stopped her movement from him to place a hand at her neck. With a thumb under her chin, he raised her face toward his.

In question, Taite let her gaze meet his. *I adore him,* she thought.

"A kiss before we have to face your dad and the world," he told her huskily.

****

Taite stared at the inside of the barn wall and at the sprayed words splattered across it. She felt physically ill. The black colored graffiti not only seemed to threaten, but it screamed *you fool, you fool.*

Was she being played?

Did they think to drive her crazy?

She was stupid for believing Pierce with all the evidence stacked against him. It was as her dad had always lectured: people do evil things for the want of money.

With sudden rage washing over her, Taite swiveled toward the barn doors when they slid open.

"Taite, honey, we have to go."

Pierce stopped dead in his tracks when his eyes caught sight of the graffiti sprawled across the barn wall. His gaze moved from the wall and the sprayed words of—*Money, money, who wants your money, Taite?* —to her father, who stood so stiff and straight.

Her father turned toward her, and he silently challenged her to question Pierce. To demand answers.

"Where did you say you had to go last night, Pierce?" Taite hoarsely asked. Pierce's eyes widened before they sharply narrowed. He didn't answer. He appeared to be in shock.

Oh, please. Spare me the wounded act. Taite wanted to scream out her thoughts. *He was good, she'd give him that.* Straightening her shoulders, Taite with determination returned his gaze. Her legs trembled and threatened to give way at the highly charged silence between them.

"Well?" she finally spit out.

The scorn and contempt that she directed toward her husband was more at herself than Pierce. Was she so pathetically desperate to believe that her husband loved her, and not her money, that she was willing to be played? How long would it have taken him before she would have added him back into her will? He must have laughed his head off at her gullibility.

"Playing games, again, Pierce? Convince me that you love me and then steadily drive me insane?" With a feral gesture, Taite slung her arm toward the barn wall to point a finger toward it.

"Is that what this is about? What everything up to now has been about? Was I supposed to turn to you as you convinced me someone else did that? Maybe my father? Well?

"Answer me. Where did you go last night before you came to my bedroom?" she practically screamed.

With his jaw clenched tight, Pierce reached into his coat pocket to withdraw a slender box.

"I went to my car to get this."

Viciously, he slung the box he held in his hand against the barn wall and the sprawled graffiti.

Instinctively ducking, Taite quivered at the hostile anger that now radiated from her husband to her.

The air cracked with it.

"I didn't do this, Taite. I don't know who did or why, but it wasn't me."

Her father quickly hoisted the pitch fork leaned against his leg, and he pointed its end toward Pierce. "The game is over, boy. She believes me now. You and Caite can leave us alone. Your sport is out in the open. Neither of you will see any of Taite's money or mine. We've made sure of it."

Pierce's narrowed gaze shifted from her father to her. Abruptly he turned on his heel and exited the barn. Taite heard his car engine roar to life a few minutes later.

Her chin quivered as she looked at her father when the sound of the vehicle's engine could no longer be heard.

How many times had her father warned her and Caite about the blindness of love? So many times, Taite had lost track and had even stopped listening. Well, she should have listened. With the bitterness she felt slicing multilayered, Taite watched her father walk over to pick up the box slung so violently. He also collected up what had fallen from it. A slender gold bracelet dangled from his fingers when he straightened.

Turning the chain over, her father squinted down at it. He brought the bracelet closer to his face. Raising his gaze to hers, he seemed to hesitate for a moment. He walked toward her.

Grasping her hand when he reached her, he pressed what he held down onto her open palm and then folded her fingers over it.

"I'm a bitter, old, and foolish man, Taite," he stated.

Taite watched as his shoulders slumped, and he walked from the barn. Opening her hand, she looked down at the bracelet he'd placed within her palm.

Turning the delicate chain over, Taite read the inscription engraved on its clasp. *My love. My life. My wife.*

Her harsh cry rose to resound off the barn walls.

****

Roughly shifting the gears of his car, Pierce didn't hear the screaming grind at his less than smooth transition from third to fourth gear. He was lost to his anger. It was hard for him to comprehend after everything that had occurred between him and Taite the night before that she would jump to the conclusion, he'd sprayed that message on the barn wall.

If I'm trying to soften her, why in the hell would she believe I'd write something like that?

No matter how often he told Taite he loved her or tried to show her, Pierce was afraid his wife would continue to look at him with suspicion and mistrust. Her father's bitter outlook on life had molded his wife to view everyone around her with an odd slant. *Hell, she doesn't even trust her own sister.*

On his last thought, Pierce braked and spun the sports car that he drove. Parking the car alongside the edge of the highway, its hood now pointed the opposite direction of just a moment ago, he reached for his cell phone. The only other driver on the two-lane, rural highway blasted his horn at him as he sped past his parked car.

Moments later, Pierce eased onto the circle driveway of Taite's family home. He saw his wife standing at the barn door he'd stormed through only moments earlier. Taite, her forehead laid against the wide door, was a picture of total dejection. She jerked toward the driveway at the purring sound of his car engine.

She began to run toward him. His heart lurching, Pierce quickly stepped from the parked car. Opening his arms wide to her, she didn't hesitate as she ran straight into them.

Hugging her tightly to him, Pierce felt her heart pound heavily against his chest as she burrowed against him.

"I am sorry," she exclaimed. She hugged against him forcefully.

He lifted her face from his chest, and her eyes glinted with unshed tears as she stared up at him. He smiled at her as he tenderly raked her mess of hair back away from her face.

"We have a ways to go with this trust thing, don't we, baby?" Pierce watched as Taite hesitantly nodded up at him.

"I...I...want to trust in you, Pierce. I mean...I do trust you. But why are these things happening to me?"

At his wife's obvious fear, Pierce frowned. It was time to get to the bottom of this mess. Someone was playing with her emotions. More than that. They were terrifying her.

"I don't know why, sweetheart. But I insist we call the police and have someone out to investigate just what it is that's going on here."

Taite shifted in his arms, and she looked back at the barn as if the culprit to all her troubles was within it. She shivered. The bracelet that encircled her wrist caught his attention. Raising her arm, Pierce handled the bracelet he'd purchased for her.

"This is what I was doing the night you saw me at the mall, Taite. I wanted to get you something to show you how sorry I was for snapping at you that day. I mentioned to Caite before I left the office that I planned to buy you a bracelet. She said she knew your favorite jewelry store, and that she'd help me to pick one out. I wish now I had told you about the bracelet, but I wanted it to be a surprise. And last night—"

Taite swiftly brought her hand up to his mouth to cut off what he had been about to say. Pierce kissed her fingers.

"And last night we got sidetracked before you could give it to me," she finished softy.

"Believe me, sweetheart. I wouldn't intentionally hurt a hair on your head, and if I did, it would be as if I were striking myself."

Pierce wondered if Taite would ever totally trust him. Would she always be suspicious of his activities if he didn't explain each and every one of his moves prior to her?

"I know you wouldn't hurt me, Pierce, honest," she said as she snuggled closer to him. Suddenly she drew back. "Oh shoot, Pierce. We forgot all about poor Lacy! Let's hurry and get her, and afterwards we can call the police."

When Taite stepped from him, intent on circling the car to the passenger side, Pierce laughed and pulled her back against him.

"Calm down. I called Emma and my new babysitter. Emma and Chad plan to pick Lacy up for me. They are going to keep her the rest of the weekend and even longer if needed until we get this mystery solved."

****

Pierce couldn't seem to keep from reaching out and touching his wife. He knew his father-in-law noted each movement he made as they waited for the sheriff to come into the room.

The sheriff remained at the barn with his deputy when he and Taite's father decided to return to the house, their statements given and the sheriff's notes completed. Pictures were still being snapped of the sprawled graffiti and the surrounding area of the barn. Pierce admitted to himself, he was terrified that something could be said or done that would turn Taite from him permanently. If she did, he didn't think he could survive the loss of her a second time. She turned to give him a sweet smile and his heart lurched.

"Thank you, sir!" the sheriff boomed when the butler finally showed the man into Blake's office where they all waited.

"Mr. Carpenter, sorry it took me so long," the sheriff stated when Taite's father stood at the man's entrance. The sheriff quickly walked forward to stretch forth his hand to Blake.

Pierce stood and shook the sheriff's hand when the man turned and approached him as well. Taite, with obvious hesitation, rose when the sheriff looked toward her. Pierce laid his arm across her shoulders.

"Sheriff, this is my wife. She didn't want to go back out to the barn just yet. You met her when she had her car accident."

"Yes, yes," the man boomed as he pumped Taite's hand.

"It surprised me when my department received not only your husband's call, Mrs. Holden, but your father's as well within minutes of each other."

The sheriff smiled broadly at Taite, and his eyes skimmed over her face and hair. He continued,

"So, Mrs. Holden, your husband and dad are worried about you. Seems there is some mischief afoot, they say."

Pierce tightened his arm around Taite's shoulders at her nod in response to the man's statement. The sheriff's sharp gaze watched as she wrapped her arms around his waist to lean against him.

The man looked at Blake.

"Can I sit?" he asked. The sheriff glanced around the room as if he searched for a suitable chair for his large frame. His gaze centered on Pierce when Taite's father remained silent. Pierce motioned to the chair positioned across from the couch, and the sheriff settled onto the cushioned seat of the chair.

Pierce and Taite sat back down beside each other on the couch. Taite reached for Pierce's hand to fold her fingers tightly around his.

"I think we better start at the beginning of yesterday's events, Mrs. Holden," the sheriff stated.

He leaned forward.

"I am a little confused with the story your husband and father told me." Straightening, he withdrew a pen and a small writing pad from his shirt pocket. His eyes flicked from Taite to Pierce, and then to their clasped hands before he settled on Taite's tense face. He waited. Pen posed.

Taite cleared her throat. "Well, Sheriff, my husband and I have been separated for some time. And yesterday, you see, he came to hand-deliver our divorce papers to me. My father...my father, he'd just left to attend a dinner party of some friends and I was alone at the house. When my husband left after delivering the legal documents, I came back into the study to look over the papers and the phone rang. When I answered it, no one responded to my hello, and when this occurred several times in a row, it scared me."

When Taite fell silent, the sheriff made a motion with his pen. "Go on, Mrs. Holden."

Taite glanced sideways and Pierce nodded his head at her.

"So, I ran to lock up the house, and as my husband said he told you earlier, that was when I found the kitchen door wide-open. And then this morning my father and I found the graffiti sprayed on the barn wall. And as you know from my car accident report, months ago, someone deliberately rammed into the back of my car causing me to wreck. Someone is harassing me, Sheriff. I just don't know who is doing it or why."

The sheriff glanced at Taite's fingers intertwined with Pierce's. "You two have made up it seems. No divorce now?"

Taite's fingers tightened firmly around Pierce's. "No. No divorce. My husband decided to come back and talk to me about the divorce when the phone calls were occurring. Anyway, to make a long story short, after I calmed down, I realized it must have just been my overwrought nerves which made me think someone was after me yesterday. But...but... this morning there was that graffiti on the barn wall."

Pierce noted though the sheriff moved slowly, his eyes were sharp and they reflected an intelligence. He could tell that the man was computing what Taite had just told him with what he and his father-in-law relayed and her story was coming up short. Pieces were missing from the puzzle. Taite thought to protect him by not letting the sheriff know what she'd believed him capable of.

Pierce looked at Blake. "I think the sheriff should read the investigation you had done on me. That is the beginning of this mess, isn't it?"

Taite made a movement of distress as her eyes caught Pierce's. "I didn't want all that dragged up. The sheriff just needs to know what happened yesterday and today."

With a reassuring smile given, Pierce took both of her hands into his and turned fully toward her.

"We need to start at the very beginning, sweetheart. What if your car accident wasn't the result of a random act of violence? When it happened, you actually thought it was something I'd done. What about the note left on your windshield? I relayed that information to the sheriff too. I don't want any doubts between us, Taite."

"I don't doubt you. Not anymore."

The sheriff watched them for a moment. He shifted his large bulk awkwardly in the chair to face Taite's father. "Why did you have this man investigated?"

Blake's gaze held an edge to it as he returned the sheriff's scrutiny. "You are a smart man, Sheriff. I am sure you can figure it out. I remember you. You were a young man, just starting your career the first time we met. You know my family's history very well, don't you? You were here both times helping to investigate the deaths that occurred here."

****

Taite stared in surprise at her father at his words and his hostile tone. *Deaths?* Had her father actually used a plural? Didn't he mean death? He avoided her searching look.

The sheriff gave a nod before he flicked his gaze toward her. He turned again toward her father.

"Yes, I was here, Mr. Carpenter. And when I received yours and Mr. Holden's calls this afternoon, I pulled those files and I read through them again. You see, I remembered that the younger brother of the man who died here in your home had threatened you. If I remember correctly, he stated that no matter how long it took, you would pay. Isn't that, right, Mr.

Carpenter?"

Curious at her father's defeated expression, Taite watched as he seemed to shrink into his chair. *What man died here*? she wondered in bewilderment. She'd never heard of anyone dying on the farm besides her mother, and that had been an accident. Her father, silently, reached for the file that contained the damning pictures of Caite and Pierce and the background report on Pierce. He looked to the sheriff.

"Take this folder, Sheriff. Read it, and do your investigation on what exactly is occurring here. I need to speak to my daughter before anything else is said. Do you understand?"

Taite jerked in surprised shock at her father's use of the word daughter. He'd never called her daughter before.

The sheriff lifted a beefy hand to take the folder held out to him. His gaze locked in with Blake's.

"Yes, I think I do understand, Mr. Carpenter. Secrets have a way of creeping to the surface, don't they?"

With a huff of labored breath, the sheriff stood. He glanced at Taite and then made a motion toward the folder he'd placed under his arm.

"I will have everything checked out, Mrs. Holden.

"By the way, one of my men found footprints leading from the back of the barn to the driveway. Did any of you walk to the backside of the barn when the message was found this morning?"

With a scan around the room, the sheriff gave a nod at their negative headshakes in response to his question. He turned toward the door and when Taite's father started to rise to follow, he waved a hand at him. "I can find my way out, Mr. Carpenter."

Then his brow furrowed. "Those two hay spikes that are sitting to the side of the barn, could one be bought? My brother has been hunting for a used one. I noticed them when I climbed up to the barn loft earlier."

He gave a self-conscious laugh. "Kinda scared me when I opened the loft doors and looked down to see them. Was afraid I might fall and impale myself."

"Nothing is for sale, Sheriff," Taite's father replied. The sheriff gave another one of his signature nods, and with one last glance at the room's occupants, he turned to slowly amble away.

"Dad?"

Taite's father sighed at her unspoken question. Silently, he pulled the desk drawer beside him out as far as it would go and then reached up inside it. He withdrew a key hidden within its cavity.

"What secrets was the sheriff talking about, Dad? Who died here besides Mom?" Taite watched her father. Her heart pounded. What secrets were creeping to the surface? Did she want to know?

"Dad, I don't think—"

"The man who I killed. Your father."

My father? He killed my father?

Taite felt her breath drag heavy. She couldn't breathe. Dimly she was aware of being jerked up onto her husband's lap and his arms wrapped securely around her.

"Hell, Blake. Did you have to blurt that out to her so cruelly?"

"Taite, honey. Look at me." At her husband's stern tone, Taite raised her gaze to lock her eyes with Pierce's. He brought his hands up to cup the sides of her face.

"We will face this together," he told her quietly.

Taite nodded at her husband's reassurance. It coursed through her, gave her a needed reservoir of strength. Sitting up straighter, Taite took a deep breath. She looked toward the man she knew as father. Pierce's hand tightened around hers.

"You're my father," she said on a half sob. When her father wouldn't meet her gaze, Taite knew—knew with a certainty that the man before her wasn't who she'd always believed he was. All her childhood memories of his kept emotional distance from her and Caite and their longing for a parent's love rushed up to engulf her.

"Now I understand. I understand so much. You never did love me or Caite, did you? We were a nuisance, weren't we? We always worked so hard to have you say that you loved us. Oh, Caite. Poor Caite. She wanted your love even more than me. I had Chad's love."

Taite dropped her face into her hands. She finally understood the distance her father always maintained from her and Caite. With a lost sense of knowing who she was, Taite lifted her head to stare at the man she'd known as father, a man who was now a stranger to her.

"Tell me your story," she gritted out. Anger over took her feeling of loss and that fury swirled through her. Abruptly she slid from her husband's lap to meet Blake's startled gaze—a man who'd never called her daughter until now. *Why now?* Taite wondered, her thoughts bitter. Narrowing her gaze, she stared at the man who for some reason appeared just as lost and confused as she felt. He cleared his throat, and then he glanced toward Pierce as if he wished for Pierce to leave the room.

"We would both like to hear this story," her husband said into the thick silence.

"He stays," Taite declared.

Leaning forward, Blake stretched his hand out to her as if in a gesture of pleading, until he seemed to realize his posture, and he pulled his hand back. Taite realized his face reflected a configuration of pain and of uncertainty. He took in a deep breath.

"I wanted to love you, Taite. I wanted to love you and Caite both, but all feeling died in me the night I learned you were not my flesh and blood."

Blake clasped his hands together and he studied his fingertips.

"I am starting my story at its end instead of the beginning. Let me begin again."

Pierce placed his hand to the center of Taite's back, and he moved his thumb slowly back and forth over the space. Taite's tension eased with his reassuring motion as she waited for her father to continue.

"I married your mother when she was but a child of eighteen and me, well, I was forty-five and old enough to have known better. Twenty-seven years separated us, but we were happy those first few years, or so I believed. When I first laid eyes on your mother, I was lost. My love for her overwhelmed me. She was the daughter of a hired hand, and at the time, was dating someone who was only two years older than her." Blake met Taite's gaze.

"This someone was eventually to be your father.

"Chad cautioned me against continuing with my plans to have your mother, but I refused to listen. Your mother was so vibrant and full of life that I had to have her, and I schemed to have her.

"Until her"—Blake swallowed with obvious difficulty— "until her, I had never been in love, and my emotion for her consumed me. Early one morning with my determination set to have your mother, I went to your father and offered him two hundred thousand cash to disappear from your mother's life. He gladly took the money, Taite. Almost snatched it from my hands he was so eager for it. And he disappeared. He vanished the following morning without a word to your mother, just as he promised he would do."

Blake sighed as his memories seemed to consume him. He gazed across the room and out its large windows for several silent moments. The other two in the room with him, it appeared, forgotten. Giving a slight shake of his head, he focused once again on Taite.

"Your mother loved your father and never stopped loving him. They had made plans to get married. She was devastated when he disappeared without a word, except a note left behind addressed to her that said he had to go. Family concerns, he had said. With your father's disappearance, I worked my way into your mother's life and I thought her heart. I took her to elaborate parties and bought her expensive jewelry.

"After six months passed and with no contact from your father, she told me for the first time that she loved me and agreed to marry me. I was on top of the moon, Taite. Your mother swore that our age gap didn't make a difference to her, and it never would. We agreed that for the first couple of years of our marriage we wouldn't have children, but after those two years went by, I began to pressure her for children. Oh, I wanted children so badly."

Blake looked down at his hands. Hands now gnarled and knotted with age. Slowly, he flexed his fingers as he studied the key that he held. "Your mother seemed to always have one excuse after another as to why we should wait another year and then yet another to have a child, until five years into our marriage, I still had no children of my own."

Blake closed his eyes. With a sudden grimace given, he jerked them back open. "After your mother died, I found journals that she'd kept, journals where she'd written down all her thoughts and emotions. Reading those journals, I learned of her disgust with me and my total devotion to her. I was an old man, she wrote, but what else could she do, except to cave into my continued and pathetic wish to marry her when her true love had left her. At least with my money she need never have to worry about working.

"Your mother also wrote that she felt she would be disloyal to your father by having my children and so would always refuse me my greatest wish. Your father had told her he was sterile, you see."

With a shrug, Blake continued, his face bleak with his emotion, "Who knows, maybe he really believed that he was.

"Your mother never stopped loving him, Taite. Daily, she wrote about him in her journals. How she longed for him to return to her. How she hated my touch. Then that fifth year into our marriage, he did return. With his reappearance, he disclosed to your mother what I'd done to get him to leave. Your mother recorded in her journal that she hated me with every fiber of her being. Secretly, she met with your father for two weeks before he finally asked her to disappear with him. She was leaving me when I happened to come home before they could sneak away. That was the day your father died."

Taite watched her father bend and unlock the lowest drawer of the desk. A drawer that Taite knew even as a child had remained barred from anyone but him. Her apprehension climbed as the man she knew as Father withdrew two large manila envelopes to lay them on top of his desk. Chills swept down Taite's spine at their appearance.

Suddenly, she wished Blake would put the bulky things back into their hiding place. Taite knew that the complete story, just sketchily told to her, was within those large envelopes, and she didn't want to know about her mother or her real father or what had happened to cause both their deaths. She'd just as soon remain ignorant of their lives.

Her father stood. He looked across the room at Pierce. "I was wrong about you, Pierce. It is easy to see that you love Taite, just as she loves you."

Blake's gaze skidded past Taite to rest somewhere over her shoulder.

"I am sorry, Taite, for everything," he said and squaring his shoulders, he continued.

"I realize now that I do love you and Caite as my true daughters. And with my realization, I also know that I'm too late in that knowledge and that I am going to lose you. I'm certain I've already lost Caite."

He looked back down to the top of his desk where he'd laid the envelopes, and his hands shook with a fine tremor as he touched them. Abruptly, he hid those hands within the pockets of his slacks.

"I hope you can find it within your heart to forgive me, but if you can't, I understand. The police reports and your mother's journals tell their story, and they tell of your mother's deep love for your father."

Abruptly, Blake turned and strode from the room. He neither glanced left or right.

Taite stared after him.

"I don't want to read what's in those envelopes, Pierce," she said into the silence. Taite shuddered, unwilling to stand and to venture toward her father's desk. Looking at her husband who silently studied her, she frowned at him.

"How different would mine and Caite's lives have been if our parents had been allowed to be together?"

With a jerky motion of her hand and a finger pointed toward the doorway Blake had just exited, Taite continued, "Instead, our lives were disrupted by that sour-faced old man who just left. Caite always tried to make him admit that he loved us, Pierce. That's why she pulled such stupid stunts over the years, and it's why I have such a hard time believing anyone can love me for me. He's the reason I believed you were only after my money. No one would love us for us he always said. He pounded that into our heads."

Pierce stood and walked over to the desk and picked up the two large envelopes. He balanced the weight of them in his hands. His gaze met Taite's. He walked toward her.

"Read their story, honey."

He held the envelopes out to her. When Taite didn't move, he pressed the bulky envelopes firmly down onto her lap, and he turned and exited the room.

For several minutes, Taite simply looked at the envelopes. Slowly and with apprehension, she began to unwind the strings that secured their flaps. Settling sideways on the couch, she kicked off her shoes to draw her legs up to sit crossways on the couch. Dumping out before her the contents of the envelopes, she picked up a slender journal from the top of the pile and began to read. Skimming through the first few pages, Taite realized her mother's writing was of when she finally accepted that the man she loved and desired wasn't coming back to her.

I feel that my life is over. Why would you leave me? I still love you so desperately, even with your desertion. I don't love Blake, but today I told him that I would marry him. He loves me and wants me for his own. He tries to please me, always wants the best for me. He dotes on me. My love, please forgive me. At least with the old man's riches I will never have to worry about a roof over my head. Isn't that what you always said? "Go where the money is, darling. Go to the money." My parents are ecstatic. Daddy said that he was glad you were gone. "Good riddance!" were his exact words to me. He says you were nothing but trouble. How I love you, trouble. I have to go now. Mom says that Blake is on the phone. Can I endure?

Slowly closing the journal, Taite felt an overwhelming sadness wash over her. Her mother had married out of desperation, but Blake had married for love. Her mother's own words conveyed his devotion to her. *Did my mother use that love to her own advantage? Was it greed on her part when she consented to the marriage, or just a lonely young woman who had needed his love for her at the time?*

Shaking her head at her troubled thoughts, Taite read a second and then a third journal. With disquiet felt when she finished skimming through that third journal, she laid it aside to pick up another journal dated the year before her mother's death. She opened it to its first page.

He keeps bugging me about children. I AM NOT HAVING CHILDREN WITH THAT OLD MAN. Where are you, love? It has been four long years and still not a word from you. My mother and father have both passed away, both within weeks of each other. I have to admit something just between you and me, love. I don't think that I can endure his touch much longer.

With a grimace, Taite tossed the journal she held onto the couch past the end of her bare feet. The more she read of her mother's journals, the more she realized her mother had been a very self-centered and selfish individual. Her mother had had an abundance of love given to her, and she'd turned her nose up at it. She'd squandered what she could have had on someone who—Taite was positive from what she'd read—was just as selfish as her mother seemed to have been.

Taite's heart contracted sharply at the thought that the man who had raised her as his own had read those same journals and had realized the contempt of the woman he'd loved so intensely. *His pain emotionally crippled him,* she thought with sadness.

Picking up the police reports, Taite tiredly scanned through them. She was relieved after reading the documents that her father's death had actually been a tragic accident resulting from a fall. Blake had been cleared of all charges.

Her mother's cause of death nine months later deeply shocked her though. It was no accident, but suicide. *And attempted murder.* Her mother had wanted not only herself but for her children to die that day, too.

Looking up from the pages of the paper that shook within her hands, Taite gazed unseeingly across the elegantly decorated room and a tear slipped down her cheek.

Could a woman who tried to kill two innocent babes have ever really loved any children she birthed? Even if she'd known they were procreated from the man she loved? Taite puzzled. She realized her mother believed the babies she carried were Blake's, the man she hated, but to punish two babies because of that hatred?

Jumping up from the couch, Taite, with jerky movements, slipped on her shoes and then haphazardly began to stuff everything she'd read back into their resting place.

Banging her knee sharply against the corner of her father's large wooden desk when she walked up to it, she quickly bent to roughly shove the bulky envelopes back into their hiding place. She slammed the drawer shut as her tears spurted.

Yanking her father's old, comfortable chair back, Taite slumped down into it, and she cried wholeheartedly. Cried because her knee throbbed, and yes, she cried because the man who'd raised her had given his very soul to a woman who hadn't deserved it. A woman who'd trampled on his heart and who'd thrown it with contempt back into his face. No wonder he couldn't feel love for her or Caite. How could he? And yet, he had raised them as his own?

Abruptly raising her hands, Taite wiped at her face with her fingertips. *No more crying,* she thought fiercely. She'd cried more in the past year than she could ever remember doing as a child. *Life can be a bitch, a real bitch, but you go on,* she realized with resolve, and she would not let what she was experiencing sour her on life as Blake and her mother had done.

"Dad!" Jumping from her chair, Taite raced from the room. "Dad!"

Her father's butler stepped into the hallway. His expression held a steadied blankness. "The sheriff is back, Mrs. Holden. Your husband and father are up at the barn with him."

With quick strides, Taite hurried past the man's watchful gaze and on out the front door of the home.

The sheriff's patrol car was parked in the driveway and at an angle that prevented anyone else from driving up into the area. Opening the gate to the walkway that led toward the barn, Taite hurried up its rock-paved pathway.

When she opened the barn door, her husband and father both turned toward her. Taite's gaze met Pierce's. The sheriff was nowhere in sight.

At her father's strained expression when she glanced toward him, Taite quickly walked to him, and she grasped his gnarled hands within hers. She gave his fingers a hard and loving squeeze. He winced and Taite eased her grip.

"You are my dad, and I love you," she whispered.

For a moment, Taite thought her father was going to crumble, but then he straightened his shoulders and his familiar stern expression once again settled over his features. He cleared his throat.

"The sheriff checked up on—*ahem*—your father's brother. Do you remember that the sheriff mentioned him? He says that he couldn't have been the one to have placed this graffiti here or the one who ran you off the road. The man has been incarcerated for the past five years, and he's not eligible for parole for another two. He has also found religion while incarcerated, says that he's forgiven me for what happened between me and his brother."

"Then who, Dad?"

Taite's hands were patted before her father turned to place them within Pierce's for him to hold. "I don't know. But the sheriff will figure it out."

Taite shivered with unease. Pierce pulled her up against his hip and wrapped an arm securely around her waist. With her father and husband by her side, Taite watched as the sheriff lumbered up to them after he walked into the barn. His breathing was heavy from exertion when he reached them.

"I wanted to take another look at those tracks we'd seen earlier. Whoever was here seemed to know the farm and its layout, Mr. Carpenter. The individual parked just far enough away that his or her vehicle remained securely hidden, and that individual hiked from there to the barn.

"We had an incident just a few days past where two local teenagers were caught in the act of defacing a barn. I mention them as a possibility because they used a first name in that incident also. Just as your daughter's was used here. This incident may just be coincidental with everything else occurring to Mrs. Holden."

****

"You don't honestly believe that it's coincidental though, do you, Sheriff," Pierce said when the sheriff glanced his way.

The sheriff peered down at his boots, dusty from his hike through the wooded area behind the barn. Bending, he attempted to wipe the dirt from previously buffed tops. Straightening, he squarely met Pierce's gaze.

"You're right, sir. I don't believe this is connected with that case."

"And you think I'm involved, don't you, Sheriff?"

Taite gasped. "Don't say that, Pierce."

She swiveled toward the sheriff. "My husband is not involved with this, Sheriff. I am positive of it."

Will she begin to doubt me again even with her defense for me? Pierce wondered. His thought gave him an aching hurt. He didn't know if he could take again that trapped expression of hers that she'd shown before. Pierce shifted so their gazes wouldn't meet. He didn't believe he could bear it if she turned against him again.

He'd wanted to gather her up into his arms and kiss her emotional pain away, which was so obvious, when she'd entered the barn in search for her dad.

The sheriff remained quiet. Pierce knew the man had already summed him up and tagged him guilty.

"Sheriff, I think you are on the wrong track. I don't believe this is my son-in-law's doing."

"Yet you did this morning, didn't you, Mr. Carpenter?" the sheriff responded as he turned toward Blake.

"Yes, but not now," Blake slammed back at him.

Taite sagged against Pierce as she smiled at her father. Pierce knew she presumed her father's harsh tone brooked no room for argument from the sheriff.

The sheriff gave his signature nod.

"Okay then," he said.

Turning he headed for the barn doors. They all followed and stepped out into the evening air.

A shot rang out. The sound of it shuddered through the air.

The wood behind Taite's head splintered.

Grabbing her arm, Pierce yanked her behind him. His blood pounded and his heart drummed as he scanned the trees from where the shot had seemed to originate.

"Down! Down!" the sheriff shouted, pulling his revolver from its holster, as his large body plopped to the ground. He fired off a protective round aiming toward the vicinity that the shot came from.

"Dad!" Taite screamed when her father didn't move as she and Pierce dove to the ground and to cover. Her father seemed immobilized as he scanned the land and trees beyond them.

Pierce leaped back up to force his father-in-law to the ground. Blake grunted when he hit the dirt at his shove.

"10-18! 10-18! Backup needed at the Carpenter place. Mile marker 100. West four." After the Sheriff's yelled orders into his police radio, the sudden quiet which surrounded the area was deafening. No one moved but scanned the horizon around them. A car engine, revving up, sounded beyond the distant trees and then nothing. Hesitantly, the sheriff lumbered upward.

Pierce stood up beside the man and reached down to help Taite to rise from her prone position.

What in the hell is it that is happening here? he wondered wildly as he kept an eye on the distant trees. Why would anyone want his wife dead? With shaking hands, Pierce brushed the dirt from Taite's face. Her whole front was covered with it.

"You okay?" he asked.

"Yes," she responded and she glanced down at her father. He didn't rise from his prone position.

"Dad, are you okay?"

Sirens wailed as three police cars squalled onto the driveway.

Her father began to chortle, but didn't attempt to rise. Pierce, Taite, and the Sheriff looked at each other and then back down to where Blake lay. Blake waved a hand at them to stand back when they all bent to help him up.

"I just needed to catch my breath," he said once he quit laughing and he'd risen. "My son-in-law took an opportunity to get even with me, I think. I can't say that I blame him though, what with my convincing my daughter that he was only after her money."

"Sir, I had nothing to do with this shooting." Pierce's posture was stiff.

Blake slapped him on the back. "I'm not talking about the shooting, son. I am talking about how you slammed me to the ground just now."

He gave into his genuine merriment again before he sobered.

"Son, you probably saved my life."

Blake smiled tentatively at Taite. "I wouldn't have wanted to miss the opportunity to get to know Taite and her sister, if they will let me.

"Will you let me?" he asked on a husky note.

"Ah, Dad..." With tears welling, Taite stepped into her father's arms.

He looked at the sheriff and Pierce over the top of her head. "Guess we better get out of this clearing before our shooter comes back, hmm?"

"Sheriff?"

The sheriff looked up at the man who called out to him. He yelled back, "We're fine. Our shooter has escaped though."

His gaze moved to the three individuals who stood by his side. "Rest assured. We'll find the culprit."

He dusted at his shirt with the palm of his hand.

"In the meantime, Mrs. Holden, stay close to home this weekend. I'll post an officer at the end of your drive. Put our number on speed dial in case of trouble."

Turning, the sheriff lumbered down the rocked pathway to the driveway. He spoke for a few minutes to his officers before they all left.

****

Dishes clinked as Pierce handed the gravy bowl he held to his wife. When their fingers touched, his gaze met hers.

"Where is that daughter of yours, Pierce?"

Turning from Taite at Blake's question, Pierce focused his attention on his father-in-law.

"Emma has her. I called and spoke to Lacy just a few minutes ago. She's enjoying being spoiled."

"Emma is keeping her for the whole weekend. We didn't think it would be a good idea for her to be here. Not with everything that's happening," Taite added as she smiled at Pierce.

She turned to look fully at her dad. "Chad was very upset with you that you hadn't called to tell him what happened this afternoon."

"I'll call him later and fill him in. But first, I want to get in contact with Caite and let her know what's occurred. I don't think she needs to come home until this mystery is solved and I'll tell her so. The last we spoke, she said she wanted to come home."

Taite exclaimed in obvious surprise at her father's comment, "You and Caite have been talking?"

"Not so much talking as Caite calling me every other day wanting to know how you're doing. She's been worried about you, Taite. She has spoken repeatedly about how awful it was that you lost your baby in the accident."

Pierce saw Taite stiffen. She'd brushed off his attempt at opening the subject the other night. He could tell she still hurt at the loss. She carefully sat her wine glass down before her onto the top of the table. Her gaze connected with his for a moment before she looked back at her father.

"It's time that Caite and I make amends. We've never been extremely close, but I'm to blame for that just as much as her. Caite needs to be told about our mother and father, and she needs to read the journals. Maybe it will help her to settle down and to understand our childhood better."

Taite's father solemnly agreed with a nod of his head before he said, "For now, though, you just make up with your sister. When the sheriff solves this mystery of who's trying to harm you, we can explain to Caite then I'm not her father. That isn't something that you should tell her over the phone."

"You're right, Dad."

Pierce silently listened as father and daughter talked quietly between themselves. He was proud of Taite. She was strong, stronger than he had believed. Not once that afternoon had her faith in him faltered. And when hit with the knowledge that the man who had raised her wasn't her father, she'd emerged even more strongminded than ever to make the most of her life. She was determined to forgive and to embrace what life had to offer.

Taite reached across the table to grasp his hand as she continued to talk with Blake. Pierce felt a peace settle within him. He was terrified at all that was occurring to her, but together, they would see it through.

Why anyone would want to harm Taite was beyond him. She'd told the sheriff when he'd inquired that she had no enemies that she could think of. Someone, though, held a grudge, and that someone was angry enough to try to kill her over it. Her car accident was no random act of violence. It couldn't be. Not after her being shot at today. Everything pointed at a planned and orchestrated assault against her.

"Mrs. Holden."

When Taite turned, the butler stepped on into the room and indicated the phone he held in his hand. He approached the table.

"Your friend, Mickey, is on the line. He seems agitated. Do you wish me to take a message?"

Taite glanced at Pierce but pushed back her chair and stood.

"No," she replied as she reached for the phone.

"I'll only be a moment," she said in passing to Pierce.

Pierce felt his anger stir. He trusted Taite. She and Mickey were, as she'd told him, only friends. However, he didn't have to like the man, and ultimately, he blamed Mickey for Taite's belief that he'd had an affair with Caite. If his wife hadn't believed Mickey, the whole ugly past few months could have been avoided altogether.

The wine glass stem that Pierce held between his fingers snapped startling him. As the top of the glassware toppled to the table, he quickly reached for it.

When Taite's father roared with laughter, Pierce stopped trying to mop up the mess he'd made. Taite's father stood and walked to where he sat. Blake patted him on the shoulder.

"She loves you, son. No need for worry."

Chapter 20

"Taite, there are two men who have blocked the entrance to your driveway. They say they work for you!"

"Calm down, Mickey. Just hand your phone to one of them."

Taite heard Mickey yell that Taite Carpenter, the owner of the house, wanted to speak with them. She then heard a voice yell back for Mickey to keep his hands high where they could be seen.

"Take the damn phone," Mickey yelled.

"Mrs. Carpenter?"

"No, Officer, this is actually Mrs. Holden, Mr. Carpenter's daughter."

"Ma'am?"

"Officer, the man you've detained is a friend of mine. Let him pass."

"Just doing our job, ma'am."

"I know, and thank you. Will you hand the phone back to my friend now?"

"Hell, Taite. What is going on here?"

Mickey's cell phone seemed to be dropped.

Taite could hear his distance curses and she smiled.

"I am leaving," he loudly stated a moment later, startling her.

"Why aren't you coming in?" she exclaimed.

"I just came by to let you know I was back in town from my parents'. It seems best if I don't stay and visit."

"I can explain the plain-clothes officers, Mickey, if that is your concern. Come on up to the house." When Taite was met with silence, it dawned on her why Mickey had decided not to visit. He'd seen Pierce's car.

"Oh, Mickey, please don't be angry with me. I have so much to tell you. Pierce and I have worked out our differences, and I got shot at."

"What do you mean you got shot at—are you okay? You weren't hurt, were you?"

Taite laughed. "No. Terrified, but I wasn't harmed. And since we don't know who shot at me, Dad is paying for 24-hour security guards posted around the property."

"It would've been nice to have known that they were here before I got ambushed," Mickey replied stiffly.

"No one knows they're here, Mickey dear, except family. The whole point is to capture whoever is out to terrorize me. And I didn't expect you back so early anyway."

"Well, I'm glad that you're okay. However, I still don't think I want to come in. And I can't say that I'm happy you and Pierce are back together," he paused, "I'm confused by it, actually."

At Mickey's sharp tone, Taite sighed. "I'm happy, Mickey. Can't you be the same for me? Please."

"I can't. Not when you're with him. Don't ask it of me. We'll talk later," he said and then abruptly disconnected the call before she could respond.

Dejection felt at Mickey's unwillingness to accept her decision, Taite walked into her father's study where she knew he and her husband would have gone after their meal. She would try to call Mickey first thing in the morning, maybe by then, he'd be in a better frame of mind to talk. Taite hoped he would come to accept her choice to believe in Pierce. *He will*, she thought, her spirits lifting when Pierce smiled at her. Mickey was a good friend. He'd stand by her.

"Is Mickey back in town from his parents'?" her father asked.

Taite went to sit down beside Pierce. He draped an arm across her shoulders. "Yes, he's back. Actually, he was out front in the driveway when your plain-clothes officers stopped him. He decided not to come in."

Taite watched Pierce's eyebrows raise in question.

"Can't say that I'm sorry about that," he said dryly. "Are you ready for bed, sweetheart? It's been a long day, and I need to be up before daylight in the morning for the commute into town."

"Do you really need to go into the office tomorrow? Can't the staff handle what needs done?" Taite knew, even as she asked it, that Pierce needed to oversee the happenings in his office. It was a newly acquired business, after all, that he was trying to build into a profitable venture for himself. She just felt securer with him by her side. In all honesty, though, with the officers stationed around the farm, there was no need for him to stand guard over her.

"Don't mind me. I'm just being a baby," she quickly amended as guilt descended at her bid to keep him close to her. He needed to be back at his office and attending to its daily operations or he'd never have mentioned going into work.

"If I thought there was any danger in leaving you, I wouldn't go, honey," he responded.

Taite stood. "I know that. Goodnight, Dad. We'll see you in the morning."

Pierce rose to stand beside her. "Goodnight, sir," he said.

Taite's father smiled and waved a hand at them. "See you both in the morning. I think I'm going to stay up a while longer myself. I'm going to call Caite. You need to make sure you call her yourself, Taite. Clear the air between you two."

"I plan to, Dad."

"What did Mickey have to say?" Pierce asked as he and Taite stepped from the study and he closed its door behind them.

At Pierce's tight tone, Taite glanced at him. She wondered if he was upset with her for taking Mickey's call. He hadn't seemed to be when she had come into the study.

"I really didn't get a chance to talk to him. As soon as he realized that you were here, he didn't want to come in."

Pierce frowned and sharply responded, "I'm sure he was afraid I'd confront him with his lies if he had."

Taite sighed. Her husband wasn't mad at her, however, his anger at her friend simmered in him. "Mickey really did believe you and Caite were having an affair, Pierce. He wouldn't have come to me with it if he hadn't.

I plan to call him tomorrow and ask if he will come here and visit with me privately."

"No."

Taite stopped on the stairway, and with reservation, she observed her husband's set face. "Pierce, even if Mickey believes you and my sister had an affair, I don't. Let me explain my trust in you to him, and let me do it in private, please. Then if he can't accept that I love and trust you completely, I'll tell him that he and I can no longer be friends."

"I don't want that man anywhere near you without me, Taite."

"Don't you trust me, Pierce?"

"Honey, it isn't a matter of trusting you. I don't care for or trust him."

Reaching out, Taite caressed her husband's jawline. "Let me talk to him alone, just this once," she pleaded.

"Taite..."

"I'll make it plain to Mickey that in the future, it would be best if he and I only saw each other when you can be present."

Seeing that Pierce was softening, Taite leaned forward, her gaze locked with his. "I love you," she said softly.

Pierce leaned down to kiss her. Taite returned his kiss with all the pent-up longing she'd experienced when they were separated. She clung to him.

Suddenly, he pulled back, breaking their embrace, and he turned to walk them up the stairs toward their bedroom. Taite didn't think she could have spoken if she'd wanted to.

"Meet with Mickey just this once, Taite," Pierce said as he opened their bedroom door and then clicked it shut behind them. At her quick nod of agreement, he reached for the buttons on her blouse and backed her up against the bedroom door. Returning his soft smile with one of her own as he slipped the thin material from her shoulders, Taite eagerly stood on tiptoe to wrap her arms about her husband's neck.

****

"Pierce, here."

Taite pictured her husband in his business suit.

"Hey."

"Hey, sweetheart," Pierce responded back. "Can you hold just a moment?"

"Sure," Taite replied. When Pierce had first answered the phone, Taite thought he'd sounded faintly irritated. In the background, she could hear him give instructions to someone concerning a customer who wanted to list a home. A female voice responded back when he grew quiet. Taite could hear her husband's muted answer to what appeared to have been questions directed at him. She heard the female respond again, and then the sound of a door shutting.

"So how is my favorite sexy lady this afternoon?" Pierce suddenly asked.

"Fine, I just thought I better check in with you, like you told me to when you called for the third time this morning," Taite replied. She couldn't stop her smile.

"Am I smothering you with my worrying?" Pierce responded.

Taite's smile stretched wider. "No. I rather enjoy it. However, there is no need for you to be worried, Pierce. Not with all the off-duty officers my father hired. Was that the new girl you were talking to? How is she working out?"

Pierce's sigh was deep. "I wish you could be here to train her, honey. I just don't have the patience. She came highly recommended, but for some reason that I can't understand, she thinks she has to clear every step she takes through me."

"Give her time, Pierce."

"I miss you."

"I miss you, too."

"Do I have to ask, or are you going to tell me how Mickey handled us getting back together? He did come by the house, didn't he, as he said he would?"

Taite leaned back in her father's chair as she fidgeted with the pen she held. She laid the pen down onto the top of the desk in front of her as she thought about Mickey's reaction to her announcement that afternoon.

"You there, honey?" Pierce asked.

"He…he said if I was stupid enough to still be in love with you and to trust you, then I deserve whatever happens." Tears sprang up into her eyes.

"That son of a bitch. Taite…Taite, are you crying? I knew that I should've come back home when he agreed to meet with you this afternoon. Honey, don't cry."

"I didn't recognize him, Pierce. He was so angry with me when he couldn't get me to change my mind about you. Dad came into the study after hearing him yelling. Mickey finally calmed down and even apologized to me, but he told Dad that he felt Dad and I were making a big mistake in believing in your innocence. And that as long as I was with you, he wouldn't be around. So…so I guess that is that." Taite sniffed.

For a moment, there was static silence on the other end of the phone line.

"You believe in me, don't you, honey?"

With surprise at Pierce's question, Taite straightened. If there was one thing she did believe in, it was her husband's innocence. It was not her husband who was out to harm her.

"I believe in you, Pierce. I know you love me. I won't ever waver in that again."

"As soon as I can run by and spend some time with Lacy tonight, I'll be home."

"Don't rush on my account, Pierce. Lacy needs to see you."

How could I have ever suspected Pierce of trying to kill me? Taite wondered, as she realized what a truly caring and loving man her husband was. How could a man who so obviously adored his little girl be a killer? Could a predator truly, love? Taite guessed so, although it seemed highly unlikely.

"I called and talked to our Lacy today."

Pierce laughed. "She loves to babble on and on, doesn't she?"

Taite smiled as she recalled the little girl's excited telling of getting to make cookies with Emma and Chad's sisters. "I love her, Pierce."

"I know you do, sweetheart. I'll see you tonight."

Chapter 21

Taite snuggled closer to Pierce. With a huge yawn and then a mischievous smile given, she placed the palm of her hand over his ribcage. Suddenly, she gave those ribs a firm rub with her knuckles. With a howl, he jerked sideways and rapidly caught her hand. Lunging upward, he rolled toward her and within that same fluid movement, jerked her arms up over her head to expose her own ribs. His expression was determined as he positioned half his body on top of hers to hold her down. Taite laughed happily.

"Do your best. I am not ticklish like you are."

"Not ticklish?"

He didn't sound convinced.

"Not in the least," she responded. Oh, she was ticklish, but not in the vicinity of her ribcage. And she wasn't about to tell her husband where her one and only problematic spot was.

Pierce slowly lowered his head; his and Taite's gazes connected. Taite smiled as she dared him on. She mimicked a kiss toward him. Pierce's chin connected with her side. She didn't move. He tried her other side.

She gave another air kiss. He undertook the sides of her neck and then the bottoms of her feet.

"Hmmm…?" she heard him issue, and she laughed. He trailed his fingers down her legs. Taite tensed when those lean fingers grazed her one and only ticklish spot.

Pierce paused and looked up at her, and his eyes were bright.

"What have we here?" he murmured. Then he smiled. That smile was positively wicked.

Taite tensed.

"Pierce...we need to get up."

"So, you are not ticklish? Well, maybe not here." Her husband stretched upward to kiss her neck.

"Or here." He ran his fingertips down her ribcage. He lightly brushed at the bottoms of her feet.

"Nope, not there either. Hmm...."

"How about here!"

Before Taite could react, Pierce had her flipped onto her belly and a beeline made for the backs of her knees.

"Stop!" she screamed even as her laughter erupted.

"Stop, I am begging you, please," she gasped.

Taite's tears flowed.

She chortled so hard her sides hurt.

Finally, the tickling eased. His mouth and tongue taken from the back of her knees.

Pierce's laughter rumbled as he jumped from the bed. "Come on, beautiful, time for a shower. Your father will be returning soon."

Wiping the waterworks from her cheeks, Taite rolled to her back and she pouted up at him.

"You're mean, do you know that?"

Pierce smiled down at her as his gaze traveled over her. "Beautiful indeed, but you deserved it," he replied.

With a laugh, Taite jumped from the bed to stand beside him. A late evening romp with her husband, while her father was gone, had been a nice surprise.

When Pierce returned home that evening, they'd discussed the events of the day and how Lacy was doing at Emma's and Chad's. Her father joined them shortly before he had stood. She and Pierce looked at each other with the same thought when he stated that he had to meet with someone concerning a horse. He'd asked Taite to inform the cook to delay their dinner for a couple of hours.

With a carefree laugh, Taite raced toward their bedroom as soon as her father exited through the front door. Pierce followed behind her at a more leisurely pace. The butler watched their actions with a frown and a shake of his head. Taite hadn't cared what he thought. She was happy.

The phone on the bed's nightstand rang, the shrill sound pulling Taite from her thoughts. Pierce picked the phone up as she reached for her housecoat.

When she started to take a step toward the bathroom, he looked at her with an arrested expression. Curious, Taite paused.

"Inform the sheriff to wait in the study for us. My wife and I will be with him in twenty minutes. Thank you, Jim."

Setting the phone down, Pierce smiled. "Well, honey. Maybe we have some good news. The sheriff is downstairs wanting to speak with us. Your sister walked in with him, too, Jim said."

"Caite is home! She never let on the last time I spoke with her that she'd come back in the country. Dad told her just the other night to stay put until whoever is terrorizing me is caught."

Pierce gave a shrug. "You know your sister. Has she ever listened to anyone?"

"Never," Taite replied. She hurried toward the bathroom to wash.

When her husband didn't move, only watched her, she paused. She gave her hair a toss over her shoulders. "Are you going to just stand there? You did tell the butler twenty minutes. I, myself, would like to know what the sheriff has to say. Wouldn't you?"

Pierce's smile spread. "You're a saucy little thing this afternoon."

He walked over to where she stood. Slapping her firmly on the butt, he drawled, "I like it."

****

As Pierce watched his wife, he felt content. She walked with her shoulders back as if she hadn't a care in the world. She'd told him that as long as he was by her side, she knew they could conquer anything they faced. He hoped so. He prayed the sheriff had good news for them. Pushing the door to the study open, Pierce indicated for Taite to proceed before him. She did with a devilish smile directed his way. Following behind her, Pierce watched the sway of her hips before he glanced up and realized the sheriff watched him watch her.

"Sheriff," he said as he walked toward the man. Pierce stretched a hand out to him. The sheriff stood, and with a firm clasp gave two sharp pumps before he turned toward Taite, as if to speak to her.

Taite had eyes only for her sister.

Caite stood, but fidgeted as her gaze darted between Taite and himself. When Taite smiled at her, her fingers stilled their nervous flutter. Slowly, she returned her sister's beam of welcome.

"The sheriff brought me to the house. I was stopped at our front drive."

Pierce wondered at Caite's nervous behavior. Her father had informed her of the officers he'd hired. Neither Blake nor Taite had relayed their belief that he and Caite were having an affair, or of that other unthinkable thing: their wish to do away with Taite. They'd all agreed that both beliefs were a misunderstanding, which should be forgotten by all and never mentioned again for all their sakes.

Could it be the unknown threat to her sister that makes her so edgy? Maybe Caite has a sister's love for Taite after all, Pierce thought with some surprise.

"How have you been?" Taite asked after she and Caite hugged. She didn't give Caite time to reply before she rushed on, "I am so glad to see you, Caite, but really, you should have stayed away until this mess of whoever is out to get me is cleared up."

Taite turned toward the sheriff to give him a smile. "Maybe your timing is perfect though. The sheriff is here with news for us. Isn't that right, Sheriff?"

She motioned for everyone to sit.

When she glanced his way, Pierce caught the sliver of apprehension within the depths of her gaze. He walked to her side to clasp an arm around her waist, and they turned together to take a seat.

He looked at the sheriff as they settled back against the couch. "Sheriff, we hope you have good news."

"I do actually, Mr. Holden. And a shocker of an ending to this mystery, which was quite a surprise to me, I have to say. That first day that I was here, Mr. Holden, do you remember I mentioned that two teenagers had been caught defacing a barn?"

Pierce nodded.

"Well sir, seems that this whole shooting and graffiti thing was the result of a teenager's prank."

Caite seemed to wilt.

Taite's fingers curled around Pierce's.

"A…a…prank, Sheriff? All of this was a prank?"

For a second, Pierce wondered if she had actually feared he'd somehow been involved. Her fingers tightened on his.

The sheriff smiled. "I am glad for your sake that someone isn't actually after you, Mrs. Holden."

"How did you figure out it was this teenager, Sheriff?" Pierce questioned.

"I didn't figure it out, Mr. Holden. The kid wasn't even in my radar of possible suspects."

Pierce leaned forward curiosity eating at him. "I don't understand?"

"The kid walked into my office, big as you please, and placed the weapon and empty cans of spray paint down onto my desk. He looked me straight in the eye and said that he wanted to confess to a crime."

"And everything checked out?"

The sheriff nodded. "Everything, from the weapon used to the bullet that we pried from the barn wall, to the black paint, and even the footprints left behind the barn. He described how he shot over your head, Mrs. Holden, and how we all hit the dirt at his shot. The boy described everything down to the last detail."

"I don't understand, Sheriff. Why did he do it?" Taite asked.

Caite leaned forward, her expression arrested.

The sheriff stood, his look severe. "On a dare, Mrs. Holden, a damn dare. Pardon me for my language ladies, but there seems to be a new game afoot with the male teenagers these days. Each must prove their manhood to their friends by showing that they can commit a crime, which doesn't actually harm someone, however, they have to come as close to it as possible and for it to be as risky as possible.

"The kid stated that he'd thought he was lucky when you and your father had come out to the barn that morning. He'd been ready to give up waiting for someone to show. He said it was then just a matter of waiting for you to call me for him to take a shot. He said that he hid up in a tree and actually watched us investigate the area."

In disbelief, Pierce leaned back against the couch. A dare? All of their worry and disruption to their lives these past few days, over a teenage dare.

"What about my wife being forced off the road, Sheriff? What about that note left on her windshield?"

"Still don't have a lead on that, Mr. Holden. Maybe it was as you told your wife, a disgruntled driver that Mrs. Holden accidently cut off."

"Well, at least the boy came in and confessed," Taite said into the quiet that fell over the room. "He must feel remorse for what he did if he confessed. That is good, isn't it?"

She looked at the sheriff.

"Yeah, well, I guess it could be seen as good, Mrs. Holden. I can't help but speculate though that I will probably see that young man again in the future. You have to wonder about kid's minds these days. Just as you have to wonder about the insanity of someone trying to hurt another over being cut off in traffic."

The sheriff looked at Pierce as he included both him and Taite in his next statement. "If you will come to the station, we can start the process of filing charges against the boy."

Taite looked at Pierce, her gaze pensive. "I don't want to file charges, Pierce. And I am sure Dad won't either since I don't wish it."

It angered Pierce, what the punk had done to their lives. Even if the kid wasn't supposed to hurt anyone, he sure as hell could have. He could've blown his wife's head off!

"That boy could have killed you, Taite."

"But he wasn't actually trying to kill me, Pierce. And he did confess to what he had done."

As their gazes clashed, Pierce's angry and Taite's pleading, the sheriff coughed. Pierce sighed and looked at the man, every instinct inside was telling him to file charges, but he wouldn't go against Taite's wishes.

"It looks as if we won't be filing charges, Sheriff."

The sheriff didn't comment as he returned his gaze. With a nod of his head, he stood and walked from the room.

"The sheriff can still file charges, Taite," Caite commented.

Taite gave a small shrug. "I guess that will have to be his decision to make. The whole incident appears to be the result of a young boy who just made a wrong choice. If he was willing to confess, he must be aware that what he did was wrong. I wouldn't feel right filing charges against him when no one was actually hurt."

At Pierce's grunt, Taite turned toward him. "Okay, not physically hurt anyway."

"You're too soft, Taite," her sister drawled.

Waving her hand at them both, Taite smiled. "Enough, I am just glad the ordeal is over. Now our lives can return to normal. This was a pleasant surprise, you showing up here today, sis. I am so glad that you came back home."

The study door opened. Taite's father walked into the room, a huge smile on his face. "Met the sheriff as he was leaving, and he told me the news. I informed the officers that we no longer need their protection.

"Caite!" he exclaimed upon seeing Caite curled up in her chair. "Glad to see you home, girl."

"Dad," Caite responded as she stood. She hugged her father back when he reached to embrace her, although her movements were stiff and awkward, as if she wasn't comfortable with the gesture of affection between them.

From what Taite had told him, Pierce realized Blake had probably never embraced either of the women before, even as children. It looked as if Taite's family was healing.

"Where are you going, Pierce?" Taite asked when he stood. She took her gaze from her father and her sister.

"I thought I would go to Chad's and Emma's and pick up Lacy."

Taite scrambled up from the couch. "I'll go with you."

Pierce shook his head. "Don't you want to stay here and talk to your sister?"

He looked at her meaningfully. Her sister still needed to be told of their real father and what had happened all those years ago. Taite easily grasped his meaning and slowly sank back down. Pierce leaned down to kiss her goodbye.

"I'll be back in no time," he stated softly. She nodded as she smiled up at him. Pierce thought that he'd never seen her look more beautiful or more radiant. She was relaxed and confident and basking in her family's healing. He smiled down at her for a moment.

"We're all looking forward to seeing your little girl again, Pierce," her father said from across the room. Pierce inclined his head at Blake before he walked away.

Chapter 22

Taite couldn't stop smiling. *Life is precious*, she thought, as she watched her father and sister heal their long-held estrangement. Taite knew deep in her heart that Blake had loved their mother unconditionally. Yes, he may have been underhanded in the way he'd been able to win her, but her actual father and own mother, in Taite's mind, were the real culprits in this saga. Their biological father had been more than willing to accept Blake's offered payment over marrying their mother, and their mother had tried to kill her own children because of hatred and selfishness. Taite sincerely hoped that Caite, when told of their real father and his subsequent death, would be able to understand Blake's side of the tangled story.

The room fell silent.

Glancing at Blake, Taite realized that he watched her expectedly, and she knew he wanted her to open the awkward subject of their mother and biological father. Taite watched as her father wiped his hands down the tops of his slacks and then he coughed. His eyes darted to the picture of their mother. Taite couldn't understand why he kept it hanging behind his desk all these years. She'd even told him just the day before that he should take it down. He'd responded with a robust "no".

Taite's heart went out to him and his nervousness. For so long he hadn't allowed himself to feel anything, had in fact kept his emotions under tight lock and key. How terrifying it must be to him, to know that he could be hurt all over again if Caite rejected him. If she accused and blamed him for everything that had transpired.

Taite didn't think Caite would reject him. As long as she could remember, her sister had been seeking Blake's approval and love.

"Caite, I have something—"

A sharp rap sounded on the study door, Taite stood and walked to it. Opening the door her father's butler gazed back at her with a harried expression.

"Is there a problem, Jim?" she asked. He nodded.

"I am sorry, ma'am," he stated quietly. "But your friend Mickey is at the front door, and he's demanding to speak with you. He wouldn't be put off. Quite rude he was about it, too."

Frowning, Taite turned to look at her father. It had been made plain to Mickey that he wasn't welcome. "Caite, did Mickey know that you were going to be here today?"

Caite jumped from her chair as if a jolt of electricity shot through her. "No! Is he here?"

"He's at the front door demanding to speak with me. The last time we spoke he left here mad, even said that we were no longer friends and some other horrible things. The only reason I can see why he would be here now, is because he knows that you're here."

"I don't want to see him ever!"

Taite and her father both looked at Caite in sharp surprise. She paced back and forth behind the chair she'd been sitting in.

"Geez, Caite, what's wrong with you?" Taite asked her.

Jerkily, Caite shoved her hair back from her face. "Please, Taite, just tell the butler to inform Mickey that he's not welcome here."

"Well, isn't that a nice howdy-do, you bitch."

Taite whirled at the harsh words drawled out from behind her. Mickey grabbed hold of her arm and halted her movement backward away from him. The handgun he held and jerked upward made a loud popping sound as he pulled its trigger. Her father's butler, a hole appearing between his eyes, and a stunned look crossing his face, crumbled to the floor. Taite inhaled to scream. Her shock electric.

"Don't even think about screaming, ladies," Mickey snarled as he made a threatening and sweeping motion with his weapon across the span of the room. Taite swallowed her terrified scream. In disbelief, she stared at the man who lay on the hallway floor. Blood pooled around his head, and as if hypnotized, Taite watched its spread on the wood planks. She couldn't pull her eyes away from it. *Oh, his family! His family!* was all she could think.

Reaching back with a foot, Mickey kicked the study door shut on the awful scene.

"Sit down, old man," he stated, his tone sharp, and his face hard-set as Blake started to rise.

"It is Sunday, and being Sunday, I know that all your staff has the day off except for that butler. And well now, he isn't going to help you is he, old man?"

Oh, Dad, don't try to be heroic, Taite thought, as she watched her father hesitate in indecision for a moment. Mickey tightened his hold of her arm, and his fingers bit into the flesh as he pulled her close to him. His gaze met hers before going back to her father's.

"I would hate to have to hurt Taite when I don't want to. But I will," he said quietly as if he issued an endearment. He guffawed when her father's eyes grew wide.

Blake sat back down.

"The shooting at the barn was you, wasn't it, Mickey, not that teenager?" Caite asked sharply.

"You promised me after Taite's car accident that you would stop our game." Caite waved her arm in a sharp loop, as if she wanted to dispel her words, her eyes wide as they met Taite's.

Taite's chest tightened in her disbelief. She had thought Caite and Pierce were involved, but the whole time it was Caite and Mickey?

"Did you have something to do with my car accident, Caite? With me losing my baby?"

"No!" Caite shouted. "It was all Mickey."

"You knew it was Mickey who ran me off the road, and yet you never said anything!" Taite cried, not wanting to believe—unable to believe that her sister had withheld that type of knowledge.

Dimly, Taite recognized that her father looked at Caite with the same expression of horror that she was feeling, his face blanching as he fumbled in his shirt pocket for his heart pills. She watched as he shook out a pill, and with trembling fingers placed the pill in his mouth and under his tongue.

Feeling her knees start to give way, Taite determinedly locked them in place. Mickey still tightly held her arm.

"Yes, darling, your sister knew," he told her.

"Tell her, Caite. Tell Taite how you planned her downfall," he shouted across the room as if Caite were a long distance away.

"You bastard, you promised me it was over," Caite screamed back. She wouldn't look at Taite or their father. Taite felt hostility rise against a sister who'd always competed with her in everything, and it seemed even willing to kill over it.

"Oh no, sweetheart," Mickey snarled back. "I didn't promise our game was over. In your arrogance that I was your whipping boy, you just assumed, I had agreed to stop."

At the hatred and mockery that laced Mickey's words, Taite swiveled toward him. She didn't recognize the hard-faced man she'd considered her dearest friend for the past two years.

"Don't look at me like that, Taite," he rasped, and he pulled her to him, his touch possessive. Tenderly, he cupped her cheek. "Don't look at me like that, honey. I can't take it."

Repulsed at his touch, Taite jerked backward. She winced when Mickey quickly fisted her hair and cruelly twisted the strands around his hand. He yanked her back into his embrace.

"Leave her be," Caite cried as Taite whimpered at the pain.

"Shut up, bitch," Mickey responded without taking his eyes from Taite. Huskily, he asked, "Why couldn't you love me, Taite? Why?"

In numbing bewilderment, Taite stared up at him. "I...I...don't understand you, Mickey?"

She tried to loosen his hold of her hair. He twisted the knot harder. Taite dropped her hands.

"That is the problem, darling. You've never understood, have you? Tell her, Caite."

"Tell her yourself, you bastard."

Mickey turned to point his gun at their father.

"Mickey, don't! I'll tell her," Caite screamed.

"I thought you would, darling," he drawled, although he didn't lower the weapon he held.

"Mickey, please," Taite whispered.

"Please what?" he whispered back. His leaned forward and his lips brushed against the outer shell of her ear. Taite wanted to cringe back away from his touch but forced herself to remain still.

"Don't you beg for me, Taite!" her father shouted.

"Please don't hurt my father, Mickey."

"But he's not your father, darling. Oh, I can see your surprise."

Mickey laughed. Then his gun exploded.

Taite's ears rang with the weapon's proximity, and the sounds of the room were muffled for a moment as she and Caite screamed. Their screams resounded against the walls of their father's study as their father tumbled from the chair that he sat in. A river of red spread on the floor beside his head. He didn't move, lifeless.

Mickey jerked at Taite's fisted hair.

"Shut up. Both of you!" he snarled.

Taite couldn't.

"Stop the damn noise, Taite, or your sister is next."

"Oh, you plan to shoot me, Mickey?" Caite shouted as Taite hastily swallowed back her horrified shrieks. Her whole body trembled.

Caite's head snapped back when Mickey swiveled toward her, his gun directly pointed at her chest. Even as she seemed to brace herself for his shot, she sneered at him, and then she laughed when he didn't shoot. Her laughter was harsh as she baited the man before her.

"Who will be the substitute for you if I'm dead? That's what you're thinking, aren't you, you son of a bitch? You low life, son-of-a-bitch."

With a surge of adrenaline, Taite bent to bury her teeth into the top of Mickey's hand. He issued a hiss of pain and the gun used to kill her father slipped from his fingers to clatter onto the hardwood floor. Jerking her head back up, Taite managed to clip him hard under the chin with the top of her head. Staggered by the sudden jolt of pain that seared through her temple, she managed to scream for Caite to run as Mickey fell backward, his look as dazed and confused as she felt.

Caite bolted around Mickey, but she grabbed a tight hold of Taite's hand as she went by and pulled Taite with her.

They both scrambled past the study door and then paused for a second at the butler's prone body before they turned to run all out for the mansion's front door.

Taite snagged a tight grasp of her purse from the hallway table as she ran by it.

"My car keys, Caite. I don't have them," she cried when she and Caite skidded to a halt before their vehicles. Frantically, Taite rummaged inside her purse. Her keys must still be lying on the hallway table. She turned to run back into the house.

"Taite!"

At the bellowed and enraged call from within the interior of the home, Taite halted, and her eyes met Caite's as wild panic consumed her.

"I should have grabbed his gun after I head-butted him," she choked out. "We have to make a run for it, Caite, through the pasture. Go!"

Caite swiftly turned.

Clasping her purse to her side, Taite blindly searched for her cell phone as they ran. Her fingers finally closed over the precious lifeline. Caite suddenly grabbed her arm to pull her to a halt, and she pushed her through the open barn door instead of them running past it as expected. Taite stumbled, then righted herself as she turned toward her sister.

"No. We keep running, Caite," she gasped her breathing labored. "We're going to be trapped in here."

Caite firmly closed the barn door. There was no lock on the inside.

"No, we're not. Not if we hide up in the loft. We can pull the ladder up after us and huddle at the back of the loft. Without that ladder, Mickey can't reach us. And once he realizes it, he'll decide it's best to leave while the leaving is good."

Caite's own breathing was labored.

Her eyes suddenly teared.

"Damn fucking bastard," she choked. She hunched her shoulders as she rapidly blinked.

Taite's heart jumped in her chest upon her name bellowed again. The sound was too close.

"Go," she urgently whispered as she pushed Caite toward the loft ladder. Grabbing the pitchfork leaned against the barn wall, Taite lugged it up with her as she hastened up the steps behind her sister.

They both turned to heave the wooden ladder up behind them once they reached the loft floor.

Quickly, they scrambled to the back of that upper space.

****

Pierce's laughter was deep as he watched his daughter's antics. Emma and Chad encouraged her on.

"Watch, Daddy," Lacy cried as she rolled across the brown-carpeted floor once again. When her small heels hit the cream painted wall on the opposite side of the room she jumped to her feet.

"See, I do cartwheels and cartwheels," she cried in her little girl lisp.

Reaching for his cell phone, Pierce replied, "I can see that, honey. It's a good trick."

Pierce knew from his ringtone that Taite was the one calling. He'd stayed and visited with Chad and Emma for over an hour now, and she was probably wondering where he was.

"Hey, sweetheart."

"Pierce."

At Taite's whispered, panicked tone, Pierce straightened in alarm.

"I hear him coming in." He heard his wife whisper to someone.

"Taite, what is going on?"

At his sharp tone, Chad and Emma fell quiet as did his daughter. Pierce jumped to his feet. When his eyes connected with Chad's, the older man quickly stood.

"Taite?" Pierce repeated at her continued silence.

"Pierce...Mickey...Mickey...Dad's dead. Shooting...not the teenager."

Suddenly, the phone went silent.

Pierce quickly turned toward Chad. "Call the police. Tell them there's an emergency at the Carpenter place. Something about Mickey and about Taite's father being dead and that the teenager the sheriff thought was responsible for the shooting isn't the one."

Emma gasped.

Abruptly, Pierce turned to leave. *Twenty minutes! Twenty minutes from Taite*, was all he could think. Chad hollered for him to wait as he sprinted to his gun cabinet. He yelled for Emma to call the sheriff.

Unlocking the cabinet, Chad jerked out two rifles.

"Take one," he ordered Pierce, even as he snatched up a box of ammunition.

"I *am* going," he roughly responded when Pierce started to object as he turned.

With a glance toward his big-eyed, but quiet daughter, Pierce turned on his heel and at a hard sprint, headed toward his car. He was surprised when Chad jumped into the car at the same time he did. If he hadn't, he would have left him behind.

****

Her hand shaking, Taite reached out to place it on her sister's arm, trying to calm her. Her sister shook worse than she did. Silently, they looked at each other. Taite's cell phone had lost its power. She wasn't diligent at keeping it charged. A shaft of light filtered across the barn floor below them.

Caite dropped her gaze from Taite's. Holding their breath, they watched through the slatted wood floor as Mickey walked into the barn, and reaching out, he flipped the lights on. He glanced around the interior of the barn. As of yet he hadn't looked upward. Taite shifted. She and Caite were squatted over a thick board left behind from a recent repair.

"I am sorry, sis. Sorry for everything," Caite quietly choked out.

Taite swallowed. If they survived this, could she ever forgive her sister for withholding the knowledge that Mickey was the cause of her miscarriage? She didn't know. Not until she heard what this game was that Mickey and Caite had played.

With deep-seated hurt, Taite felt the painful loss of her child once again. Mickey, her best friend, her sister's lover, the cause of all her hurt and sorrow these past few months? Her bitterness swelled as she watched that same man searching for her within the lit interior of the barn.

With a suddenness that made Taite jump backwards, Mickey jerked his head up. It seemed that his gaze caught hers through the slatted wood floor, although Taite knew that he couldn't see her. With his devilish, lopsided smile that she'd always thought of as endearing, yet now seemed evil, he stared upward.

Where is the tender, caring man I knew? That laughing Mickey. The "I'm here for you" Mickey, she wondered.

"Taite," he drawled. "I know you and your sister are hiding up there. Come down here."

Taite shook her head, refusing, even though she knew that Mickey couldn't see her silent response to his words. Her gaze caught Caite's wide-eyed stare at her.

From day one of meeting Mickey, Taite had considered him a dear friend. A wonderful man who'd always encouraged her and who'd always made her laugh at life's hardships. What had gone wrong?

Breaking eye contact with her sister, she yelled, "We're not coming down, Mickey. I called Pierce! He's on his way here even as we speak."

Caite shifted, and her movement showed her unease.

Mickey cursed. "All this is your fault, Taite. If you hadn't taken that bastard back, we would never have come to this end. I have forgiven you for headbutting me under the chin. I know you didn't mean to cause harm. Now come down here to me like a good girl. If you leave with me now, no one else will needlessly have to get hurt. Come down. Come with me before Pierce gets here and tries to keep us apart."

Taite's gaze locked with her sister's. She knew that her eyes must be bulging.

"He's a certifiable nutcase, sis," she whispered. Caite ducked her head, and silently, she peered down through the floor gap.

"Caite!" Mickey yelled up at them, somehow sensing her movement.

"We started this thing together. Don't you want to end it together? Make your sister come down here to me. Hell, I thought I was doing you a favor when I killed your old man."

"Shut up you, bastard!" Caite screamed. She lunged to her feet. Taite frantically tried to reach out to hold her back. Slipping from her grasp, Caite ran to the edge of the loft.

"Shut up!" she screamed down at Mickey.

Taite jumped to her feet when she saw Mickey raise the gun he held. He pointed it at Caite.

"Mickey, don't," Taite cried running to step in front of her pacing sister, blocking his path to her.

"Don't, please."

"Ah, darling, are you still protecting Caite? Tell her what you've done, Caite," he yelled, his eyes hard. He didn't lower the weapon he held.

White-faced, Caite stepped out from behind Taite even as Taite tried to stop her. She looked down at Mickey, and Mickey smiled back up at her.

"Tell your sister what you've done, Caite. Let's see if she will want to protect you then."

Turning toward her, Caite raised her hand out to her in a helpless and defeated gesture. "He's right, sis. You wouldn't want to protect me if you knew everything that I've done to you."

Taite shook her head in denial.

Caite began to sob, and suddenly, she whirled toward Mickey.

"You bastard," she screamed. "The game was over!"

Tears coursed down Taite's cheeks as she stared at her sister. Her confusion was tearing her apart. Had her sister wanted her money after all? Had Caite planned to kill her, only to back out?

Sensing Mickey's movements below, some sixth sense made Taite dive for the floor just as a bullet whizzed over her head.

Caite just seconds behind her let out a wild scream.

"Hey, up there. Guess what? I can climb on top of these hay bales stacked down here and shoot you. How about it, girls? You going to put that ladder down, or do you both want to die?"

Mickey continued his scrambled ascent and then he paced across the top of the hay bales stacked against the other side of the barn wall. He fired a shot over Taite and Caite's heads again.

He glanced toward the barn door. Jerking his head back toward them when the door remained closed, his gaze caught Taite's when she raised upward.

He jerked his arm up, his face set with firm decision.

Jumping to her feet, Taite yelled out, "I want to come down to you. Don't shoot, Mickey. I'll put the ladder down.

"Help me, Caite," Taite gasped, her mind settled on the decision made. A decision which might get them both killed. As Caite's gaze met hers—for the first time in their life as twins—Taite felt that psychic phenomenon that she'd read about that occurred between identical twins. She knew Caite was cognizant of what she had in mind.

With a slight nod, her sister rose from her prone position, and she turned to help Taite heave and shove the bulky ladder back into its previous position.

Mickey leaped from the stacked hay bales and sauntered toward the ladder when its base hit the floor of the barn. He motioned for Taite to climb down from the loft.

Taite took a step down onto the ladder's first rung and then scrambled back up to the loft floor.

"I...I...can't, Mickey. I can't come down." She wrung her hands, an action not altogether an act.

His foot resting on the bottom rung, Mickey's gaze devoured her. "Come down here, Taite," he growled up at her.

"Promise that you won't hurt me or Caite."

Taite sensed Caite's small steady movements behind her. Mickey seemed aware of only herself as he stared up at her.

"I promise, Taite. Now get down here," he replied.

Stepping forward to the edge of the loft, Taite took two slow steps down the ladder rung but then scrambled back up to the loft.

"Fuck it, Taite! Get down here."

"I am sorry, Mickey. I...I...want to come down, but you have me so scared."

Mickey kicked at the ladder. His face hardened as he stared up at her.

"Both you and Caite stand back," he ordered.

Taite took a step back. Caite stood directly behind her.

In no time, Mickey's head and shoulders cleared the top of the loft. His gaze met Taite's. Then his eyes widened.

"Where's your sister?"

As if on cue, Caite jumped out from behind Taite just as Taite swung her foot and kicked the gun from Mickey's hand. Caite plunged the tips of the pitchfork that she held into his broad shoulder.

With a hoarse cry, he swayed backwards.

The heavy ladder banked at his action.

Mickey, after his initial surprised reaction, remained stock still for an instant before he leaned forward toward Taite. The ladder tilted again to settle back in its former resting place.

Taite felt her panic rise. She wanted to reach out and give the ladder a shove sideways yet she was too scared to get within arm's range of Mickey. Caite didn't move. She seemed frozen. She hadn't used enough force to cause Mickey and the ladder to fall backward to the floor as planned.

His face white, Mickey cursed. His gaze met Taite's. "I should have killed you the day I ran you off the road."

Without thought, Taite snatched hold of the pitchfork still held in Caite's hands, and in one fluid motion, she slammed its forked metal-end against the side of Mickey's head. His lunge backwards caused the ladder to tilt, and Taite continued its backward descent with a sharp shove at it with the farm tool she held.

The heavy ladder thudded as it hit the stacked hay, and Mickey's back slammed against the hard floor of the barn. His arms flopped out beside him as his hold to the sides of the ladder were jerked loose by the force of the contact. His eyes open, he gazed upward. He didn't move.

Taite fell to her knees. The roar of sirens outside the barn resounded, and then silence reigned as engines were killed simultaneously.

"Taite!"

The adrenaline rush held Taite within its grip. She couldn't move. Her breathing sounded loud.

"We're in here!" Caite yelled. "The barn! We're in the barn!"

The barn door slammed open. Taite watched Pierce's gaze take in Mickey's sprawled form before he jerked his stare upwards at her sister's sudden burst of hilarity. A second later, his gaze caught Taite's and held.

In a daze, Taite turned to look at Caite.

Her sister's amusement continued. Then her wild laughter abruptly stopped.

"I hope the son of a bitch is dead!" she shrilled down at the police who swarmed into the building behind Pierce.

"Taite, honey, are you okay?" Pierce asked. He started toward the ladder Mickey lay under when she didn't respond. She couldn't. Her throat was too tightly closed.

Taite watched, still on her knees, as the sheriff walked to Mickey's lifeless body. He helped Pierce to set the ladder aside. Bending down on one knee, he felt for a pulse on Mickey's still unmoving form. He moved his hand along the back of Mickey's head. Taite thought she heard a low groan in response to the sheriff's probing fingers.

The sheriff reached for his radio, and she heard him order an ambulance.

"He's alive," the sheriff said to no one in particular.

"Thank goodness," Taite breathed, relief felt that she and Caite hadn't killed Mickey. She didn't know if she could have lived with the knowledge that she'd actually been responsible for someone's death, even his.

With a gasp, Caite angrily whirled toward her.

"I want him dead!" she shrilled. Just as sudden as her demand for death was spoken, her shoulders slumped, and she seemed lost and confused. "You are the good one, aren't you, sis? You always have been. I...I...guess you must be if you're relieved that bastard is still alive after all he's done to you."

Caite's hands shook as she raised them to push her hair back from her face. She stared at a silent and bewildered, Taite. She took a deep breath and then let it out slowly.

She heartbreakingly whispered, "I absorbed all our mother's hatred on her deathbed, didn't I, Taite? While you, you absorbed all the love Chad had for you when he breathed life into you. The Good and Evil of nature split between us that day, Taite. Good versus Evil....and evil picked me."

Taite returned Caite's glazed stare with one of her own. What was her sister talking about? Caite knew the story of their birth and their mother's hatred for them? *But how*? Her sister hadn't read the police reports or their mother's diaries. *Or had she*? Mickey had known that Blake wasn't their father. How had he known?

With determination, Taite stood.

Those questions could be answered later, just as all the others would be. "You are not evil, Caite."

When Caite didn't respond, Taite walked to her and she grasped her sister's shoulders to give her a firm shake. "You are not evil. Do you hear me?"

Caite's eyes lost their vacant look as she seemed to work to focus on what Taite had said.

Hugging Caite to her, Taite whispered, "You are not evil, sis."

Caite held onto her tightly as her tears flowed.

"I love you, sis. I really do," she chokingly responded.

"I love you, too, Caite," Taite said, her throat so tight her words could barely be whispered.

"We have a lot to work through, don't we? You and I," she continued, and pulling from their embrace, she smiled tentatively at Caite.

Her sister nodded in agreement as she wiped at her eyes with the back of her hand.

"Are you going to be okay?" Taite asked with concern.

"Everything is going to be fine," Caite huskily responded. She smiled brightly as she squeezed at Taite's fingers, and she made a motion behind her.

"Your husband is here for you," she stated softly.

Turning, Taite smiled wide and ran into Pierce's open receiving arms.

****

Closing his arms tight around his wife, Pierce pulled Taite securely to him. He looked her over for injuries.

"I'm okay, Pierce."

"I have to make sure for myself, sweetheart." Relief surged through Pierce at the realization that Taite was unhurt.

"I love you," he hoarsely murmured. Tilting his wife's face up toward his, he tenderly kissed her mouth. Taite's arms wrapped about his waist as she swayed against him.

It was several moments before either of them became aware of their surroundings again or anyone else. Raising his gaze from Taite's smiling response to his light tap of a finger upon her nose, they reluctantly parted. Pierce's gaze met Caite's, and his eyes widened in alarm.

Taite quickly turned.

"Caite!" she cried.

Pierce took a step forward, intent on rescue.

"Don't come any closer, Pierce," Caite demanded as she stood perfectly balanced on the balls of her feet.

The doors to the loft were open, and Caite was poised on the framework of that opening. The open sky loomed behind her. She looked so beautiful and so heartrendingly identical to his wife that Pierce felt his insides twist in raw fear.

The outside wind that passed through the open doorway gently lifted the copper-colored strands of Caite's hair. She had an almost ethereal and otherworld quality about her.

"Caite, step back inside this barn," he commanded, his fear overwhelming him. Caite ignored him as she looked past him to her sister. Her gaze was pleading and sad.

"I...I...can't live with what I've done, Taite. I prodded Mickey on with our game. But he went too far, and I told him I wanted it to stop. I was jealous of you. I wanted to hurt you. Forgive me. Forgive me for the grief that I've caused you and for Dad's death."

Pierce took a scared step toward Caite when her face took a resolute twist. With disbelief, he watched as with a sudden lift of her arms, she arched backwards. *No!* he thought. He tried to run.

As if time slowed to a crawl, in one graceful swoop, Caite fell through the air and floated, it seemed, downward.

Pierce heard Taite screaming as he ran.

In a sick daze and at his wife's continued high-pitched screams, Pierce turned from the scene below him. His bicep muscles contracted as he released his clenched fingers from their tight hold to the barn loft doorway. His stomach contents bucked and churned as he took several stumbling steps back from the open space before him. A space he'd damn near fell through in his attempt to grasp hold of Caite as she jumped.

Pierce glanced toward Taite.

"Let me go!" she hoarsely screamed. She clawed at the sheriff's hands. The sheriff held her by the waist as she strained to escape his arms. Pierce gave a quick nod. The sheriff released his tight hold of her. When Taite ran hell bent toward the loft doors, Pierce quickly grabbed her and yanked her to him. She screamed in anger as she wildly struggled against his restraint.

"No!" he told her as she continued to struggle.

"No," he repeated firmly when Taite looked up at him, her expression determined.

"Let me go," she shrieked. Her tears streamed down her cheeks. In sudden defeat, she abruptly stopped her struggles and laid her head against his chest. She shuddered in grief. Pierce's heart broke.

The sheriff walked to the loft's edge.

"May God Almighty have grace on her soul," he uttered, his tone soft.

His gaze met Pierce's. Pierce knew the sheriff's insides churned. Caite's beautiful form, impaled by the hay equipment parked up against the side of the barn, was something Pierce would never be able to erase from his memory.

Chapter 23

When the last words were said over her sister's grave, Taite turned toward her father. The wind whipped harshly around them. Silently, he gazed back at her. Taite knew she looked terrible. The horror of her sister's death had taken its toll. With sympathy felt for her father, she realized that he didn't look much better than she did.

The bullet Caite believed had killed him had only grazed his temple, knocking him out. Taite leaned toward him.

"Let's go home, Dad," she said softly. She watched as his eyes teared up and he rapidly blinked them back He quickly stood and then awkwardly stumbled backwards a step. Taite took hold of his arm to steady him.

Pierce walked with them when they started forward, ready to leave the crowd behind them. Taite raised her hand to Chad and Emma who stood across the way visiting with a group of people. Chad's unmarried sisters stood beside them. With a sad smile given toward her, Chad nodded at Taite. He placed his arm around Emma's shoulders. Chad knew that she and her father needed this time alone.

Walking slowly toward their car, Pierce opened the car door for Blake when they reached it. As her father folded his thin form into the back seat, Taite swallowed back her tears. When she shut the car door after he settled, Pierce patted at the center of her back.

Looking up at him at his gesture of comfort given, Taite felt her love for her husband swell to overflowing. She and her father had been numb with grief at Caite's suicide, and Pierce, understanding their shock, had handled all the necessary police reports and the arrangements for Caite's burial.

The funeral had been beautiful and packed with Caite's friends and coworkers. *And why shouldn't Caite have had tons of friends,* Taite thought defensively. Her sister had been a vivacious individual. She'd just become lost and confused for some reason.

"Ready, honey?" Pierce asked.

"Why? Why, Pierce?"

Understanding her question, Pierce shook his head. Taite stared up at him, unmoving.

"I don't know why, sweetheart," he told her. He gently touched her cheek. "I don't know why."

With a deep sigh, Taite turned.

****

Taite walked into her father's study and abruptly sat down on his couch. "The sheriff is here, Dad."

It had been two months since they had buried Caite, and life was slowly continuing. She and her father were trying to bring their lives back to a semblance of normalcy. Pierce and she had finalized the purchase of their new home that morning. The same home that she had wanted her husband to look at with her before her car accident and the near destruction of their marriage.

Pierce had found the paperwork she'd gathered on the home and her notes. Realizing the house was the one she had told him she'd wanted him to see and that it was still unsold, they had gone and looked at it together, and he had loved it.

Blake looked up from his paperwork when Pierce walked into the study still dressed in his work suit. The sheriff followed him into the room behind him.

"Hello, Sheriff," Taite said as Pierce walked toward her. The sheriff hesitated. She motioned to the empty chair beside the couch.

"Please, take a seat."

Leaning back on the couch, Taite nervously picked at the crease of her trousers. Pierce grasped hold of her hand when he sat down beside her, stalling her actions. *He looks tired,* Taite thought when their gazes connected. The following week she was scheduled to start back to work at the office. She was ready.

Pierce had stated the evening prior that he could use a good salesperson, someone who knew the business as well as he did if she really wanted to come back to work. In spite of everything that had happened over the past few months, they both thought it would be better for her to stay busy.

The sheriff settled his large frame onto the chair that Taite had indicated. He coughed for a moment as if to clear his throat. After several shifts of his legs, his heavy frame grew still, and he met their gazes.

"Mr. North has started talking. He gave a full confession yesterday. I was pretty shocked by what he owned up to."

Stiffening, Taite lifted a hand toward the sheriff to halt his words. She looked at her father. Did either of them want to hear what Mickey had confessed? With a sigh at her father's nod, Taite looked toward the sheriff. "Go ahead, Sheriff."

The sheriff glanced at Pierce. "Mr. North's story starts before you came into your wife's life, Mr. Holden, but it was your arrival which caused things to escalate to the point of Ms. Carpenter taking her life."

Pierce glanced at Taite, and his fingers tightened around hers.

"My husband, Sheriff?" Taite inserted.

"My husband wasn't involved with Mickey trying to kill me or with my sister taking her life."

Waving his beefy hand in the air, the sheriff shook his head. "I know, Mrs. Holden. No worries there. I'm sorry. Let me start over. Mr. North revealed that he fell in love with you the first moment he laid eyes on you. However, once he realized you were not romantically attracted to him, he thought your sister, Caite, was heaven-sent. He says he actually believed he was in love with her, for a while anyway. He said that now in hindsight he never should have allowed a relationship to develop with Caite. It only strengthened his love for you, and your sister was aware of it. And she used it to her advantage, sometimes, even pretending to be you for him to get him to go along with her when she wanted something done."

Lunging up from the couch, Taite yelled in anger, "Mickey is lying! Caite would never have pretended to be me. That's disgusting. I am not going to sit here and listen to you malign my sister now that she's gone."

"Sit down, Taite," Blake ordered.

Angrily, Taite swiveled toward her father. "You can't believe this, Dad."

"We need to hear what Mickey had to tell the sheriff, Taite, and then we can decide if we want to believe it. And yes, Caite would pretend to be you. She did it when she swindled money from Chad."

Taite brought her hands to her face to cover it from the others. "I can't listen to this. I just can't."

Pierce stood. He looked at the sheriff and then his father-in-law. "Taite and I will be back shortly."

"Come with me, honey," he stated grasping hold of her elbow.

Angrily, Taite jerked her elbow from her husband's hand. Marching from her father's study, she continued until she reached their bedroom. Flopping down onto the top of their bed, Taite glared at Pierce when he shut the bedroom door behind her and then turned toward her.

"I am not going to listen to my sister being blamed for that man's actions."

Stripping his tie, Pierce silently folded it and laid it on top of the dresser. Wordlessly, he slipped off his dress shoes. He reached out to remove Taite's shoes. When he stretched out beside her, he gathered her to him.

Stiffening, Taite pulled back from him.

"Stop," he commanded sharply as he tightened his arms around her to pull her up to him once again.

Taite immediately stilled and she gave a sniff. She felt her tears threaten. "I can't bear to hear Caite slandered. I won't stand for it, Pierce, especially since she's not here to defend herself."

"Is she being slandered, honey?" he responded. "Or are we finally going to hear why your sister felt she had to commit suicide? Something bad occurred between Caite and Mickey, and it spilled over onto us. Both were in a sick relationship. You need to face the fact that your sister was emotionally ill."

Furiously, Taite slapped at her husband. "Mickey made my sister sick. Don't you blame Caite. If it hadn't been for him, she wouldn't have committed suicide!"

With obvious anger, Pierce grabbed at Taite's flaying hands and he tightly held them down on top of the bed covers between them. Rising, he leaned over her.

"It's time for you to stop denying what your sister did. Hell, Taite, Caite more or less confessed to you that she drove Mickey to his actions."

"But...but she also wanted him to stop. She said that Mickey had gone too far. She said that, Pierce!"

"She was still involved in hurting you, damn it. Don't do this, Taite. Son of a bitch, don't deny your sister's involvement in what happened to you. Hell, what happened to us."

His features drawn tight, Pierce's gaze searched hers.

Taite felt her chest tighten as raw pain gripped her. It tore through her as the truth of her sister's ugliness washed over her. Gasping, she cried out in agony, and once she started crying, she couldn't stop. She struggled for air as she felt her husband gather her close to him as he crawled back onto the bed with her, and quietly, he stroked her hair and her arms as he let her pour out her grief. Gradually, Taite's anguish quieted.

Bending, he kissed her wet cheeks. He continued to gently, and softly, kiss her cheeks and her eyelids.

"I love you, baby," he whispered.

Reaching up, Taite wrapped her arms around her husband's neck. His love for her a place she could draw strength from.

Chapter 24

Taite hesitated as the guard asked her to step through the metal detector. She looked toward Pierce.

"Go ahead, honey," he urged.

The sheriff and Mickey's lawyer waited for them beyond the glass partitions to the left of them. Taite could see Mickey being wheeled by a prison guard toward the visiting room where they waited. Her stomach churned. She was glad that her father hadn't wanted to come. He had listened to the sheriff's statement at their home.

"You can do this, Taite," Pierce stated softly. With resolve, Taite took a step forward. The metal detector didn't go off. The female officer smiled at her, and then at Pierce when he followed suit.

"This way, ma-am, sir," the officer stated as she buzzed them through locked doors. Taite could hear the resounding click of the security latch when it slid open and then again when it closed.

With Pierce keeping his hand to the center of her back, Taite walked toward the waiting men. She sat in a hard one-piece molded chair when a door opened and Mickey was wheeled forward toward her. A nurse walked behind the guard. Taite was vaguely aware of Pierce settling by her side.

"Hello, Taite," Mickey said when the guard stopped his wheelchair beside his lawyer. The fall had paralyzed him from the neck down. The guard turned to stand against the far wall. The nurse stayed beside Mickey.

Nausea rose in Taite as she stared at the man who had killed her father's butler and who had attempted to kill her father, too. How dare he say *hello* to her. As if...as if they were still old friends. Slowly, she drew a breath. Taite felt Pierce's hand at the small of her back, and she looked to him. *You can do it*, were his silent words as he looked back at her. She straightened.

"I wanted to hear from your own mouth what happened between you and my sister," she stiffly stated, turning back toward the man she had thought was a friend.

Mickey gave her a sad smile. "I know, Taite. When my lawyer called and said the sheriff had gone to your home with my statement, I knew you would come."

"You knew I would come?" Taite felt sick. Mickey knew her well enough to know that she would want to hear what he had to say with her own ears. She couldn't meet his gaze.

"Caite always knew I loved you, Taite. Although you never realized it," he said softly. "She could tell the first night we met I was head-over-heels in love with you. She thought it was funny. And you, you thought I looked at her that first time with lust for her, but it was you I saw, an identical replica of someone I wanted—someone who saw me only as a friend."

Taite felt her husband's hand clench against her back, and she snapped her eyes up to meet Mickey's gaze.

"When your sister returned my interest," he continued, "I think...I think that was when my sanity started to slip. I was happy with you—her, until Christmas when Caite kept driving the fact home to me that you, the real Taite, had fallen for our new boss. She enjoyed it, Taite. She enjoyed my confusion. And she wasn't content with just driving me crazy, she even thought it was hilarious when you were so distraught over your precious Sexy being hurt that weekend."

Taite stared at the man she didn't know. A man she had never known. "It was you who caused the injuries to Sexy over the Christmas holidays?"

His eyes pleaded for her to understand his motive.

"It wasn't me, Taite. It was someone I didn't recognize. Caite taunted me so mercilessly that weekend about Pierce getting laid by you that I lashed out by hurting your pet. She enjoyed your misery, laughed over it, just as I enjoyed your misery later when she and I joined together with the plan to bust you and Pierce up."

"How were you to break us apart?" Taite whispered although she already had a good idea.

"At your wedding, Caite saw your changed will on your father's desk. She had me hint around that day, within your father's hearing, that since you were so in love with Pierce that I wondered if Pierce could be trusted. Caite knew your father's suspicious nature and counted on his hiring an investigator to check Pierce out."

"And then you and she worked to set me and Pierce both up, didn't you?"

Mickey nodded at Taite's disbelieving question.

"I hate you, Mickey."

Taite watched as his eyes teared, and her skin crawled in reaction. *Would he be so bent on confessing, if his injuries hadn't permanently bound him to that wheelchair?* No longer would he walk or even be able to go to the bathroom without help. In that moment, Taite felt no sympathy.

"I went over the edge, Taite. Caite only wanted to end your happiness with Pierce, and she truly believed I had stopped our game."

"Your game," Pierce growled with obvious disbelief. "Your game cost three lives and nearly a fourth."

Mickey glanced Pierce's way, but quickly averted his gaze. "I am sorry, truly sorry."

Pierce snorted, but didn't respond.

Taite leaned forward. "How did you know Blake wasn't mine and Caite's father?"

"Do you remember a maid by the name of Sal?"

"Sal?" Taite dug in her memory but couldn't recall anyone by that name who ever worked for her father.

"This maid told Caite she was a bad seed. That everyone knew she was evil. And that it was all proven in your mother's journals."

"How old was Caite when this happened?" Taite asked with horrified disbelief.

"Six, I think she said. Caite hunted until she found those journals. She said by age eight she could read everything that had been written, and she devoured them."

"Sally! Sally was the maid's name hired to watch us when we were six. Dad fired her for slapping Caite. Caite used to call her Sal as an insult."

Mickey coughed. For a moment they all watched as he seemed to choke, but then he breathed in. The nurse that had come in behind the guard wiped away the spit that drooled from the corners of his mouth. Mickey's face turned a mottled shade of red as his eyes met Taite's.

"Don't you feel sorry for me, Taite," he growled.

Taite stood as did Pierce and the others. Her conversation with Mickey was over.

"I don't," she stated before she turned away.

Good and Evil had split between them, Caite had said of their violent birth, before she'd committed her final act of destruction. Taite sighed. *Yes, it had*, she thought sadly. *It most certainly had. And it was an unfair division.*

****

Taite's father looked up when she and Pierce walked into his study where he was reading the local newspaper. Laying the paper down on his desk, he studied Taite.

"Did seeing Mickey help to heal you, Taite?"

Walking to her father, Taite leaned down and kissed his cheek.

"I love you, Dad. And, yes, it did." She joined Pierce on the couch as her father watched her. He seemed to relax.

"Are we ready to get on with our lives? Can we, Taite, do you think?"

"We have to, Dad." Taite responded as she looked to Pierce.

"I have a daughter to raise and a husband to love."

Pierce directed a slow smile her way.

Taite, loving him as she had loved no other, returned that smile.

The End

About The Author

L. J. Vant and her husband make their home in the great state of Oklahoma. Blessed with a vivid imagination L. J. is never short of a story brewing and it wanting to be written down. Besides writing, she loves working in her yard and flowerbeds. With a Masters in Applied Psychology, she is always people watching and wondering what is going on inside of them.

CPSIA information can be obtained
at www.ICGtesting.com
Printed in the USA
BVHW092054170422
634551BV00004B/66